little black dress
· IT'S A GIRL THING ·

Dear Little Black Dress Reader,

Thanks for picking up this Little Black Dress book, one of the great new titles from our series of fun, page-turning romance novels. Lucky you — you're about to have a fantastic romantic read that we know you won't be able to put down!

Why don't you make your Little Black Dress experience even better by logging on to

www.littleblackdressbooks.com

where you can:

♥ Enter our **monthly competitions** to win **gorgeous** prizes

♥ Get **hot-off-the-press** news about our latest titles

♥ Read **exclusive** preview chapters both from your **favourite** authors and from brilliant new writing talent

♥ Buy **up-and-coming** books online

♥ Sign up for an essential slice of romance via our **fortnightly email** newsletter

We love nothing more than to curl up and indulge in an addictive romance, and so we're delighted to welcome you into the Little Black Dress club!

With love from,

The ☐

D0774209

Five interesting things about Kate Lace:

1. When I left school I joined the army instead of going to university – there were 500 men to every woman when I joined up – yesss.

2. While I was there I discovered that there were more sports than hockey and lacrosse and learnt to glide, rock climb, pot hole, sail and ski. I also discovered that I wasn't much good at any of them but I had a lot of fun.

3. I met my husband in the army. We've been married for donkey's years. (I was a child bride.)

4. Since I got married I have moved house 17 times. We now live in our own house and have done for quite a while so we know what is growing in the garden. Also, our children can remember what their address is.

5. I captained the Romantic Novelists' Association team on University Challenge the Professionals in 2005. We got to the grand finals so I got to meet Jeremy Paxman three times.

By Kate Lace

The Chalet Girl
The Movie Girl
The Trophy Girl
The Love Boat

The Love Boat

Kate Lace

little
black
dress

First published in 2009
by LITTLE BLACK DRESS
An imprint of HEADLINE PUBLISHING GROUP

A LITTLE BLACK DRESS paperback

1

Cataloguing in Publication Data is available from the British Library

ISBN 978 0 7553 4792 6

Typeset in Transit511BT by Avon DataSet Ltd,
Bidford-on-Avon, Warwickshire

Printed and bound in Great Britain by
Clays Ltd, St Ives plc

Headline's policy is to use papers that are natural, renewable and
recyclable products and made from wood grown in sustainable forests.
The logging and manufacturing processes are expected to conform to the
environmental regulations of the country of origin.

HEADLINE PUBLISHING GROUP
An Hachette UK Company
338 Euston Road
London NW1 3BH

www.littleblackdressbooks.com
www.headline.co.uk
www.hachette.co.uk

To Ian – as always

Acknowledgements

I am indebted to Pete and Jan Barnes for introducing me to their wonderful sailing club at Porthpean and for taking me out on their boat across the bay to Polkerris. Also I owe thanks and possibly a drink (which might be more welcome) to Jan Jones for her encyclopaedic knowledge of flotilla holidays and yacht chartering and to Desmond Fforde who told me the names for certain technical bits and pieces on boats. If I've got any details wrong it's because I wasn't paying sufficient attention and I'm a numpty and it's no fault of theirs. I must also thank Claire Baldwin, my wonderful and patient editor and the art department at LBD for my fab covers; I love them. And finally, a big 'thank you' to all my mates in the Romantic Novelists' Association who are just inspirational.

Poppy Sanders waved her piece of A4, with the name Garvie clearly printed in thick marker pen, at the passengers who poured out of Arrivals into the main airport concourse. Despite the air-conditioning, which functioned reasonably well for a provincial Greek airport, they all looked warm and weary as they lugged their cases and herded small children. She smiled expectantly at any of them who gave her notice a cursory glance. Dressed in her navy and white WorldFleet shore uniform she looked cool and efficient and, she hoped, welcoming. Wouldn't it be wonderful, she thought as she scanned passing faces, to get another group like the one she'd said goodbye to that morning? But having seen the manifest she knew this was unlikely; she could tell by the names and ages that this was a family group with the parents allowing each of the teenaged children to bring along a friend for company. Knowing their usual clients she imagined a merchant banker and his wife and their well-spoken, public-school-educated offspring and their cultured friends.

A family group erupted through the sliding doors from immigration, baggage reclaim and customs. They were led by a large, buxom bottle-blonde in stilettos and a mauve velour tracksuit who bore a passing resemblance to Barbara Windsor. Behind her came a gaggle of teenagers all shouting each other down. They seemed to be arguing over the relative merits of Millwall and Crystal Palace and feelings were obviously running high judging by the fruity language. Poppy watched them for a few seconds, thinking that whichever tour operator they were booked with was going to have their hands full with that lot; lots of energy, totally boisterous, up for a good time and going to have it come what may. Smiling, she looked back at the sliding doors.

'Oi!'

Poppy snapped back to the real world and turned her attention to the owner of the voice.

'Yeah, you!'

Oh my God. Barbara Windsor was addressing her. Her heart plummeted and her smile lapsed. 'Mrs Garvie?'

'That's righ'.'

Poppy swallowed. Shit. The boisterous bunch were hers. The Garvies were not quiet merchant bankers seeking an idle holiday vegging out after the cut and thrust of City life, and she was the lucky rep whose work was going to be cut out keeping this lot from wreaking too much mayhem around the Med for a fortnight. Great. But Poppy was nothing if not a pro, and it was her job to give her charges a fantastic holiday. She wasn't employed by WorldFleet to enjoy herself but to make sure the clients did. So she smiled broadly, extended her hand and said, 'Welcome. I'm delighted to meet you.'

The vision sniffed. 'Likewise.' She stuck out a hand. 'Veronica, but everyone calls me Ronnie.'

'Poppy,' Poppy reciprocated, shaking it, and clocking

the extravagant nail extensions as she did so. She didn't think Ronnie Garvie was going to be doing much hands-on sailing over the next fortnight. Not that she had to; the yacht came with a perfectly able skipper as well as Poppy herself, who was mainly the cook/cleaner but also helped out on deck when necessary. 'Is all your party here?'

Ronnie glanced over her shoulder and did a quick head count. The argument was raging just as fiercely, although there was now a distraction caused by someone's mention of Arsenal, considered a poofs' club by one of the others, an opinion which wasn't going down well. Despite the racket, however, the argument was still good-natured. The language and the shouting got more intense. Other family groups with younger children were looking worriedly at the scene of the altercation, presumably concerned at the vocabulary their offspring were likely to pick up.

'Shut it, you lot,' yelled Ronnie, over the din. 'There's kids around what don't need to hear your foul language.' Silence fell instantly. The other parents looked relieved.

Impressive, thought Poppy. In the quiet that followed Poppy made a quick assessment of the group. Apart from being noisy and boisterous and totally inappropriately dressed, she didn't think any of them looked as if they were really cut out for the sort of holiday Mr and Mrs Garvie had booked. The kind of sailing holiday that WorldFleet offered generally appealed to clients who had a genuine wish to do a bit of hands-on sailing around some of the most beautiful islands Greece had to offer, in between eating gourmet food and enjoying the cultural delights of the cradle of civilisation. The group of teenagers and young adults in front of her had the appearance of people who would have been much more at home on a large cruise ship with wall-to-wall entertainment, eat-as-much-as-you-like buffets, discos, bars and the company of other youngsters. She hoped they wouldn't be bored to sobs by the yacht. It wouldn't be much fun for the six kids if they were, and given the money that had been shelled out it would be a rotten shame.

Ronnie turned back to Poppy. 'Just Mick to come. We'd better wait for 'im. 'E's the one wiv the cash. But more cash than dash as 'e's last.' She laughed raucously at her own joke. At that moment a rotund bloke sloped out of the doors, chugging at a can of lager, with a grin as wide as the Thames estuary plastered across his face.

'Ahoy, me hearties,' he hollered across the width of the concourse as he caught sight of the rest of his group and ambled over to join them.

'Come on, Mick, we're all waiting for you.'

He increased his pace a bit.

''Ere 'e 'is. Righ', let's go. Let's not waste any more time. We've got an 'oliday to enjoy.'

'Good,' said Poppy, already wondering how she was going to keep up with the energy of this family. It was shaping up to be a long fortnight.

She led the way out of the little airport into the shimmering heat of a Greek afternoon. In her wake came her eight new guests dragging their mountains of inappropriate luggage. The brochure asked guests to bring soft bags that could be easily stowed; obviously this lot either didn't think such a request applied to them or hadn't bothered to read the small print. Poppy sighed as she wondered where the hell they were going to put it all.

The minibus, also in smart WorldFleet livery, was parked close by, and as soon as the driver saw Poppy coming he leapt forward and relieved two of the female guests of their cases. The others began to stack theirs near the rear door.

'An' 'ere's mine, mate.' Mr Garvie dropped his bag on to the pavement and in so doing slopped some of his lager, splashing the driver's shoes.

The bus driver took one look at Mr Garvie and his can of drink and told Poppy in rapid Greek that either the can went or the minibus would – without its complement of passengers. He wasn't having his precious vehicle made sticky with beer. He stopped stowing the rafts of rip-off designer suitcases in the back and glared at Mick.

'Mr Garvie,' began Poppy politely.

'Call me Mick,' he said, stifling a belch.

'Mick,' began Poppy again. 'I'm afraid the company has a strict rule about food and drink on this vehicle. So could I ask you to finish that,' she nodded at the Carlsberg can, 'before you get on board?' She smiled sweetly.

Mick inclined his head towards the driver and said conspiratorially, 'Come on. 'E's cross I didn't offer 'im one, isn't 'e?'

'We don't allow our employees or anyone associated with this company to drink alcohol on duty,' said Poppy carefully.

Mick looked at her and shook his head. 'Well you're goin' to be a righ' larf.'

Poppy very nearly shot back that she was the cook, not the comedy turn, but managed to restrain herself. They were here on holiday and they had every right to expect to enjoy themselves, and she had to make sure they did. So she smiled warmly and suggested that if he was hot he'd be cooler on the bus, especially if it got going so the air-con could kick in. 'Besides,' she added, 'there's a complimentary bar on board with loads of cold beers waiting for you.'

Mick nodded. It sounded good to him. He drained his beer, tossed the tin into a nearly litter bin and shuffled on to the bus. Poppy followed.

'This is nice, innit? Classy,' said Ronnie, running her fingers over the soft grey leather of the executive minibus seats.

Poppy nodded. Maybe her first impressions were wrong. Maybe this family could and did appreciate the finer things in life and this was exactly the sort of holiday they wanted. Maybe they'd done something similar before. She hoped so, because she didn't want the yacht and what she and Jake had to offer to be a disappointment to them. That would be such a shocking waste.

She thought about her last group: four middle-aged, polite, urbane and charming couples who took a delight in the scenery, their surroundings, the food she'd cooked and the itinerary the skipper had planned. They'd been so easy to please and so laid back, their fortnight had flown past and she and Jake had really enjoyed looking after them. It had almost been like entertaining friends. But Poppy didn't think this trip would be quite such a doddle. No way.

She gave her standard introductory spiel about the length of the journey to the little port they were heading for where the yacht was berthed, the area they were passing through and some information about the weather conditions they might expect for the next few days. She smiled at her guests as she finished and noticed that the girls were plugged into their iPods, the boys had their eyes shut and the parents were staring vacantly out of the window, completely ignoring her.

'Any questions?' she ended brightly.

'Yeah,' said one of the teenagers, opening his eyes. 'Is there any beer on board your boat or do we need to stop at an offy before we get there?' He obviously hadn't caught Poppy's comment to Mick a few minutes earlier.

'There's a fully stocked bar on the yacht, which you are welcome to use. Of course, if there's a particular drink or brand not provided I'll be delighted to try to obtain it at the first opportunity, although I think you'll find we've got most things.'

'You got cream de menf?' said Ronnie.

Poppy nodded.

'And what abou' chocolate milk to go wiv it?'

Poppy's eyes widened involuntarily and her eyebrows shot up her forehead. 'I don't think so,' she said, forcing a bubble of startled laughter back down her throat. 'I can get some. I expect one of the supermarkets in the village will stock it. Or I'll be able to chill some drinking chocolate for you.'

'Good,' said Ronnie. 'And you'll 'ave to try it. It's ever so yummy. Just like drinkin' After Eights.'

Poppy thought she'd rather fry her own eyes but, hey, each to their own.

There were no more questions so she settled down in her seat to watch the familiar villages and sights pass by. Last year she'd lost count of the number of times she did this trip and it hadn't palled, but the Garvies seemed utterly uninterested in it. A shame really as there was always something interesting to see: a tortoise ambling along the edge of the road, a herd of goats standing on their hind legs to get at the lower leaves of an olive grove, or some stunning butterflies flitting round the tubs of flowers that the tavernas used to brighten up their stretches of pavement.

Poppy loved the journey; it was all so different from her native Cornwall, and even after fifteen months she still couldn't believe her luck at landing this job.

If she hadn't been tidying the yachting magazines at the minuscule sailing club where she worked she'd never have seen the ad for hostesses for a company specialising in flotilla and yacht charter holidays. It had not previously occurred to her that she could turn her hobby into a means of earning a living, but suddenly it had seemed possible. She scanned the advertisement, then ripped out the page and stuffed it in her pocket before putting the magazine at the bottom of the pile in the hope that the club commodore wouldn't notice the small act of vandalism. He got bees in his bonnet about anything and everything, and Poppy was certain that he'd make a fuss if he found out.

With the clubhouse bar ready for the weekend crowd to pitch up, as they did every Saturday, for their gin and tonics, gossip and fish and chip lunches, Poppy took herself off to the privacy of the stock room to read the ad properly. Well, she concluded, the pay was pants but everything else was perfect. Besides, if she was housed and fed and provided with a uniform, what on earth would she have to spend money on?

For a few minutes she wondered how her parents

would take it. She knew that they relied on her to help out in their pub in the high season, but she also knew that she'd suffocate if she didn't do something with her life before long. She loved the village, she loved the sailing club and most of all she loved her parents, but there was a whole world east of the Tamar. Hell, she'd never even been to Plymouth, let alone London, while most kids of her age seemed to have swanned round the world on gap years. And where had she been? The Isles of Scilly. She snorted and made her mind up; it was time for Poppy Sanders to see the world.

That had been Easter the previous year and look at her now: at home in the village where their shore base was situated, on first name terms with more taverna owners than there were Greek islands, fully conversant with a large section of the Mediterranean coastline and reasonably fluent in the local lingo. Okay, she still had to conquer the rest of the world, but Greece was a start.

Another argument started up at the back of the minibus, this time about cabins. Poppy sighed deeply. Let joy be unconfined. She took her mobile out of her bag and began to text Jake back on the *Earth Star*.

'Brace urself 4 this crowd,' she tapped. 'Not quite like the last lot.' She pressed send. She hoped that the message might make Jake lighten up a bit. He was always so darned serious; polite, great skipper, planned wonderful itineraries with the guests, but always utterly distant. Her character analysis was suddenly interrupted.

'Can you stop the van?' said Ronnie. 'I fink our Jade's goin' to hurl. She's a martyr to . . .'

The sound of noisy vomiting interrupted her.

'. . . motion sickness.'

And they've booked a yachting holiday? thought Poppy. Great. Just wonderful. As the cleaner as well as the cook, she knew what she'd be doing for the next fortnight.

Jake, the *Earth Star*'s skipper, watched the minibus draw up on the quayside. Poppy's text had left him wondering just exactly what this group would be like if they weren't 'like the last lot'. Not that it mattered; it was his job to be completely professional with whoever had chartered the yacht. He was there to sail the vessel and Poppy was there to feed and look after them. She seemed to think it was important to be friends with the guests too, but Jake wasn't interested in socialising beyond what he was expected to do as a host.

He saw Poppy climb out looking weary. That wasn't like her: she was always so upbeat. Her buoyant good humour was one of the things that made her a good workmate. That and her fantastic cooking, although she wouldn't have got this job without that talent. Being able to cook was more important than being able to sail. He supposed that being brought up in a pub had a lot to do with it, because although there were others in the company who could knock up equally delicious meals she always seemed to do it faster and cheaper and more efficiently. One day she'd make some man a wonderful wife. But not him, not with his track record with women.

Much better he kept the whole species, including Poppy, at an emotional arm's length. He put his thoughts from his mind and prepared to greet the new holidaymakers.

'Hello,' he called. He turned on some charm for the new guests. 'Good transfer?'

Poppy's eyes rolled and she gave an almost imperceptible shake of her head.

Spiros, the driver, got out of the minibus and launched into a full account of the journey, sparing no details about the bout of travel sickness, and ending with 'and I'm not taking them back to the airport!' before he stamped off to find a raki to calm himself with before he set about cleaning up his precious vehicle. Jake, whose Greek was only adequate, got the gist. So that explained Poppy's mood. He glanced at the girl Spiros had fingered as the one who had 'ruined' his van.

The girl, still very pasty, leant weakly against the side of the minibus. She'd cleaned herself up and changed into a fresh top, but a faint whiff of vomit still hung around her so no one was inclined to approach too closely, least of all Jake who had a man's aversion to all bodily functions that weren't his own.

Poppy introduced Jake to his new guests, while the Garvies and their friends stared open-mouthed at the huge sailing vessel that was to be their home for a fortnight.

'And this is the *Earth Star*,' said Poppy, waving a hand at the boat. 'Now I know you're all anxious to get on board and explore, and maybe to freshen up after your long journey, but before you do I'm afraid I have to ask all the ladies to take off their high-heeled shoes. We don't allow them to be worn on board as they damage the decks. I'm sure you all packed lots of deck shoes and flip-flops so if I could ask you to wear those instead for the duration of the holiday . . .' She smiled hopefully.

Ronnie shrieked. 'Wot? No 'eels? My legs look fat wivout me stilettos.'

Jake glanced at her velour-clad tree trunks and bit back the observation that her legs looked fat because they *were*. Poppy turned away and Jake was annoyed to see that she was shaking with laughter. Very unprofessional. He ignored Ronnie's protestations and Poppy's lack of self-control and suggested that once they had removed their shoes they might like to follow him on board for a cold drink and a quick briefing about life on a yacht before he brought their luggage down to their cabins.

'Oh, drink,' said Ronnie, toeing her stilettos off in an instant and beetling up the gangplank. Her family went after her in an unseemly rush, leaving a pile of abandoned shoes on the quay. Jake and Poppy were just about to follow the group when shrieks and squeals of delight cannoned out of the saloon. The cries of 'Bling!' and 'Lush!' seemed to indicate that the inside of the yacht was meeting with as much approval as the outside had.

'They like the boat, then,' said Poppy with a grin.

'As well they might.'

When Poppy and Jake arrived down in the saloon, their new guests, with the exception of the travel-sick daughter now sitting alone and pale at the table, were already opening cupboards, nosing round the cabins and generally exploring their new living quarters. Jake restored order with charm, persistence and by dint of opening the bar and offering drinks: cold beer or his lethal welcome punch. The poorly girl was still on her own so he nobly sat next to her. She smiled wanly at him, but despite obviously still feeling a little queasy she didn't refuse the proffered punch and began to gulp it down.

Jake cleared his throat and tapped the table. Once he had the family's attention he got Ronnie to introduce everyone to him.

'This is Lynette and 'er fiancé Kyle.' Ronnie pointed out the oldest of the three girls and the tallest of the lads. Lynette flashed her engagement ring at Poppy and Jake and they both dutifully admired it before she snuggled up to Kyle proprietorially. Obviously she didn't want Poppy making a move on her bloke, although Jake thought that Lynette might be overestimating Kyle's attractiveness to other women.

'And that's Jade and this is 'er friend Raquel, an' last here's my Darren and 'is friend Wayne. An' this is Micky – me old man.'

'Wonderful,' said Jake warmly. 'And now we all know each other I'm sure we'll all get along like a house on fire for the next two weeks. Now, before we do anything else I'd just like to run through a couple of rules to make sure both you and this beautiful boat stay safe. First,' he looked round at his audience, 'I need to have a word about the heads.'

The two younger boys snickered and nudged each other over the distantly smutty connotation of the word *head*. Luke ignored them – it wasn't the first time and it was bound not to be the last.

'The heads are what we call the loos on a boat. However, because whatever goes down them mostly ends up in the sea we have to ask you to be very careful in their use. So nothing goes into them unless you've eaten it first.'

Judging by the looks on the Garvies' faces this was a difficult concept. Jake sighed and prepared to spell it out. 'You can't put paper, tissues or anything else down the loo. Girls, this especially applies to your sanitary waste.'

Jade gave a cry of horror. 'You mean . . . !'

'Exactly. You will find a bin by each head for anything that isn't entirely natural. Now I know you may find this distasteful at first . . .'

'I should cocoa,' said Ronnie. 'It ain't distasteful, it's disgustin'. We 'aven't paid all this bleedin' money for this boat for us not to be able to use the toilets like normal decent folk.'

'But this is exactly what normal decent folk do on boats of this size,' said Jake firmly. 'When you go snorkelling you don't want to be splashing around with, well . . .' He let the implication hang in the air. 'Sorry, folks, but that's the way it is.'

Ronnie sighed heavily. 'If you say so. Well, we'll do as you ask, but I can't say I'm 'appy.'

'Good. Honestly, you'll get used to it. And Poppy here would just like to check that none of you is vegetarian.' Jake looked around the faces of their guests and it seemed from their blank looks of amazement that vegetarianism was almost as much of an alien concept as the use of the heads. 'And now we've got that cleared up, I suggest that Poppy and I fetch your luggage while you choose your cabins.'

'Oi,' said Ronnie. She pointed at the two youngest boys. 'You two can help Jake and Poppy get the stuff.'

'Oh, no,' protested Poppy. 'It's not necessary. Really.'

'I'm not 'avin' no one say my lot don't know 'ow to behave like gents and let a girl do the work.'

'Honestly, we're paid to do this,' insisted Poppy.

But Ronnie was having none of it and shooed her son and his friend out to give a hand with the bags. Given the quantity that the Garvies had brought with them the assistance was welcome, although Jake hoped no one from management saw them allowing the guests to help. That was definitely a no-no.

As they lugged the kit on board, he was glad the yacht was as spacious as it was, as stowing the empty cases was going to be a mission. If all else failed he knew there was probably a place at the shore base where they could store them but it would be inconvenient and would take time to cart everything up there. Besides, Jake had hoped to get going this evening and pootle down to the next little resort. Setting sail gave their guests a feeling that they were truly on a yachting holiday rather than being tied up in a berth, and if they had to hang around too long the magic of sailing into the sunset would be lost. Ah well, he thought, their loss.

While their guests began to unpack and freshen up Poppy got busy in the kitchen. Jake was on hand to answer questions, dispense more drinks, show them how various gadgets and gizmos worked and explain some of the finer points of shipboard life. There were cries of delight at some of the cunning design features and shrieks of laughter as they swapped chat and jokes and got into the holiday spirit – a process not hindered by the quantity of drink they were putting away.

It was about an hour later that the group began to reassemble in the saloon. Poppy passed round some delicious smoked salmon and cucumber canapés and Jake had mixed up yet another batch of his lethal punch. It was designed to get everyone relaxed, although given the amount that had already been shipped Jake thought that if they got any more relaxed they would go completely limp.

He managed to get them to gather round the chart on the main table in the saloon while he took them through some ideas for their two-week itinerary. 'However,' he finished, 'this is your holiday so we can go wherever you'd like me to take you. Within reason, of course. We haven't time to nip across to the Bahamas.'

'But if we had longer we could,' said Poppy. 'This boat might look pretty but she's perfectly capable of going round the world.'

'So can we go to Faliraki?' asked Lynette hopefully.

'We could, but it's a long way. You wouldn't do much else if we went all the way across to Rhodes.'

'But it's Greek, innit?' insisted Lynette. 'So it can't be far.'

'Probably a bit far for us to think about,' said Jake, who had no desire to take the yacht there.

'What about Kavos?' asked Raquel.

'On Corfu?' said Poppy.

Raquel nodded eagerly. 'My mate went clubbing there. Said she had a blindin' time.'

'It's certainly okay as far as distance goes,' said Jake carefully. 'The only trouble is it doesn't have a harbour and the only little port available is quite a walk from the town. Still, I imagine you might be able to get a taxi. Or we could anchor off the shore and you could take the launch.'

'So the uvver people there wouldn't see us rocking up in this,' said Lynette, clearly disappointed. 'They'd just see us arriving in that little boat.'

' 'Fraid so,' said Jake.

A large sigh escaped all three girls simultaneously. Obviously they'd fancied swanking about on their private yacht and if they were going to be berthed right out of the town, or arrive in the dinghy, their entrance would be much more muted. *No point then* was clear on their faces.

'Well, I'm glad. We 'aven't come all this way just so you lot can spend your days sleeping off the nigh' before, now 'ave we?' said Mick, who had found a jaunty yachting cap in his luggage and was now sporting it.

Judging by the look on the girls' faces this was exactly what they had planned to do if the conditions had been right.

They began to discuss all the options Jake had put before them, together with their own ideas, which seemed to revolve around how they were going to extract the most fun out of their fortnight. Two different factions emerged: those who wanted to spend as much time as possible in ports and those (only Mick really) who wanted to spend as much time as possible sailing. As he'd obviously been the one who'd paid for the holiday Jake suspected that democracy wasn't going to figure much in the final decision, and to judge by the increasing volume and shrillness of the girls, neither did they.

'Tell you what,' said Jake, 'why don't I decide the next day or so and then when you've had a chance to think about other options we can come up with a plan for the rest of the holiday. After all, we've got two whole weeks, and I'm sure we can find something to suit everyone. Meantime, how about we raise the anchor, you lot take your drinks up on deck and enjoy the evening sunshine, I'll get the engine going, and we drift down the coast a bit till dinner? If the wind is up enough we'll set the sails and you'll see what a wonderful feeling it is.'

'That sounds just lush,' said Mick, leading the way on deck.

Poppy disappeared into the spacious galley and began to finish off their supper while Jake weighed anchor, started the engine and cast off. As he steered a course out of the little port past dozens of small vessels and fishing boats, he reckoned that this group might not have sophistication but what they lacked in that department they more than made up for in energy. Keeping them entertained was going to be hard work.

Poppy was in the galley making a Greek salad and simultaneously frying off some calamari when she heard Ronnie ask tentatively from the doorway if she could lend a hand.

'Honestly, it's not necessary. It's my job and you're here to enjoy yourself.'

Ronnie looked faintly disappointed.

'Wouldn't you rather be out on deck with the others?' prompted Poppy.

Ronnie shrugged. 'To be honest, I'm not mad about boats. I'd rather be down 'ere. The sea scares the livin' daylights outta me.'

Poppy put down the knife she was using to slice up the cucumber and stared at Ronnie. 'Really? Why?'

'Cos it's so big and wet.' There was a short embarrassed pause. 'An' I can't swim,' Ronnie added quietly.

'But we have life vests. If you wore one of those when you were up on deck you'd be safe. And if you sat in the cockpit there's no way you could fall overboard. I know the Med can be a bit iffy in a storm but mostly it's like a big bath. It certainly is today – and likely to remain so for a week at the very least.'

'It's still big and wet and I wouldn't be able to touch the bottom.'

Poppy had to admit that Ronnie didn't look too happy. She was hanging on to the edge of one of the counters like a limpet, and considering the boat was hardly pitching or rolling at all Poppy wondered how she would react when the swell reached even a moderate size. She felt a surge of sympathy for her guest as she continued to chop up the ingredients for the salad, giving the calamari an occasional quick flick with a fish slice. The hob remained level thanks to the magic of gimbals, but not being equipped with a similar self-balancing system herself Poppy had to keep altering her stance to keep hers as the yacht rolled over a slightly larger wave or Jake tacked and they heeled over in the other direction. Over and above any noise Poppy was making in the kitchen the swish and slap of the waves against the hull was clearly audible, along with the creak and squeak of the boat as the waves rolled beneath it. Poppy found it all very soothing, but she could tell Ronnie wasn't at ease at all.

'Why don't you get yourself another glass of punch and come back and chat to me while I get this finished?' she said. 'I think Jake left the jug on the saloon table.'

Ronnie tottered off, stumbling once or twice as a sudden movement of the yacht caught her unawares, and came back with a brimming glass and the remains of the plate of canapés. She shoved them in Poppy's direction then heaved herself on to a stool Poppy had hooked out from under the counter.

'What about a drink for yourself?' she asked.

'Not while I'm working,' said Poppy. 'Company regs.'

'What, not even a fruit juice or nuffink?'

'Actually, I'd love an orange juice. There's a carton in the fridge.' Poppy pointed out the relevant door and reached into yet another cupboard for a glass.

'Cor, this is just like a real kitchen, innit?' Ronnie slugged the juice into the glass and sploshed in several chunks of ice before passing it to Poppy.

'And better than some land-based ones I've worked in,' said Poppy, taking a grateful gulp.

'So is that what you did – caterin' – before you got involved in this lark?'

Poppy explained about her parents' pub and her job in her local sailing club.

'Well I never. I'm a pub kid too. My parents owned a boozer an' all, a real spit and sawdust joint. Mind you, we never did food. Just as well really. My mum would 'ave probably poisoned most of the punters. Terrible cook my mum. An' I'm not much better. Maybe I could learn a fing or two off of you while I'm 'ere.' She looked hopefully at Poppy.

Poppy took the squid off the gas and tipped it on to some kitchen paper to mop up the oil.

'But you're here to have fun, sunbathe, relax, visit the sights . . .' As she spoke she deftly sliced up some bread and then got out the ingredients to make salad dressing.

Ronnie looked less than enthusiastic. 'This 'oliday is Mick's idea. 'E's always wanted to be an old salt like Napoleon.'

'Er – Nelson?'

'Whatever. And the kids fort it was a lush idea because he promised them a real posh boat an' they could bring their friends an' . . .'

'And you didn't like to rain on their parade,' offered Poppy.

'Somefink like that, yeah.'

Poor old Ronnie, thought Poppy, railroaded into the sort of holiday she obviously wasn't going to really enjoy in an environment she was unhappy about.

'So what would *you* like to do most in this fortnight?'

'Mick says I ought to learn to swim for starters, but I dunno.'

'Would you like to?'

'I'd feel a bit of a tart at my age. Do they make water wings for grown-ups? My kids don't know I can't swim. They'd laugh their bleedin' socks off if they found out.'

'They needn't know.'

' 'Ow's that goin' to work, then?'

'Jake could take everyone off in the dinghy for a picnic or something and leave you and me at some quiet beach and I could teach you. I mean, I doubt if I'll get you so you could compete in the Olympics but I could teach you enough for you to have fun in the water. And this is the place to do it. The water's lovely and warm and seawater is much more buoyant than the stuff you get in your local pool. And if you liked it we could do some snorkelling together.'

Ronnie shook her head. 'I dunno about that. I don't fancy going under water.'

Poppy explained that she wouldn't be under water, just her face, and the breathing tube meant she could just gaze about at another world. 'You wouldn't believe how beautiful it is under the surface. Honest,' she added encouragingly.

'An' you reckon I could do tha'?'

'I absolutely promise that you could.'

Ronnie's face brightened up. She nicked a calamari ring and popped it in her mouth. 'Well,' she said, after she'd swallowed it and smacked her lips in appreciation, 'if you're as good a swimmin' teacher as you are a cook, I'll be giving Rebecca bleedin' Adlington a run for her money soon.'

Poppy began to gather together cutlery and glasses to start laying the table.

' 'Ere, I can do that. Might as well make myself useful rather than gettin' under your feet,' said Ronnie, taking the things out of Poppy's hands.

'But you shouldn't.'

Ronnie put the things firmly down on the counter. 'Now you listen 'ere, my girl, let's get one fing straight. Me and Micky 'ave paid for this boat which means that for the fortnight it's ours and you and Jake 'ave to do what we ask.'

Poppy raised an eyebrow; she wasn't quite sure she understood what Ronnie had in mind. 'Well . . .' she began.

'Yeah, all right. Within reason.'

Poppy nodded, relieved. All sorts of bizarre scenarios had flashed through her brain.

'Well, I want to 'elp out. Okay?'

Poppy knew when she was beaten. 'Thanks,' she said with a warm smile.

A few minutes later Ronnie was back in the galley. 'Now what can I do?'

'Sit down and have a canapé and another drink,' suggested Poppy.

'Nah, I fink I've 'ad enough. I fort it was the boat

rocking that was makin' me feel all wobbly but I fink it must be what that Jake 'as put in that punch.'

Poppy grinned. Jake's punches had a deserved reputation.

She flipped open the oven and took out a blind-baked pastry case. As she eased it out of the tin she asked Ronnie something that had aroused her curiosity. 'So tell me,' she said. 'If you hate the sea, why did you agree to a yachting holiday?'

'Well, I told you Mick wanted to play at bein' Nap— Nelson. It's been 'is dream for so long and, well, now we've got the dosh I couldn't say no, could I?'

Poppy shrugged. 'I suppose not.'

'Micky 'ad a tough life when 'e was little. 'Is mum and dad were dirt poor and 'e always said that if 'e ever made any money 'is kids would want for nuffink.' It was Ronnie's turn to shrug. 'So 'e did make money – shitloads of it – and when he said we might 'ave an 'oliday on a boat we all fort it was a blinding idea. I fort 'e meant a proper cruise so I went along wiv the idea an' all. Actually,' she added, 'I fink the kids fort 'e meant a cruise too but when 'e showed them a picture of this yacht they didn't care. I didn't 'ave the 'eart to tell 'im it was my idea of a bleedin' nightmare.'

'Then we've just got to make sure that your nightmare turns into a dream.'

And Ronnie smiled at her with such warmth that Poppy felt the last of her earlier reservations disappear completely. Ronnie was a diamond. The kids might be spoilt, noisy and hard work but there was nothing wrong with Ronnie. Poppy knew the pair of them were going to get on just fine.

The next day Jake took them north to a pretty port near the border with Albania.

'And if you want to we can nip over to Corfu tomorrow evening and you girls can take in the delights of Kavos,' he said as he and Poppy secured the mooring lines.

Jade, who was lounging on the leather cushions in the cockpit, perked up. She was still looking pale and had complained about feeling seasick, but the pills Ronnie dished out to her seemed to work and she hadn't actually been sick that day at all.

'So how far is it?' she asked cautiously.

'Just a few miles,' replied Jake.

'I don't mind that then. Only I don't like it when we're moving for a long time.'

'I know,' said Jake. 'How are you feeling now?'

'Better now we've stopped. This place is pretty, ain't it?'

Jake nodded as he jumped off the boat on to the quay-side to give Poppy a hand with securing the gangplank.

Ronnie came up on deck, bringing with her a big jug of iced tea and half a dozen glasses on a tray. 'Poppy made this earlier specially for you. She says it's very settling for a gippy tummy. She fort you might like it once we got 'ere, but there's enough for everyone.'

'That was nice of her,' said Jade, looking at the two crew as they worked. She raised her glass to Poppy and shouted her thanks. 'She's dead sweet, isn't she?' she said, turning back to her mother.

'She's a great cook, that's for sure.'

Ronnie settled herself on the seat next to Jade and tipped her face towards the sun. 'What do you reckon to 'er and Jake? Have you noticed 'ow they're always looking at each uvver – but, you know, behind each uvver's backs, like they're dead shy.'

'Can't say I have.' Jade looked at Poppy faintly enviously, and then at Jake. As she did, she saw Jake watch Poppy as she made her way back over the gangplank at the stern of the boat. Maybe her mum was right. She sighed and half wished Jake looked at her like that. He was lush. Wouldn't it be phat to have a bloke fancy you in secret. 'I wouldn't kick 'im out of bed, if I was 'er.'

Ronnie shook her head. 'Don't tell your dad, but neither would I.' She chuckled at the thought. She opened her eyes and contemplated Jake with his tanned skin, glossy dark hair and smiling blue eyes. Then she turned her attention to Poppy and had to admit that she was a looker. Ronnie adored her kids and thought the sun shone out of all their orifices but even she could see that Lynette and Jade weren't in Poppy's league. For a start, Poppy was slender. Ronnie knew that her girls carried just a teeny bit of puppy fat which was bound to disappear as they got older – well, it did, didn't it? And Poppy's sun-bleached blond hair had a shine and a bounce to it which made her girls' look quite lacklustre in comparison – all that bleach took its toll, as Ronnie knew from personal experience.

And she didn't appear to use any make-up, although with a tan like hers she didn't need any. Ronnie comforted herself with the thought that all the sun and wind and outdoor living would probably give Poppy skin like rhino-hide by the time she was in her forties. But it wasn't much consolation right now with all the blokes sniffing round her like dogs and none sparing even a glance at her daughters. Even Raquel, whom she knew Jade envied for her curves and her big brown eyes, was outclassed by Poppy.

Still, she thought, Poppy might have the looks but she didn't have any dough. Poppy was working her arse off on this boat, not like her girls, who were living in the lap of luxury.

'So you think her and Jake are just friends,' said Ronnie sceptically.

'Reckon so.'

'Or maybe they're not allowed to.'

'Maybe. Maybe he's gay.'

Ronnie's eyes flew wide. 'Nah!'

The boat rocked as the rest of the younger members of the group came aft from the deck at the bow where they'd been sunbathing. Raquel was looking rather red. Ronnie poured out the iced tea and handed the glasses round.

Darren took a slurp and then spat it back into his glass. 'What the bleedin' 'ell is this muck?'

'Iced tea an' it's lovely,' said Ronnie stoutly. 'Poppy made it specially.'

'It's rank,' said Darren. Kyle and Wayne nodded their agreement. 'I'm going to get a beer. Anyone else?' They put their barely touched drinks back on the tray and sloped off down to the bar in the saloon, leaving the girls alone.

'Where's your dad?' asked Ronnie.

'Gone to look round the village,' said Lynette. 'Said he needed to stretch his legs.'

There was silence as they sipped their iced tea and soaked up the mid-afternoon sun.

'You know, I'm not sure I really like this,' said Jade as she took another sip.

'Nah – me neither,' said Raquel.

'To be honest, I'd rather have a cold beer,' said Ronnie. They giggled. 'I think I'll tell Poppy not to bother another time.' Lynette fetched four cans and they slurped the contents contentedly.

'This is the life, innit?' said Ronnie, stretching out on the soft seat.

Around them the warm air was filled with the noise of halyards slapping against aluminium masts as the other, smaller yachts swayed gently in the calm waters of the little port. Delicious cooking smells wafted across the quayside from the numerous tavernas that did business along it and groups of holidaymakers ambled by casting admiring glances at the boats moored there. As theirs was the biggest by far Ronnie was able to revel in the knowledge that she was the object of a certain amount of envy from the passers-by. She quite fancied going for a walk herself, but if she did no one would know that she and this lush boat belonged together. On shore she'd be just another tripper; on the boat everyone could see she was loaded!

The four women lounged around in the sunshine like a pride of well-fed lionesses. Occasionally one or other of them would stir herself enough to fetch another cold can from the fridge in the bar. The boys had joined them briefly but complained it was too hot and retired to the air-conditioned cool of the saloon from where, now and again, the sound of a raucous card game drifted on to the deck. Jake and Poppy had disappeared to get provisions, and Mick hadn't returned from stretching his legs. Peace descended over the women as the warmth and the beer induced slumber.

It was more a pulse than a noise, to start with. Then the pulse became a throb and then a dull roar. Ronnie roused herself and turned to see what was disturbing the tranquillity.

'Fuck me!' she said, her jaw dropping.

The girls, curious, followed her gaze and made similar exclamations in turn as into the bay came a motor yacht the size of a small cruise liner; four decks, a large launch swinging casually on davits, a clutch of radar domes and satellite dishes on the bridge and a helipad at the stern left no one in any doubt that this craft belonged to someone in the super-rich league.

'Bling or what,' said Raquel, awestruck.

'Who the fuck's got a boat like that?' said Ronnie. 'Al Fayed? A film star?'

'A mafia boss?' offered Raquel.

The throb of the engine died away as the captain throttled back. The yacht drifted silently further into the bay before the rattle of the anchor being lowered reached them. The vessel was being moored outside the little harbour, since it was far too big to consider squeezing in with the flotilla of smaller boats. It would have been like a huge shark stranded in a pool with a bunch of sardines.

'Looks like whoever it is is stopping 'ere for the night,' said Ronnie. 'Maybe we'll find out who it belongs to,' she added hopefully. She stared dreamily at the new addition to the view – the sleek, aerodynamic lines and the high-tech steel and smoked glass superstructure being much more attractive, in her opinion, than anything nature had to offer.

The lads reappeared on deck and were equally impressed with their new neighbour. Over another can or two of lager they speculated about who might have the sort of cash to afford such a yacht.

'Let's take the launch and 'ave a closer look,' said Kyle. 'See if we can spot the owner.'

'I don't think you ought,' said Ronnie. 'They may not like you snoopin' around. Rich geezers can be funny like that.'

'There's no law against lookin',' said Darren. He stood up and swayed a little.

'Bloody boat,' he muttered as he dumped yet another empty can on the growing pile littering the cockpit table. Slightly unsteadily, he and Kyle hauled the little launch alongside the *Earth Star* and jumped down into it. The launch rocked alarmingly.

'Are you two sure you know what you're doing?' said Ronnie, peering over the side of the yacht at the two lads.

'Mum, if we can drive a car we can drive this,' said Darren. He tugged on the starter cord and the outboard sputtered. 'Anyone else want to come?' he called.

'I will,' said Raquel. The others, made idle by beer and sun, shook their heads.

The three, revitalised by the activity and the prospect of a jaunt, set off noisily out of the harbour. The rest watched the little dinghy disappear out of the port in a less than straight line and then returned to their beers and sunbathing.

*

Jake and Poppy had finished ordering provisions from the little supermarket, tucked down a shady back street, and had paused in their return to the yacht for a cold glass of orange juice. Strewn around the table were half a dozen plastic carrier bags filled with fresh salads, fruit and vegetables. Like most of the people enjoying the hot afternoon sun on the quayside they had clocked the arrival of the huge yacht.

'Wouldn't mind working on a gin palace like that,' said Jake.

'I bet it's overrated. I should think anyone who has got the money to blow on something like that is probably a right bastard.'

Jake frowned. 'And what makes you think that?'

'Stands to reason. If it's from business you'd have to be completely ruthless to get that rich, a total shark. Either that or the owner's earned it through drug money or crime or something.'

Jake laughed. 'So Richard Branson and Bill Gates come into that category?'

'Well, not them, obviously.' She grinned. 'Okay, it could belong to someone perfectly decent, but I bet it'd be a lot of work to be crew on that. The guests would probably be very demanding and you'd never be able to let standards slip.'

'Like you do, you mean.'

Poppy kicked him under the table. 'I do *so* not! Anyway, what do you think that cost?'

Jake shrugged. 'Dunno. A hundred mill?'

Poppy whistled. 'So I don't suppose even the Beckhams could run to it.'

'You'd have to be fabulously rich to own a boat like that,' agreed Jake.

They both stared at the massive boat, then Poppy pointed a finger. 'Isn't that our launch heading towards it?'

Jake shielded his eyes and stood up for a better look. 'Well it's certainly Raquel and Darren in it. And Kyle, I think. Shit, what on earth do they think they're doing?'

They both stared in horror as the little craft careered straight towards the ship.

'Do they know how to handle it?' said Poppy.

'Well, I haven't shown them. But surely . . . Even they . . .'

Jake shut up as the little launch cannoned off the side of the giant yacht and Raquel was catapulted over the side into the sea.

'Shit!' yelled Poppy.

Jake went dead white before he took off like a grey-hound after a hare. Leaving their bags of shopping strewn around their table the pair of them raced off to the *Earth Star* to grab the inflatable life raft. WorldFleet management would not be impressed if a guest on one of their yacht charters drowned and Jake and Poppy both knew that the consequences would be dire, even if the kids had been behaving recklessly. The fact that the crew had had nothing to do with the incident would cut no ice if things went badly wrong. None of the kids was wearing a life vest and neither Jake nor Poppy knew if Raquel could swim.

They charged up the gangplank and raced to where the life raft was kept on the foredeck. They were about to pull the toggle to inflate it when they saw that Darren and Kyle had managed to haul Raquel over the side into the dinghy, which apparently hadn't been made unseaworthy by the force of the impact.

'Panic over,' said Jake, still very pale. Poppy noticed he was shaking, his demeanour making a lie of his words. Poppy hadn't thought that Jake was the sort to react badly in an emergency, but he seemed really shocked by the incident.

'You all right?' she asked, concerned.

Jake swallowed and appeared to bring himself under control. 'Yeah, fine. Just, you know, someone going overboard like that – it can be serious.'

'Obviously.' But she had detected that his reaction was more than just professional concern; something had really rattled him. 'But . . .' She stared at him, still worried.

'I'm fine,' he snapped.

Poppy sensed she was intruding so she backed off. Whatever it was that had got him so rattled wasn't something he wanted to share.

'What's going on?' said Ronnie who had joined them, her curiosity roused by the pair of them pounding past her at full speed.

Jake, obviously still scared and angry about what might have happened, turned furiously on her and was about to tell her exactly what he thought of her kids and their friends when he seemed to remember that he was dealing with a guest and ought to be more diplomatic. He took a deep breath and gave her a quick résumé of the events of the previous few minutes.

'The little bleeders,' said Ronnie. 'Just you wait till I get my 'ands on them.'

'The main thing is no one was hurt,' said Poppy tightly.

'Stuff *no one was 'urt*,' screeched Ronnie. 'What about that bleedin' boat?' She waved a taloned hand in the direction of the super-yacht. 'Fuck knows what it'll cost to put righ' if them kids 'ave damaged it. An' two of them ain't even mine!'

'There'll be insurance,' said Jake.

Poppy, however, wasn't sure how the owner would react to finding that his shiny pride and joy had been trashed by a boatload of teenagers. No doubt they'd find out how he felt soon enough.

Ronnie looked faintly mollified at the thought that insurance might pick up the tab. In the meantime she watched the little dinghy approach the port again with three subdued-looking kids, one of them wet through.

Before they got close to the *Earth Star*, Ronnie was leaning over the safety rail and telling them exactly what she thought of them, thus providing a good five minutes of entertainment for the passers-by on the quayside plus a free lesson in Anglo-Saxon thrown in.

'And you can go and apologise right now,' she finished off.

'Actually,' Jake interrupted, 'I think it might be best if Poppy or I did that. We might have to involve WorldFleet's insurers.'

Ronnie glowered at the three shame-faced teenagers. 'Well you're bleedin' lucky, you lot. If I had my way you'd be eating so much 'umble pie you'd 'ave it coming out your bleedin' ears. An' you'd better say sorry to Jake an' Poppy 'ere for giving them a right fright.'

The three mumbled apologies to Jake and Poppy. They were then told to go to their cabins and wait till Mick came back. Ronnie went back to the cockpit muttering threats about what she'd do to them if they disobeyed her on this as the kids slunk off below decks.

Jake and Poppy jumped into the dinghy to examine the damage. The fibreglass was quite badly chipped and cracked where it had connected with the huge motor yacht but all the damage was above the waterline so the harm was only cosmetic.

'So are you going to go or shall I?' said Poppy as they sat on the thwarts.

'I suppose I'd better.'

'Oh,' said Poppy, disappointed.

Jake looked at her in surprise. 'You mean you *want* to go and grovel?'

'Hell, no. But I want a look at that yacht.'

Jake shook his head in amazement. 'So sucking up to the rich owner and persuading him or her not to sue our sorry little arses from here to kingdom come is the price you're prepared to pay to satisfy your curiosity.'

Poppy nodded enthusiastically. 'That's about the size of it.'

'More fool you.'

'Just because you're not curious.'

'Shallow is the word you're looking for.'

Poppy shrugged. She wasn't fussed. 'I'm a woman – or haven't you noticed? Of course I'm shallow.' She batted her eyelashes at him provocatively.

'Cut the crap, Poppy. It doesn't suit you.'

She pouted. God, the man could be so moody sometimes. Well, two could play at that game. An angry silence settled over them.

Jake relented first. 'I was only winding you up. You can go. You're right, I'm not that curious.'

Instantly Poppy forgave him and a broad smile spread across her face. 'Really? You'll let me? Oh, fantastic. I'll give you a hand with the shopping first if you like.'

Jake shook his head. 'I expect I can manage. Now get yourself over to that boat and try to stop them from taking WorldFleet to the cleaners.'

'Aye aye, skipper.'

Jake jumped out of the dinghy and untied it. He wished Poppy good luck as she started the outboard and set off towards the super-yacht.

Poppy manoeuvred her little craft carefully alongside the huge boat. She clocked its name painted in large letters on the stern: *Wet Dream*. How tacky, she thought. The owner obviously had more money than taste – shedloads more. Then she saw where the kids had collided with it. It looked as if the damage to the big motor yacht was even more cosmetic than the damage to the dinghy. As far as she could see the paintwork was just scuffed and scratched and could probably be sorted out with an orbital sander and a quick touch-up with some gloss. However, the owner might not see things that way and she prepared herself for a tough dressing down. She'd promised Jake she'd do this so she couldn't turn tail and run away.

She called out for permission to come aboard but got no response. Not surprising, she thought. The yacht was so blooming big anyone for'ard would need a radio to communicate with someone at the stern. She was faintly surprised that there weren't any crew around but now they'd moored she supposed they might be allowed some time off and be relaxing in their quarters.

She tied the painter up to one of the chrome stanchions at the stern. There was a little side deck just above water level to help the rich owner and his guests to board the vessel from the sea as easily as possible. From there a set of stairs led up to the main deck and the saloon – or she supposed they did. They certainly led to a deck and a bank of huge, tinted plate-glass windows but what was behind them was anyone's guess. Hell's teeth, she thought, this yacht was vast. Huge! Whoever owned it must be completely minted. She just hoped that as well as minted they might be kind. And forgiving. Shit – what if they weren't?

Timidly she knocked on the window. 'Hello,' she called. 'Permission to come aboard?'

'A bit late seeing as you already have,' replied a man's voice from above her.

Poppy leant back and looked up. The first thing she saw was a pair of feet, thrust into a pair of worn deck shoes that were about level with her head. She moved her gaze up his very tanned and muscular legs, past his baggy and tatty shorts to the T-shirt with a *Wet Dream* logo embroidered just over his left nipple. Poor sap, she thought. But the owner must pay the crew well if they were prepared to go around with that emblazoned on their kit. She thanked her lucky stars the logo she was expected to wear said *WorldFleet*. She couldn't – actually she *could* – imagine the sort of comment she'd get walking along the harbour with *Wet Dream* splashed all over her clothes! She couldn't make out anything more about him as his head was silhouetted against the blazing sun. She tried squinting but the glare was just too bright.

'Yes?'

She jerked back to reality. 'Yes, sorry. Um . . .' She paused. 'I came to apologise.'

'Really? Wait there.' He disappeared. A minute later he stood in front of her. She noticed that his clothes, despite obviously being the crew uniform, were tatty and stained. However, stuff the tatty clothes – she clocked his face. Wow! With his deep tan, sun-bleached hair and brooding, blue eyes Poppy reckoned if a casting director saw him he'd be snapped up for the film industry. What a hunk.

'I came to apologise to the owner,' she said when she had managed to marshal her thoughts.

'Really? What about?'

'I'm crew on the *Earth Star*. Over there.' Poppy pointed at the yacht in the harbour.

The deckhand shrugged. 'So? Do you want a round of applause?'

'No . . . I . . . It's . . . There was a bit of an accident.'

The deckhand raised an eyebrow. 'You mean when that boatload of yobs hit us amidships?'

Poppy felt herself colouring up. 'Yes,' she mumbled.

'Lucky for you they didn't do much damage.'

Poppy nodded. 'I had a look just now and I think it's mostly cosmetic. But I ought to talk to the owner about it. He might want to claim on the insurance or something.'

'The owner's not here.'

That explained the scruffiness of the deckhand. When the cat's away and all that. 'So how can I get in touch with him?'

'It doesn't matter.'

'Look, I know the damage is only slight but I really think . . .' Poppy shrugged. Whoever this guy was, it seemed a bit much that he was making decisions for a very rich and powerful person without any reference to him at all.

'Do you want a drink?' the man asked suddenly.

Poppy shook her head, confused. 'Um, not really.'

'Well I do. I'm hot and tired and I was about to get one for myself when you pitched up.' Without another word, he turned on his heel and disappeared through one of the sliding glass doors. Poppy, who still needed to know how to contact the owner, padded after him.

Inside, the yacht was a minimalist heaven of pale wood, cream soft furnishings and a few large paintings. Poppy didn't know much about art but she could swear one of them had to be a Van Gogh. Maybe it was just a print, but then, as she looked at it and noticed visible brush strokes, she thought perhaps not. The man led the way through a stunning dining room and down a companionway which descended a couple of decks. She noticed that, apart from the two of them, there didn't seem to be anyone else on board.

'The crew quarters,' her guide said as he stepped through a door.

Poppy began to feel anxious. Was she being naïve following this man, a complete stranger, down into the depths of this vast, empty yacht? She hesitated.

'I'm not going to jump on you, if that's what you think,' he said, sensing her unease.

'No, of course not,' she said with a bravado she didn't feel. Although being 'jumped on' by a man with looks like his wasn't likely to be so bad. Poppy reckoned she wouldn't have to lie back and think of England – thinking of the Isle of Wight would allow her to cope, or even just Rockall.

She followed him through the door and into a vast galley. She'd thought the one on the *Earth Star* was pretty spacious but this one was enormous.

'Wow!'

'Sure you don't want that drink?'

'Well, perhaps a coke.'

The man went to a huge fridge and extracted a couple of cans. He tossed one across the galley to Poppy, who caught it deftly.

'Thanks . . . um . . . ?' She looked at him enquiringly.

'Charlie.' He raised an eyebrow at Poppy.

'Poppy,' she reciprocated as she popped the can. 'So why just you on this huge empty ship? A bit *Marie Celeste*, isn't it? Or have the rest of the crew gone ashore?'

'I'm just delivering it. The owner keeps it berthed in Syracuse a lot of the time but he likes to holiday in the Greek islands. He asked me to bring it over from Sicily for him.'

'Cool. When's he coming himself?'

'Flying out next week. By which time I should have the hull looking like new again. A bit of sandpaper, a touch of paint . . .'

'Even so, don't you think he should know?' Poppy was grateful for Charlie's offer but was a firm believer that honesty really was the best policy.

'He'll be fine.'

'You're very confident.'

Charlie shrugged. 'I've known him a while.'

'What does he do, this Mr Big?'

'He owns companies – lots of them.'

'And makes money.'

Charlie nodded. 'You could say that.'

'Just a quid or two.'

Charlie nodded again. 'One or two.'

Poppy swigged from her can. 'Look, if you're sure about the damage . . .'

'Honest. It'll be all right. Trust me.'

He moved across the galley to stand closer to her.

Poppy suddenly wondered if his comment about not jumping on her still held true. He was dangerously close – and dangerously sexy.

She put her can down on the counter and moved away a step. She felt a tiny bit safer now the distance between them wasn't quite so small. Charlie looked amused – as if he'd guessed her worries. Of course she was being stupid and jumpy. To prove that she trusted him she said, 'Okay then. How about I buy you a drink – a proper one – when I'm off duty this evening?'

'Yeah, I'd like that,' said Charlie, looking at her over the rim of his can. 'What time?' He moved closer again.

Poppy swallowed. 'Tennish? At the taverna at the end of the quay. The Blue Dolphin.'

'I'll be there.' He blinked lazily and flashed a film-star smile at her.

Shit, he was gorgeous. But as she gazed at him she realised that he knew precisely what effect he was having on her. But then if you were that good looking, having girls fall for you, finding you irresistible, would be a daily hazard.

'Right, I'll be off then. Thanks for the Coke.'

Charlie's mobile rang. He looked apologetic as he answered it. Poppy mouthed 'goodbye' and made her way back to the dinghy. She had a slightly hysterical feeling she might just have been saved by the bell. It wouldn't have been a fate worse than death, but she certainly had had the feeling that Charlie was about to try something on. Blokes didn't stand that close to girls in places the size of the *Wet Dream*'s galley because they were afraid of empty spaces.

'So how was it? As ostentatious on the inside as it is on the outside?' Jake wasn't really interested but he could see that Poppy was bursting to tell him.

She described it for him. 'And I swear there was a Van Gogh in the saloon.'

'Unlikely. The damp wouldn't do it any good.'

'Anyway, Charlie—'

'Charlie! You're on first name terms with the owner?'

Poppy shook her head. 'No. He was hired to bring the yacht round from Sicily to here, so not the owner at all. Anyway, Charlie reckons he can sort out the damage so the owner need never know.'

Jake was sceptical. 'And what if he can't? What then?'

'We'll be long gone,' said Poppy glibly. 'Besides, I did try to get him to give me the owner's details, and as he refused to let me have them I suppose it's his problem. I can have another go, if you like. I said I'd buy Charlie a drink this evening so I can do it then.'

'Did you now?' For some reason he was annoyed that Poppy was going to see this stranger again.

'Well, I felt we owe him that at least. Besides, he's nice.'

Jake didn't answer. Poppy worried him. She was so

naïve, so trusting, she thought everyone could be her friend. Well, life wasn't like that. He knew that – he'd learnt it from bitter experience.

He knew from the way she'd behaved towards him when they had first been teamed up together that she'd really liked him. The last thing he'd wanted, though, was any sort of relationship, so he'd made sure he'd done nothing whatsoever to encourage her. He'd hurt her, he knew that; it had been a bit like being unkind to a puppy, but it would be fairer on Poppy in the long run if she had nothing to do with him outside their professional relationship. That being the case, he wasn't in a position now to carp if she wanted to go on a date with someone else. Even if he did think it was unwise, even foolish.

'Do you want to come along?' she asked as an after-thought.

Jake shook his head. It would be unfair to shadow Poppy like some sort of minder when she went for a drink with this bloke. She was a grown-up, for heaven's sake, and if she wanted to date some random man it was none of his business. Besides, they were presumably going to one of the tavernas along the waterfront so it was hardly a date – just a drink with a new acquaintance. Yet, irrationally, he was still irked at the idea that Poppy was taking an interest in someone else. And because he felt like a dog in the manger he became even more annoyed.

'I don't suppose you'd have invited him out if his boat had been some tatty old tug,' he observed meanly.

'It's not *his* boat, is it?' she replied with irritating logic. 'And I invited him out because he's rattling around by himself on that huge great monster, and – well, as I said, he's nice.'

Jake gave up. So what? In the morning they'd be sailing on somewhere else while Charlie and his gin palace waited for the owner to come swanning out on holiday. He felt glad that Poppy and Charlie wouldn't be able to see each other again. Working for someone as rich as that he was bound to be a slimy bastard and Poppy was just too blinded by the glitz of the motor yacht to see it.

When Poppy skipped off to her assignation later that evening Jake felt his niggle of annoyance return. Why should he feel so grumpy that his colleague was off to meet someone when she was off duty? Just because they worked together didn't give him any say in how she chose to spend her leisure time. It wasn't even as if they were particularly friendly. Well, that was his fault, of course; he didn't like to get too close to anyone these days. Better that way. So now Poppy was looking for friendship elsewhere. Why did that make him feel fed up?

Charlie was already at the taverna when Poppy got there, a cold lager on the table in front of him together with a small bowl of local olives. He rose to his feet as she strolled up: a gesture that made Poppy feel rather sophisticated although the feeling disappeared when she noticed he was still wearing the same tatty shorts and stained polo shirt as he had been earlier.

'What can I get you?' he asked.

'But I said I'd buy you a drink,' she countered, 'as a thank you for offering to cover up our guests' little mishap.'

'Call me old fashioned, but I happen to think that it should be the men who ought to buy fit girls their drinks.'

Poppy felt suddenly self-conscious at being called fit

by Charlie so she said lightly, 'Actually I wasn't going to call you old fashioned; I was going to call you Charlie.'

'Ho ho. And wit too.'

Poppy shook her head. 'Now you're taking the piss.'

'You still haven't answered my question. What would you like to drink?'

Poppy gave in. What the hell? Besides, her earnings were minute and she would bet her bottom dollar Charlie got a lot more than she did. 'A white wine and soda, please.'

Charlie caught the waiter's eye and ordered while Poppy nibbled on an olive.

'Jake's worried about the owner not knowing about the damage,' she said, helping herself to another one.

'Jake?'

'The skipper of the *Earth Star*.'

'He needn't be. It'll be cool.'

'Jake doesn't share your confidence,' said Poppy gloomily, thinking of his likely reaction. He was such an old grump, which considering he could only be about thirty was worrying. She'd tried to get him to see the lighter side of life but he never seemed to want to and the more she tried the worse he got.

She'd asked some of the other WorldFleet hostesses if he'd always been like that and as far as anyone knew he had. Admittedly the collective memory could only go back about five seasons to when he'd started working for the company, but right from the start he'd always had a reputation for being aloof; perfectly pleasant, always polite but not a party animal. A definite loner.

When she joined him on the *Earth Star* she hadn't exactly been expecting him to make a move on her, but she was aware that quite a few blokes fancied her (well, loads actually) and his indifference was slightly hurtful, besides doing nothing for her self-confidence. She'd stared worriedly in the shower-room mirror every morning for a week, checking out her reflection for signs of becoming old and unattractive. Getting her bum pinched by a complete stranger when she bent over to examine some aubergines in the supermarket had restored some of her self-belief, and the remainder had bounced back when a new crew member for the summer season had made a complete fool of himself during an impromptu barbecue by declaring undying lust for her.

Confidence back in place, she came to terms with the fact that it was just Jake whose buttons she didn't press. And although she could have been tempted to risk an illicit relationship with him, and thus break most of WorldFleet's crew regs, she now accepted that it wasn't going to happen. His loss, she thought. Although she knew that if it *did* happen she'd be chuffed to bits; he was a total hunk. But never mind. Stuff Jake. She shoved such thoughts to the back of her brain and turned her attention back to Charlie. She batted her eyelids over the rim of her spritzer.

'So when you're not ferrying huge yachts for members of the super-rich club, what do you do?'

Charlie cocked his head on one side and looked as if he was thinking hard. 'Hmm,' he mused. 'Tough one. Loaf would be a true answer.'

'So does ferrying boats pay that well? I mean, obviously the owner isn't short of cash . . .' She was aware Charlie was staring at her. 'Sorry,' she mumbled. 'I'm being rude. What you get paid is absolutely none of my business.'

'Oh, I don't care about that,' said Charlie airily. 'I was wondering about you.'

'Me? Why on earth?'

'Because you're single, you're a pretty girl, so why not?'

Her brow furrowed as she returned his stare and she thought about how to answer him. How smooth was that? Too smooth, maybe. But undeniably flattering, especially when she considered how devastatingly good looking he was.

'Oh,' was all she could manage. After a moment, she went on, 'There's not much to know, and what there is isn't very interesting.'

'No? Well, I think you're wrong. From what I know—'

'Which is bugger all.'

'Actually I know quite a bit about you.'

'Yeah, right.'

'One, you're called Poppy. Two, you're a fantastic cook—'

Poppy held up her hand. Hey, had he been asking around about her? That seemed rather sinister. Suddenly the game stopped being fun. 'How do you know that?'

Charlie grinned, apparently not the least bit aware of her worries. 'When you charter a yacht like the *Earth Star*, having gourmet food dished up is part of the deal. As it's just you and Jake crewing, one of you is the cook and my guess is that it's you.'

Poppy had to admit that his assumption was correct and felt a small ripple of relief. She really ought to relax, she told herself, and just enjoy the attention. See, not a scary stalker at all. 'So you know my name and that I can cook. Big deal.'

'Three, you like to drink white wine spritzers and four, you like olives. Five, I suspect you're also a great sailor. Six, you have blond hair and seven, you've got blue eyes. Eight, I reckon you must weigh about nine and a half stone and nine, you're five six? Five seven? And ten, you take a size ten. So, I reckon that's quite a lot I know about you.' He looked smug and Poppy couldn't help but laugh. Funny *and* good looking. Quite a combo.

'So, if you're so smart, what's my favourite colour?'

'Blue,' answered Charlie without hesitation.

Poppy nodded. Okay, she'd give him that one but she was still curious to know how he'd guessed so unerringly. 'How on earth?'

'The colour of the sea. Stands to reason. That makes eleven things.'

'All right, smart-arse. Where do I come from?'

Charlie pursed his lips as he thought about it. 'Hmm. Somewhere with lots of water because you sail. Not Norfolk.'

'Why not?'

'Well, I've heard about people from Norfolk and you don't look the least inbred.' Charlie looked at her more closely. 'Although . . .'

'Shut up!' But she couldn't suppress a giggle.

'Anyway, I'm right about the water, aren't I?'

'Might be.'

Charlie sipped his lager as he considered her. 'How about Portsmouth?'

'Stone cold.'

'Brighton?'

'Even colder.'

'Plymouth.'

'Getting warmer.'

'Penzance?'

'Hot.'

'St Ives?'

Poppy shook her head. 'I'll have to tell you. I come from Polzeal.'

'And where the fuck's that? And by the way, that's now a round dozen Poppy-facts I've got.'

'Cornwall. A place about the size of a dot with a sailing club, a pub, a few cottages and about a million visitors for eight weeks of the year.'

'It sounds exciting.'

Poppy laughed. 'Oh yeah. The place is just jumping. Two months of mayhem then ten months of nothing. Anyway, you've just proved you can't read minds. Derren Brown you ain't.'

Charlie shrugged. 'I can probably live with that.' He sipped his beer. 'So what have you found out about me?'

'This is assuming I've given you a second thought.'

Charlie looked shocked. 'Such cruelty!'

Poppy laughed and realised she was having heaps more fun than she'd had in an age. Jake was always so wary and so dismissive when she tried a bit of light flirting. What was wrong with flirting, for God's sake? It didn't mean 'commitment' or 'relationship' but Jake didn't seem to see it like that. Thank goodness Charlie wasn't like him. She could do a lot worse than spend an evening with this guy. She could happily string him along for another couple of hours and get to know him a whole lot better. She cocked her head and considered Charlie. So what *did* she know about him?

'All right,' she said after a few seconds. 'I know you

don't give a stuff what others think about you and you're quite confident.' Charlie raised an eyebrow to encourage her to explain. 'Well, you didn't bother to change to come out with me and you're completely sure you know how the yacht's owner is going to react.'

Charlie nodded. 'Can't fault the logic there.'

Poppy grinned and took a mock bow. 'And I reckon you don't care about money or you'd be doing a better paid job than ferrying yachts around the Med. You must have your master's ticket and I would have thought you could get a proper job if you wanted one.'

Charlie looked amused. 'So I like to loaf around. I told you that and there's nothing wrong with it. Working for a living is vastly overrated!'

Poppy giggled again and realised she was going to be sorry when they sailed tomorrow. Although if he was sailing around the Med, and she was too, maybe their paths might cross again. Maybe she'd offer him her mobile number to make sure they did. It would be a shame to lose track of him altogether. Or maybe that would be a little pushy.

Perhaps she ought to settle for this one date. After all, given the circumstances there was no way this date was going to lead to anything, although if it did she wasn't going to bitch about it.

J ake was sitting in the cockpit of the *Earth Star*, sipping a cool lager and watching the activity on the quayside. He was alone on the boat, the Garvies having gone ashore to explore the little port's one and only nightclub. Solitude was something he usually relished; yachts, even ones the size of the *Earth Star*, were cramped. It was rare you could get away from the others on board, unless you went and shut yourself in your cabin – a luxury denied the skipper until they moored each day. But despite the solitude, the gentle lapping of the waves against the stones of the harbour wall, the hypnotic plink-plink of the halyards against the masts of the surrounding vessels and the soporific rocking of the *Earth Star*, Jake felt tense.

Along the harbour he could see Poppy and That Man laughing and joking. Charlie? A right Charlie, he thought sourly. What was Poppy doing throwing herself at this bloke? To Jake he looked a completely unprincipled opportunist. As he sipped his beer it didn't cross his mind that he had absolutely no reason whatsoever on which to base his judgement. Come to that he had no reason to believe that Poppy was 'throwing herself' at Charlie, but he wasn't thinking rationally. He was worried about

Poppy. He didn't trust Charlie as far as he could throw a grand piano. He was too good looking, too perfect, and he'd rocked up in that . . . ship. As far as Jake was concerned Charlie looked exactly like the sort of bloke who might try to get Poppy drunk, then shag her and dump her. Poppy didn't need that sort of bloke in her life. No way.

Angrily he drained his beer and crushed the can. It was none of his business, he told himself. Poppy was an adult. But another voice told him it was. He was her boss; he had a duty of care. Besides, on a personal level, he thought she was a nice kid and he didn't want to see her wind up getting hurt. He contemplated going below and fetching another beer but decided that he needed a walk. Exercise – that was the ticket.

He stomped down the gangplank to the shore, making the yacht rock quite markedly. The boat looked as jumpy as he felt. He strode along the quay, ignoring the vendors selling barbecued corncobs, the girls flogging friendship bracelets, the artists offering instant caricatures and the taverna owners proffering menus for him to peruse. He was wound up and disturbed by his anxiety for Poppy and determined not to find anything to enjoy in the velvet-dark night, filled with laughter and delicious smells.

There was only one possible route to take along the harbour and Jake was engrossed in his thoughts. He'd left the yacht with no destination in mind and he was still so focused on his concerns and antipathy for Charlie that he just stamped along completely oblivious of his surroundings.

'Hi, Jake. Coming to join us?'

He stopped in his tracks and snapped back to reality as

Poppy's voice cut into his brain. 'Sorry?' What had she said? She repeated herself as Jake saw, from the corner of his eye, That Man stand up and extend a hand.

'You must be Jake – nice to meet you. I'm Charlie.'

Trained in good manners, Jake shook it, but reluctantly and hesitantly.

'Drink?' offered Charlie. 'To show you that there are no hard feelings about what your guests did to my boat.'

Jake bridled. *His* boat? He didn't think so. Huh! But Poppy was shooting him a warning glance. He hadn't realised his animosity was quite so obvious. Perhaps he'd better be a little more amenable. After all, litigation – or the lack of it – was still dependent on Charlie's sorting things out.

'Come on, Jake,' Poppy said meaningfully. 'Join us. It's been a long day and you look as if you could do with some down-time.'

Jake sighed. Truth was he really didn't want to join them and he didn't think Poppy wanted him to either. Judging from the body language he'd witnessed from the boat, she was getting on just fine with Charlie, despite his personal misgivings about the man. The last thing she probably wanted was him playing gooseberry. He'd left the boat to go for a walk and sitting here on the quayside wasn't going to give him any exercise. He wondered if the invitation had been issued out of pity. Poor old Jake No-Mates, let's buy him a drink.

'Come on, Jake. Take a seat,' Poppy insisted, pulling a chair out for him and motioning for him to take it.

Not to would look churlish. And maybe he'd read Poppy wrong. Maybe she really did want him there, wanted him to be on hand in case Charlie came on too strong. That thought made him make up his mind.

'Why not?' he said, trying to sound cheery. 'But let me get these.' He attracted the waiter's attention and ordered two more lagers and Poppy's spritzer. 'Cheers,' he said, still not entirely sure why he'd accepted their invitation. He tried to look happy but judging by the look Poppy shot him he hadn't managed a convincing act. 'Problem?' he challenged.

'No, nothing.' But she dropped her gaze and the conversation went no further. The three sipped their drinks in silence. That's what you get when there's a gooseberry around, thought Jake, wishing now he'd kept on walking. The saying about a fart in a space suit floated into his mind. Perhaps he ought to make an effort with some small talk to lighten the atmosphere.

'So, Charlie, is it a girl in every port for you?' He felt a sharp pain in his shin as Poppy kicked him hard under the table. What was that all about?

'Well, I've never been sure if that's cheaper or more expensive than putting a port into every girl. As I don't drink port I have no idea how much it would cost.'

Was that a joke? thought Jake. He forced a smile. 'I suppose it depends on whether you have to buy the girls or just the port.'

This time she kicked him so hard he had to bite his lip. He shot her a hurt look. What had put a spike up her arse? He was only trying to make conversation.

'Ha ha,' replied Charlie mirthlessly. He turned his attention to Poppy. 'Any idea where you're off to tomorrow?'

Jake jumped in before she could answer. 'Well, as it's a charter we leave the decision up to the guests. I think they want to take a look at Corfu.' For some reason he just wanted to get some distance between the *Earth Star* and Charlie.

'Oh, is it decided?' Poppy chipped in, sounding surprised. As well she might. She knew as well as he did no decision had been made when she'd left.

'Yes,' lied Jake. 'They finally came to a decision.'

Poppy shrugged. Well, the clients were king.

Of course she was ignorant of the fact that they'd done nothing of the sort but Jake was pretty certain he could persuade the Garvies, out of Poppy's hearing, that Corfu would be a good place to potter round for a couple of days, especially as they'd already shown an interest in Kavos. And if Charlie was still berthed here, over on the mainland, waiting for Mr Filthy-Rich to turn up, he wouldn't be able to hang around them any more.

Jake didn't address the fact that it was Charlie's hanging around Poppy that he minded, not hanging around 'them'. He blanked from his mind that it was obvious that Poppy found Charlie attractive and the sentiment seemed to be reciprocated. As far as he was concerned he just wanted to get the *Earth Star* back out to sea as soon as possible the next morning – nothing more, nothing less.

And in the meantime he would have a drink with Poppy and Charlie because they'd invited him and he had nothing better to do. And drink he did – heavily. He didn't notice the frustrated glances that passed between Charlie and Poppy, or the hints they dropped that they'd delayed Jake from his walk for quite long enough. Poppy became moodier and moodier, and her bad temper permeated the atmosphere around their table until even Jake was aware of it, despite his alcoholic daze.

They returned in stony silence to the *Earth Star* at around half past eleven, Poppy storming angrily along the quay, Jake stumbling along in her wake.

As far as Poppy was concerned Jake was a moody prick who was hell-bent on spoiling her fun. She regretted ever asking him to join her and Charlie at the taverna. Until he'd pitched up she and Charlie had been having fun; he'd been a laugh and he made her feel good, and what was so wrong with that? But she'd seen Jake striding along the quay, looking rather sad and lonely, and she'd asked him to join them on an impulse.

'Why?' Charlie had hissed at her. And ten minutes later she was wondering the same thing herself, as all he'd done for those first few minutes, and then for the entire evening, was to put a damper on everything. He'd even made a couple of snide comments about Charlie's boat and his unknown boss. What right had he to do that? She was surprised Charlie hadn't lamped him one. She would have done if she'd been a bloke.

She stamped up the gangplank, making the vessel rock at its mooring. She unlocked the hatch in the cockpit and stormed down into the saloon and through the galley to her cabin. Pointedly she shut the door without wishing Jake goodnight, although he was unlikely to notice given how much beer he'd shipped.

He was behaving more like her minder than a work colleague, she thought angrily as she slipped off her deck shoes, although a proper minder wouldn't get pissed or take against her choice of friend.

Oh, for heaven's sake! What had got into him? She sighed heavily and began to undress. If he was going to be like this for the rest of the season it was going to be a nightmare.

Her mood wasn't improved when the Garvies arrived back en masse at around two in the morning and woke her up again, yelling and stumbling and crashing into things. Obviously they'd been enjoying a drink too. And at least they had *enjoyed* their drink – unlike some she could think of.

Her cabin had grown stuffy and she had a raging thirst – she shouldn't have snarfed all those olives. By the time she'd opened a porthole and got herself a glass of cold water she was so wide awake that she knew sleep wasn't going to return readily. She lay in her bunk and wondered if she ought to get hold of head office and ask for a transfer. If Jake was going to go off on one every time she had a little fun, she didn't think she'd be able to cope. What was she supposed to do? Sit around the yacht every evening with a bit of tapestry or a book and be all demure and well behaved? It might suit some people but it wasn't going to float her boat. The only thing that made up for the endless loo-cleaning, cooking, scrubbing, swabbing, tidying and all-round dogsbodying was the chance to let off steam or have a run ashore once she'd finished dinner. If Jake was going to get all snarky about her social life . . . well, it didn't bear thinking about.

No. If that was how things were going to be Poppy would rather sack working on the *Earth Star* and get another job within the company. Surely there had to be another cook/cleaner they could transfer into her place. She'd go back to being a flotilla host if that was the only way out. Poppy chewed irritatedly on the corner of a fingernail as she considered her options and decided that she didn't have many. Stay or go. Take it or leave it.

Well, perhaps she was overreacting. Maybe his mood was just a one-off. She sure hoped so. Angrily she turned on her side, banged her pillow with her fist to fluff it up and shut her eyes. Maybe the answer would come to her while she was sleeping.

Her mood was little improved when she woke but she didn't have time to dwell on the previous evening as preparing breakfast for ten people was a job that needed concentration. She bustled round the galley, slicing fruit, opening pots of yogurt, getting the honey and butter out of the fridge, and making tea and coffee. When Jake passed her to go up on deck she ignored him but was pleased to note that he looked slightly hungover.

Serve him right, she thought sourly.

Breakfast was ready before Ronnie and Mick appeared, looking as bad as Jake, if not worse. Well, no surprise there, given the racket they'd made coming back on board. Poppy thought that it probably hadn't been just her who got woken up by their return – half the boats in the port must have heard the Garvie clan carousing and shrieking as they swayed up the gangplank in the small hours.

'Good evening?' she asked, deliberately loud and chirpy. She knew when to stop drinking and she had little time for those who didn't.

Ronnie rewarded her with a groan as she lowered herself into her seat at the dining table.

'Would you prefer it if I were to serve breakfast upstairs in the cockpit?' asked Poppy.

'The light's too bleedin' bright in 'ere, never mind outside,' complained Ronnie. Mick couldn't even bring himself to speak but just reached for the orange juice.

'What 'ave you and Jaky got planned for today?' asked Ronnie as she spooned some yogurt into a bowl and then stared at it as if she was wondering what to do with it.

'Jake said he thought you wanted to go to Corfu.'

Ronnie shrugged. 'Do we, Mick? Frankly, a lot of yesterday is a bit blurred. We might 'ave said anything.'

Mick raised his bloodshot eyes and gazed at Ronnie. 'The only place I want to go is back to bed.' And with a stifled belch he abandoned his orange juice and fled the saloon.

'I think I might have a bit of a lie-down too,' said Ronnie, leaving her yogurt and tottering after him.

By ten o'clock it was obvious none of the rest of the party was even going to attempt breakfast so Poppy cleared away. Jake wandered into the saloon, wiping his hands on an oily rag.

'Given the guests food poisoning already?' he joked. His hangover, although bad, obviously wasn't as catastrophic as the others'.

'Very funny,' she snapped back.

'What's got your goat? You were in a vile mood last night and you're no better this morning. Wrong time of the month?'

Poppy just narrowed her eyes and shook her head before she swept into the galley, taking with her the mostly untouched food. She'd got in a vile mood last night thanks to him, but he was obviously too thick to work it out. Men!

She heard him go down to the engine room in the bilges. She hoped that the bilge rats, if the yacht accommodated any, wouldn't object to the sudden lowering of the tone in their domain.

She had just finished the washing up and was contemplating whether it was worth doing anything for lunch, given the state of their guests, when she heard the engines start. It seemed that whether the Garvies wanted to or not, they were going to Corfu.

Briefly she thought about nipping up on deck to see if she could catch sight of Charlie and wave him goodbye. But it would antagonise Jake. Which made it an even more attractive idea. For a second or two she stood poised to make a move, but then had second thoughts. She wasn't going to see Charlie again. She sighed. Last night had been fun; well, it had been till Jake had joined them. And she really fancied Charlie, but he'd go back to Syracuse or wherever and she would spend the rest of the summer schlepping round this bit of the Med. What was the point? She gave up on the idea and continued stowing the clean crockery away before returning to the saloon to clean and polish. Again.

Jake had taken the majority of their guests off to Fiskardo on the island of Kefalonia on board the *Earth Star*, while Poppy and Ronnie were left in a tiny cove some miles away with the motor launch and a picnic.

'This is good, innit?' purred Ronnie as she stretched out on the sand and basked like a cat.

Poppy, in the shade of a big beach umbrella, paused in unloading the cool box. 'Well, it beats working for a living, that's for sure.'

Ronnie grinned at her. ''Ow can you say that? You work your bleedin' socks off every day. We've been on board over a week and I think I've seen you relax about once.'

'But I enjoy cooking so it's not really work. And anyway, how hard is today going to be?' She waved a hand at the limpid turquoise water and the minute, deserted beach.

Ronnie propped herself up on her elbows to admire the scene. 'You're right. Except that you're goin' to give me another swimming lesson in a minute, and that's going to be a mission, innit?'

'Absolutely not. You've nearly cracked it and Mick is

going to be so impressed in a couple of days when you power through the water.'

Ronnie screeched with laughter. 'Power through the water? I don't think so. My doggy paddle might get a bit faster though. Might even get to beat some mutt in a race. But *power*?' Ronnie laughed again.

Poppy snapped the lid back on the cool box and draped a clean tea towel over a plate of filled rolls. 'How about a quick dip before we eat?'

'Yeah, let's. I'm done to a crisp.' Ronnie looked down at her rotund, mahogany stomach. 'It always pays to get ahead with a tan before you come away, don't it? Hours I spent on a sunbed before we came out here and look at the colour I've got now.'

'Great,' agreed Poppy, although in reality she thought that Ronnie's skin looked like something that had been stripped off an old leather sofa – all saggy, wrinkled and dark brown. Poppy, who had been in the Med for well over a year and had a warm honey glow to her skin, took pains to try to protect it as much as possible. And Ronnie was the living proof that tans could be too dark. But hey, Ronnie loved her colour so it was no business of Poppy's to pass judgement.

They both tiptoed over the baking sand the ten feet or so to the water's edge, giving the occasional yelp as the soles of their feet fried. They splashed through the lukewarm water till they were up to their waists before plunging in.

'Right,' said Poppy, standing up again and brushing wet hair off her face. 'Off you go.'

Ronnie began thrashing around in the water in a fairly ungainly way, but there was no doubt at all that she was actually swimming. As she got closer to her mentor and reached out a hand to grab her for support Poppy backed away.

'Come on,' she called encouragingly. 'Keep going. You can do it. Remember what I said about kicking with your legs.'

Ronnie's front crawl calmed down a bit at that reminder and it began to look a little more like some recognised stroke. She was swimming with her face held high out of the water, her mouth set in a tight line of concentration.

'You're doing brilliantly,' Poppy encouraged her. 'Just fantastic. A few more strokes and I'll let you have lunch.'

'Good,' gasped Ronnie breathlessly.

Poppy made her swim about twenty metres before she caught her hands. 'Well done. I am so proud of you!'

Ronnie stood up in the water, panting heavily, a huge smile plastered across her face. 'It's all thanks to you, my girl. I couldn't 'ave done it wivout you.'

'Rubbish. All I did was give you a bit of a push and some encouragement. I reckon we deserve some lunch now.'

A movement at the mouth of the bay caught Poppy's eye as the two women began to wade out of the water. She turned to look and Ronnie followed her gaze,

'Blimey, 'ow pretty is that? I must get a picture of that,' said Ronnie in awestruck tones as she ran to grab her mobile.

Sliding into their bay came a little Contessa 33 with a yellow, white and green spinnaker billowing pregnantly from the mast. The helmsman brought the bow round into the wind and the mainsail and the spinnaker both fluttered and drooped as they lost the breeze. As they watched, the sails were lowered and then there was a splash aft as the helmsman threw the anchor overboard. Silently and gracefully the yacht stopped.

''Ave you seen some of the snaps I've taken of the *Earth Star*?' Ronnie asked.

'Show me.'

Ronnie handed over her phone and Poppy flicked through the album. 'Some of these are brilliant. You couldn't send the last couple to my phone? I'd love to have copies.'

'Sure. Gimme your number.'

Poppy reeled it off while Ronnie tapped it into her keypad. A few seconds later Poppy's mobile bing-bonged as the pics arrived. She flicked it open and checked out the results. 'Great. Thanks.'

Ronnie stowed her phone away, sat down on her beach towel and gazed at the little sailing boat. 'Do you think 'e's stopped here for a swim?'

'Probably.' Poppy pointed to an arm of rocks that formed one side of the bay. 'The snorkelling's pretty good over there.'

'So he won't come this way?'

'Why? You not keen on the idea of sharing this beach with anyone either?'

'Nah, you're dead wrong there, my girl, not if it's some tasty Greek geezer in tight Speedos,' said Ronnie with a dirty giggle.

A loud splash out in the bay caught their attention. Whoever had piloted the little sailing vessel into the bay had dived over the side and was now swimming strongly towards them.

Poppy sighed. 'This is our beach,' she muttered. 'We were here first.'

'Blimey, you've never holidayed at Southend then, 'ave you? Beach to yourself? Fat chance! However, I need to have a slash and I don't fancy doing it if there's a stranger on the beach. I think I'll nip into the bushes before he gets here. You don't mind, do you, Poppy?'

Poppy shook her head. 'Be my guest.'

Ronnie bustled off into the dense scrub at the back of the beach and disappeared from view.

The man swam efficiently and smoothly through the calm sea and it was only a minute or so before he hauled himself upright and waded out of the shallow water.

'Hello,' he called. 'I hope you don't mind me joining you?'

'Bloody hell,' squeaked Poppy as her insides whooshed with pleasure at seeing him again. 'Charlie,' she yelled back down the beach. 'What the hell are you doing here?'

'Looking for you,' he shouted back.

Charlie padded up the blazing sand as if he were indifferent to its red-hot temperature and stood in the shade of the umbrella gazing down at Poppy. She felt her innards doing flick-flacks.

'What a surprise,' she said.

'A nice one, I hope,' he said.

Poppy thought so, but his presence, out of the blue, was a bit of a worry. A sickening thought had flashed into her brain. Maybe there was something badly wrong with the huge motor yacht and the owner had sent Charlie to seek her out and drag her back to explain. Or sue her. Her stomach did a rather unpleasant lurch. She needed to know what he was doing there but she didn't want to sound too heavy.

'Is this coincidence,' she asked, 'or are you stalking me?' She hoped her question came across as casual and joky.

'Oh, I'm a stalker, definitely,' responded Charlie, which just made her abdominal problems worse. He grinned at her. 'I saw the *Earth Star* come into Fiskardo harbour but there was no sign of you or the launch. I reckoned you just might be having some time off and picnicking along the coast. As I planned on heading this way anyway I thought

I'd drift along and see if I could find you. I hope you don't mind? I thought maybe I could invite myself to lunch.'

Ah. That was a bit tricky. The answer wasn't really in Poppy's gift. Just at that moment Ronnie appeared out of the undergrowth and began to pick her way back over the sand to their picnic spot. Poppy noticed that a flicker of annoyance crossed Charlie's face. Maybe he'd thought she was on her own. For some reason, Poppy was faintly glad she wasn't. Neither of them was what could be described as properly dressed and Charlie was staring at her body rather obviously.

'Hiya,' Ronnie said, looking from Charlie to Poppy curiously, obviously wondering who Poppy's friend was. Poppy introduced them.

'Charlie is the skipper of that big yacht the kids hit.'

'Oh, blimey. I am so sorry about that.'

'Don't be. The damage – such as it was – is all fixed now. Nothing to worry about.' Charlie smiled at Ronnie. 'No harm done. But I was just asking Poppy if you had a spare crust for a shipwrecked mariner.'

Ronnie guffawed and whisked the tea towel off the rolls. 'Help yourself, there's heaps. Poppy always cooks enough for the air force and the navy, let alone the bleedin' army! And the more the merrier, I always say.'

She offered the food to Charlie and then, flopping back down on the sand, took one herself. 'Got anything to drink in the cool box?' she asked indistinctly through tuna and mayonnaise.

'Beer or wine?' offered Poppy. 'Didn't know which you'd prefer.'

'Chuck us a beer. Got a blinding thirst on me. All that swimming, I shouldn't wonder.'

Poppy pulled a Mythos out of the box and flipped off the cap with an opener. She passed the cold bottle to Ronnie, who rolled the chilled glass across her forehead before she took a long pull at it.

'Gawd, did I need that.' She sighed contentedly.

Charlie eyed her beer. 'I don't suppose there's another one of those in the cool box?'

'You'll 'ave to ask Poppy. She's in charge of supplies.'

Silently Poppy fished one out for their guest. She handed it to Charlie along with the bottle opener and rummaged around in the box again to produce a bottle of mineral water. 'I'm on duty, so you don't have to share the beers with me too, and there's plenty more.'

'Tough luck.' Ronnie raised her bottle at Poppy. 'Here's to the best swimming teacher in the world.'

Poppy grinned back. 'Thanks. Actually, I thought it was about time we went on to the next phase. We'll have a go at snorkelling this afternoon, if you'd like to try it.'

Ronnie nearly choked on her beer. 'What?' she spluttered.

'Truly, it's easy. It's not like scuba diving. All you do is float on the surface of the water and breathe through a tube. It's so simple. Really.' Ronnie looked doubtful.

Charlie nodded. 'She's right. Nothing difficult, honest. Well, this is jolly, I must say. I was expecting to have a lonely sandwich aboard my boat and now – two lovely ladies for company.'

'You can stop yer flannel for starters,' said Ronnie.

Ronnie and Charlie got into a conversation about snorkelling and swimming and the Greek islands round about as they chewed on their rolls and swigged their drinks, but Poppy didn't join in. She was trying to do some sums and either her maths was shit – quite possible – or

Charlie was lying. Because the way she worked things out, given the lack of wind, not enough time had passed since the *Earth Star* had dropped her and Ronnie off here for it to get to Fiskardo and be spotted by Charlie before he set off in the Contessa 33 and sailed to their beach. It really, really didn't add up.

Or maybe it was her maths. Or not. And anyway, did it matter? She was trying to find a problem where there wasn't one.

Ronnie was laughing at some comment Charlie had made, so Poppy pushed the puzzle into a recess of her mind and concentrated on her lunch. Even though she had put the picnic together herself, she had to admit it was remarkably good.

'So how come you're sailing that tiddly little boat and not swannin' around in the big ship?' asked Ronnie with her usual candour.

'The crew arrived out a few days ago so I'm not needed any more. I thought I'd kick around this neck of the woods for a week or so more and I rented that little beauty to do it in. For a bloke on his own it's plenty big enough. And besides, it's proper sailing. Being on that other boat is like being on a cruise ship, I would imagine – not that I've ever been on a cruise.'

'I always wanted to do one,' said Ronnie pensively. She told Charlie that that was what she thought this holiday was going to be about. 'When Mick said we'd be sailing round the Med I never fort he meant with sails!' She shrieked at her own gaffe. 'But never mind, eh? Poppy and Jake are giving us a fine old time and that boat has every mod con. Well, apart from the toilets.' She wrinkled her nose.

'You'll get used to them,' said Charlie.

'Never,' said Ronnie. 'I bet that big ship you were on had proper toilets.'

'Well, yes.'

'Then next year I'm going to get Mick to hire one that size.'

Charlie whistled. 'That'll set you back a bob or two.'

'I expect he can afford it.'

'So what does he do?' asked Poppy, realising that she'd never actually asked about the source of Mick's wealth.

'Scrap merchant. Well, dealer really,' said Ronnie. 'There's a lot of truth in that saying "where there's muck there's brass". Ain't we the living proof?'

'You fancy a taste of the high life, then?' said Charlie.

'You bet. Trouble is, Mick's wedded to his business. It's all I can do to get him to take two weeks off in the summer. Can't complain, though. Me and the kids never want for nuffink. He's a good husband is my Mick.'

After lunch they lazed on the sand while their meal went down and then Poppy left the other two chatting idly about this and that and went for an energetic swim across the bay. Surrounded as she was by food all day it was only too easy for the pounds to pile on and she took every opportunity to get some exercise to minimise the damage. As she swam she considered what Charlie had said about seeing the *Earth Star* in Fiskardo and working out that she had gone off on a picnic. And the more she thought about it the more she knew he was fibbing. It wasn't just that the timing didn't add up; there was no way he could have made such a deduction and guessed where to head for. It was an unsettling thought that he must have known exactly where to find her, but how? She decided to tackle him when she got back to the beach, but he was just leaving as she strolled up the sand and the moment was lost.

After he'd gone Poppy distracted herself from her thoughts by giving Ronnie another swimming lesson and persuading her to try putting a mask on and looking under the water.

Nervously Ronnie had a go, standing chest deep in the sea and bobbing down. Her face had only been under the water for a second when she bobbed up again.

'I saw a fish!' she shrieked. 'A big one. Honest!'

Poppy laughed. 'I told you it was another world. Have another look.'

After about half an hour Ronnie had progressed to floating on her stomach in water so shallow she could touch the bottom with her fingertips and gazing at the sea bed and the life beneath the waves for as long as she could hold her breath. She had refused the snorkelling tube but Poppy was sure she would be using it before the holiday was over. Maybe she'd be able to take Ronnie to some more interesting coastline to see fire worms and sea urchins and maybe even an octopus or two. She hoped so. If anything would get Ronnie completely relaxed about swimming she thought an experience like that ought to do it.

It was getting towards teatime when the *Earth Star* sailed gracefully round the point and hove to. By the time Poppy and Ronnie had puttered back to it and climbed on board it was time for Poppy to rush off to the galley to start getting the guests' dinner ready. Through the hatch she could hear the group exchanging their news of the day over cold beers and iced cocktails. Ronnie, who had finally come clean about learning to swim, was full of the fact that she had actually looked about underwater with a mask on her face, although she hadn't yet tried doing it with the snorkelling tube.

'Why not, Mum?' said Lynette. 'It's easier when you can breathe.'

'I'll do it my way, thank you, miss. I want to go at my own pace.'

'Well, suit yourself,' said her daughter, who then proceeded to launch into an account of the delights of Fiskardo.

As Poppy chopped and sliced, seared and steamed, she noticed that Ronnie hadn't mentioned Charlie's visit. Maybe the excitement of the snorkelling had put it out of her head. She was faintly grateful. Given the way Jake had behaved when they'd had that drink together a few days previously she didn't think that a reminder that Charlie was still around would be either politic or tactful.

When Poppy came up on deck to help Jake with berthing the *Earth Star* at Agia Efimia, down the coast from Fiskardo, she paid no attention to the other yachts moored around them. She bustled about tightening the mooring lines and getting the gangplank across to the quay while a few tourists, out late, watched the activity with mild curiosity. When the job was done she intended to retreat below decks again to finish tidying up the kitchen and then hit the hay. The Garvies were all set to go ashore for a late night drink but Poppy, despite a day lazing on a beach, was tired. Cooking while the yacht was sailing was always tricky and since she and Ronnie had re-joined the boat she hadn't had a chance to sit down. She'd eaten her own dinner on the run in the kitchen and the thought of lying in her bunk and letting her eyes close was incredibly enticing.

'Hey, Poppy? Over here.' Next to them was a Contessa 33 and on its deck was Charlie. Her stomach did back flips. The trouble was she couldn't quite work out if it was because his knowledge of her whereabouts was unsettling, or just total pleasure at seeing him again.

'Charlie!' Keep it light, she told herself. 'What a surprise, and twice in one day. Are you following me?' She said it with a smile but it was a bit . . . odd.

'As I was moored here first,' said Charlie, 'I think you might be following me.'

Ah. She hadn't thought of that. She shrugged. Fair point. Of course it was just coincidence. Jake had suggested they come here, the Garvies had agreed, and now here they were. All of them. And as the little port was one of Kefalonia's most beautiful it was a very likely coincidence.

'Fancy a drink?' offered Charlie. 'I owe you for that beer at lunchtime.'

Poppy hesitated.

'You again,' said Jake ungraciously, making an appearance from the bow where he'd been stowing sails.

'Hi, Jake. And nice to see you too.' Charlie, who had picked up on Jake's attitude, said it with a smile that didn't reach his voice.

That decided Poppy; if Jake was going to behave like an arse, then she was having none of it. 'I'd love a beer. May I come aboard?'

Charlie stepped to one side to allow Poppy access from the quay on to the deck and then down into the cockpit.

'You're welcome too, Jake.'

Jake looked as though he'd rather dig his own eyes out with a rusty penknife. He muttered an almost inaudible refusal and disappeared below deck.

Poppy sat in the tiny cockpit – so different from the *Earth Star*'s – and watched Charlie move into the cabin, ducking under the hatch. A few seconds later he re-emerged with a couple of brown bottles. He flicked them open and handed one to Poppy.

'Cheers,' he said, taking a swig. He sat down opposite her. 'How's it going?'

'Fine. Same old same old. The guests have fun. Jake and I work our socks off. We're sailing, doing what we love, so obviously don't need paying a proper wage.'

'But it has to be better than being stuck in an office.'

'Says a guy who doesn't look as though he can even spell office let alone work in one.'

'Yeah, well . . . And I have worked in an office.'

'Doing what?'

'Accounts, mainly.'

'You? An accountant?'

'Someone's got to do it.'

Poppy considered her companion. Playboy, lothario, loafer – yes. Accountant – never.

Jake finished all his duties for the day and walked down the gangplank on to the quay. He could hear Poppy and Charlie chatting and laughing and for some reason the sound began to wind him up. He tried to reason with himself. Why on earth should it? She was a free agent. They were colleagues, that was all. But it didn't help. And Charlie was probably harmless. He was just being paranoid about Charlie and Poppy.

He walked along the harbour till he was out of earshot and sat on a mooring bollard to admire the warm, starlit darkness. Noise drifted across to him from the sea front, which was thronged with tourists and holidaymakers. Bouzouki music from one of the many tavernas was just audible over the sounds coming from the boats and the slap of the waves lapping against the hulls, and the air was heavy with the smell of ozone, seaweed, roasting corncobs and fish. The familiar sights, sounds and smells of Agia Efimia calmed him and his tension eased.

So what if Poppy had a bit of a fling with this Charlie chap? He didn't want her. Actually, he knew that wasn't strictly true; Jake was attracted to Poppy but he'd decided some years back that he and women had no future. Where relationships were concerned Jake didn't dare risk another involvement. The only two women he'd really cared about had wound up dead, he thought bitterly. He wasn't going to get close to anyone else and go through that pain again. No way. Better to end up alone than risk another tragedy. And he wasn't going to admit to himself that he cared too much for Poppy to put her in any sort of jeopardy by tempting providence a third time.

Jake got up and began to stroll eastwards away from the main town, past the busy tavernas and their enticing smells, past a group of drunk British girls in too-short skirts and too much make-up, past the closed bakery and round the corner to the mole that protected the little harbour from the sea. Here the wide pavement was separated from the jumble of rocks and concrete blocks that formed the sea defence by a low wall.

Jake sat on it and swung his legs over it so his back was to the bright lights of the town. He gazed out to sea and listened to the swish of the gentle waves on the shore and watched the lights of the fishing boats, near the horizon, as the locals searched for octopus and squid. He relaxed further and lay along the wall so as to gaze up at the stars strewn across the sky. A satellite tracked across the Plough and he followed it for a few seconds, his mind drifting, taking him back to a previous occasion when he'd gazed at the stars.

That time he'd been lying in the garden of his home in Norfolk and trying to make sense of his mother's suicide. Even as a little kid he'd known that she wasn't the same as his mates' mums. When he went round to his friends' houses their mums didn't lie on the sofa staring blankly at the TV, or stay in their bedrooms and refuse to cook the boys' teas, so he stopped inviting his friends back – he didn't know how to cope with their awkward questions, and it was easier that way. By the time Jake was at secondary school he'd realised that fending for himself was essential and that he had to fend for her too. Maybe it would have been different if his father had stuck around, but he'd disappeared long before Jake had really had a chance to get to know him and by the time Jake was heading for his GCSEs he didn't have time to think about might have beens and what ifs. School work, caring and shopping took up all his time and he didn't have a moment to try to make sense of his mother. As he got older he gleaned from things people said and stuff he saw on TV that his mum suffered from depression. And depression, he discovered, didn't mean just feeling a bit down in the dumps. What he didn't pick up though was that his mum could have got help, so he struggled on by himself. All he knew was that she was ill and he had to look after her and, in the way that children do, he accepted his life as 'normal' because it was all he'd ever known. And because his situation was normal, as he saw it, there didn't seem any need to talk about it.

Looking back he ought to have cried for help; he ought to have told someone what was going on, and when it all went horribly wrong he blamed himself for not doing so. If he had maybe his mum would still be alive.

The week he finished school, when for once he went out with friends to celebrate the end of his exams, she filled her pockets with stones and walked into the river. She left him a note saying that now he was old enough to get a job he didn't need her any more and he'd be better off without her. She didn't say she loved him and she didn't say why she chose to end her life, so Jake blamed himself. And he'd been blaming himself ever since.

It was about eight years later that he began to move on. He had a job in Norwich which kept him fed and housed, and at the weekends he escaped from the mundane drudgery of work to the freedom and friendship of his local sailing club. In that time he had risen from being an enthusiastic amateur to become one of the club's best instructors, although even his staunchest supporters wouldn't have voted for him in a Mr Conviviality contest. Solid and safe summed up Jake, and no one would accuse him of being the life and soul of the club.

Until he met Julie. Julie, like him, wanted an escape from the drudgery of the day job and had pitched up one weekend and asked about lessons. He'd been instantly captivated by her. She was fun, lively and vibrant and he'd allowed himself to fall in love with her. When Julie had reciprocated his feelings everyone at the club noticed the transformation in him. Suddenly the man who never seemed to smile was full of bonhomie: he went to the club parties; he was even seen *dancing*. Behind his back a book was started on the likelihood of him and Julie getting married. The odds were incredibly short.

It had been Julie who'd seen the ad inviting applications to make up a crew in the Sail Fast race, a prestigious annual boat race between the country's sailing clubs. They'd applied 'for a laugh' and had been amazed when they'd both been selected. They'd both taken a month's leave to cover the intensive team training prior to the race and the race itself, and the odds for their marriage shortened still further in their absence with another book opened that they would be engaged by the time they returned. It was a cert, said their friends. What could go wrong?

When the storm hit, just off Land's End, a great deal went wrong. First of all half the mainmast was broken off by the terrible winds. With the yacht disabled and the rigging and sails fouling the rest of the gear the yacht was in desperate straits. The entire crew battled to save it as they hacked to clear the debris. In the confusion and chaos no one noticed the small figure in orange foul-weather gear slip on deck and plunge over the side. By the time the cry went up for man overboard the near-hurricane had blown them miles further on and despite a massive air-sea rescue operation Julie was never found.

Seeing Raquel get catapulted over the side of the dinghy when she and her mates had hit the *Wet Dream* amidships had brought the incident back in horrific detail. The strength of the flashback had shaken him more than he cared to think about and he knew it had been one of the reasons why he'd behaved so appallingly and got so horribly drunk that evening when he'd been out with Poppy and Charlie. Not that he'd wanted to confide in Poppy about it all. She didn't need him unloading all his baggage on to her, all the guilt that he still felt, the responsibility he still shouldered.

No one had ever said it was his fault. Accidental death was what the coroner said, but Jake had made up his mind that he was to blame. He should have taken care of Julie. He should have stayed with her. If he'd been more vigilant Julie would still be alive. His friends told him that the idea of joining the Sail Fast race had been Julie's, they insisted that the coroner was right, they repeated time and again that Jake was not responsible for what had happened, but he didn't believe them then and he didn't now.

Someone had once said that grief was the price you pay for love. As he stared up at the stars he wondered what sort of crap philosophy that was. Well, he wasn't risking either love or grief again, so now he kept every woman who crossed his path at as big a distance as he could manage. And Poppy was no exception. He just wasn't going to allow himself to fall for her.

So why was he getting so upset because she was taking an interest in someone else?

They were late setting sail the next morning as, once again, the Garvie family didn't return to the yacht until the early hours. In deference to the groans and mutterings from the various cabins Jake put off their departure until mid-morning and Poppy didn't even bother with breakfast apart from a scratch one for herself and Jake in the galley. Charlie and his little boat had long gone by the time the *Earth Star* was ready to set off with her complement of guests – all hiding massive hangovers behind equally massive sunglasses. Jake's suggestion of a leisurely sail across to the neighbouring island of Ithaca and a day of sailing, sunbathing and some lazy swimming was greeted with a little whimper of relief from Ronnie.

As the yacht got under way Jade's seasickness made an unwelcome, noisy and messy reappearance, fuelled no doubt by her overindulgence the night before. She retired back to her cabin and Poppy was left swabbing the deck. Poppy tried not to mind and to tell herself that this was all part of the job, but she'd had over a week now of clearing up after Ronnie's kids and their friends.

She loved Ronnie to bits; she was warm and funny and always grateful for everything that Poppy did, but her kids . . . 'spoilt brats' was the phrase that sprang to Poppy's mind several times a day. They seemed incapable of picking anything up off the floor, their cabins were shitholes, they never said please or thank you and frankly they treated her like dirt. She knew she was there to look after them but she wasn't their slave. Although she might just as well have been as far as Jade, Lynette, Darren and their friends were concerned.

Angrily Poppy swished the mop over the side and finished sluicing the deck down.

She wasn't paid enough for this. Or for coping with Jake's moodiness.

Maybe she ought to find a better job. Maybe she could get a position on a super-yacht like the one that Charlie had ferried over to the islands. Maybe if she asked Charlie he might be able to fix something for her – after all, everyone said that it wasn't what you knew but who.

With a resolve to get a job with a class of people who didn't habitually vomit on the deck and understood that staff had feelings too, Poppy tipped the bucket of scummy water over the side and took her cleaning kit below deck.

Jake steered the yacht out of the harbour and past the mole that stuck a finger of concrete and rock into the clear blue of the calm Mediterranean; then, with practised deftness, he loosened a couple of ropes and let a winch whirr and two sails billowed from the mast. The yacht heeled over as the hull hissed and scythed through the turquoise sea.

As they left the harbour behind, together with the complication of her third encounter with Charlie, Poppy felt a sense of relief. Charlie was gone; she wasn't going to see him again. She would look after the Garvies for the remainder of their fortnight, and then they would return to base port, clean down, change the bedding, resupply and get new clients on board. Charlie would be a part of the past, just like the Garvies, just like all their previous clients. Life would move on and the previous weeks would blur as the season rolled inexorably on.

Poppy began preparing the next meal. And as she sliced and salted, washed, shredded and drained, Jake tacked the yacht in long lazy zigzags into the headwind en route to Ithaca and their next port. The routine, the motion of the yacht, the swish and slap of the water, calmed her. Hey, maybe this job wasn't so bad after all; she could cope with Jake, and lots of people got seasick.

When Poppy re-emerged on deck with Pimm's, homemade canapés and a tray of plates and napkins, the Garvies were all looking much perkier. Even Jade had lost her pasty hue and was sitting up in the cockpit flicking through a magazine.

Poppy put her laden tray on the table in the cockpit and invited the guests to help themselves.

'Cor, these are nice, ain't they?' said Ronnie as she bit into one of Poppy's nibbles.

Jade, having lost anything that remained of her previous night's dinner, was now famished. She cast her magazine aside on the seat next to her and tucked in.

'Lee-ho,' called Jake as he prepared to come about again. Poppy watched as the boom swung over her head and the sail refilled with a slap and a crack. The angle of the deck shifted markedly as the big boat changed tack and the tray of goodies slid across the table and lodged against the fiddle on the opposite edge as the boat heeled over sharply.

The wind, now from the other quarter, caught Jade's magazine and flicked it off the seat. Poppy automatically bent down to retrieve it as it flapped about on the deck.

Surely she was mistaken. She looked at the picture on the open page closely and knew with absolute certainty that she wasn't. Why on earth would Charlie have his picture in a glossy goss mag? And why on earth had the mag wanted to print a snap of this random guy on some sunny sea front? Trying not to look too obvious, Poppy read the caption. 'Charles Pencombe, charmer, playboy, son and heir of multi-millionaire Philip Pencombe, founder of the Wing Travel empire, is pictured in Syracuse, Sicily, where his father's yacht is based in winter. Does Daddy know Charlie is about to make off in his pride and joy?' And below was a picture of the *Wet Dream*.

11

Weakly she folded the magazine shut and handed it to Jade.

'You don't want this to blow away,' she said, trying to sound normal.

Jade ignored her and the proffered mag as she continued to stuff tiny vegetable samosas and delicate vol au vents into her mouth, so Poppy muttered something about taking the magazine below deck where it would be safe, and disappeared. Seeing no one was around, she high-tailed into the galley with it and slapped it on the counter. It took her a few seconds to riffle through the pages to find the picture again; no, she absolutely wasn't mistaken.

She sat down heavily on one of the stools and thought about her new-found knowledge. So she'd been dated by a multi-millionaire. Well, get that! She wondered why he hadn't told her. Maybe he'd wanted to be sure she liked him for himself and not his millions. As if she was *that* shallow – huh! Although there was no denying that knowing about his bank balance did add a certain *je ne sais quoi* to his allure.

No wonder, she thought wryly, he was so certain that no one was going to kick up a stink about the slight damage her guests had inflicted on the *Wet Dream*. Of course he knew how the owner was going to feel about it. She sighed, and wondered if she would have acted differently with him if she'd known who he really was; been a bit more welcoming, a bit less suspicious.

She did feel a little cheated, though. It would have been nice to know she was having a drink with a multi-millionaire. Oh well, too late now. Her chance acquaintance with him was over; they'd both sailed off in their separate boats that morning, presumably for separate destinations, and her chances of seeing him again were slim to non-existent.

She shrugged. And so what? Guys like him didn't go for girls like her. Except . . . a little voice in her subconscious told her that he *had* seemed interested in her. What if she'd played her cards differently?

Absolutely not, another bit of her brain argued. She was just a bit of friendly totty who spoke the same language he did. Back in Monaco, or wherever the rich and famous hung out, he probably wouldn't give her a second glance.

She folded the magazine shut and took it through to the saloon. Charlie had flitted into her life and had, just as quickly, flitted out again. She dumped the periodical on the table and went back into the galley to carry on with making lunch.

She was halfway through slicing tomatoes for a salad when the words 'Wing Travel empire' slid into her mind. Slowly she put down her knife and leant against the work surface. Didn't they . . . Weren't they . . . Wing and WorldFleet . . . ? She fished around in her brain for the information she was sure lurked in there somewhere, but nothing surfaced. Leaving the galley she made her way up on deck and over to the wheel where Jake was braced, holding the heeling yacht firmly on her course.

'Want a go at the helm?' Jake offered.

Poppy shook her head, the wind catching her curls and whipping them across her eyes.

'I was just wondering,' she said, her voice raised to be heard over the sound of the waves on the hull and the creaking of the yacht. She paused, not sure if she wanted to voice her concerns to Jake and even less sure of how to gain the information she wanted without arousing his suspicions.

'Wondering what?'

She decided it was better to come straight out with her question rather than try to dress it up in some sort of concealing guise. 'Is WorldFleet part of Wing Travel?'

Jake took his eye off the horizon and looked at Poppy. 'Why do you ask?'

'No reason really. I was just wondering.'

'Well, they are, although there's a rumour that the parent company is planning to dispose of some of the assets – WorldFleet being one of the bits earmarked for sale.'

'Oh.'

'It probably won't make much difference to the likes of us, down at the bottom of the food chain.'

'No,' said Poppy tonelessly. So Charlie was effectively her and Jake's boss, or for the time being anyway, until Wing sold off WorldFleet if the rumour was true. She wondered what Jake's reaction would be if he knew. Probably best not to tell him. She didn't think he'd react well to finding out that he'd been rude to Pencombe's son or that she had had a multi-millionaire getting friendly with her.

So had Charlie been taking an interest in her because of her connection with WorldFleet or on her own merits?

Had he cosied up to her to find out what she thought about her working conditions and the company? Poppy groaned as she tried to remember anything she might have said about her employers. She remembered she'd bitched about the rates of pay. Probably not a sackable offence, and she really couldn't think of anything else derogatory – thank goodness.

Beside her Jake was busy trimming the sails and adjusting the course slightly so he didn't notice how engrossed Poppy was in her thoughts, for which she was grateful. Her mind drifted back to those encounters. Of course, as the boss's son, he'd have easily been able to find out the whereabouts of any of the charter yachts at any given time, as the skippers had to radio their itineraries to the shore base each morning before setting off. So at least that explained all their 'accidental' meetings – well, after the first one, which really even Charlie and all his millions couldn't have engineered.

'So now you know about Wing and WorldFleet are you planning on making an offer for the outfit?' joked Jake, the yacht now sailing to his exacting standards.

Poppy shook her head automatically. She had a lot to think about. Was Charlie's interest in her genuine, and if so why? If not, why had he been following them around the Med?

She became aware of the look on Jake's face. 'You still haven't told me why the sudden curiosity?' he said.

'Oh?' She hoped she sounded airy and careless. 'I just read something about Wing Travel in some glossy mag of Jade's and it set me wondering.'

'What did the article say? Anything about Wing's plans?'

'Not a sausage,' said Poppy, glad she could be honest answering this question. 'It was just a gossip piece about Ch—' She'd been about to say Charlie but just managed to get her tongue to skid to a halt in time. 'About charter yachts.'

'Right.'

'So it made me wonder if Wing and WorldFleet had a connection.' To her relief, Jake seemed to accept this. 'Anyway, this won't get lunch made.' She returned below deck, retrieving the magazine from the saloon table as she went and chucking it in the gash can. There was no way she wanted any of the others spotting the picture and working out just who Charlie was. With the magazine in the bin there was every chance that Charlie's real identity would remain hidden. She hoped that Jade wouldn't notice its loss or, if she did, would put it down to one of her family's snaffling it, or assume that it had just blown overboard, which it jolly nearly had.

It was late in the day when they finally sailed in to their destination and tied up on the quay. As soon as the *Earth Star* was secure Poppy examined their fellow voyagers berthed in the harbour. She tried to tell herself that she wasn't scanning the boats for the little Contessa, but she was incapable of such monstrous self-delusion, especially when she felt a rush of cold disappointment that nothing resembling Charlie's boat was in the port. She'd nursed a vague hope that she had been the attraction, and if he'd been in this port she could have been certain of it. But he wasn't there. So had he been shadowing the *Earth Star* to find out how she and Jake had been running it? If she was honest with herself that had to be the likely explanation.

But she knew she was kidding herself trying to dismiss

him from her life so easily. Not if the way her insides turned to mush every time she thought about him was anything to go by. Was it the fact that he was good looking or that she'd always felt he was faintly dangerous? She knew he would only have to snap his fingers for her to fall for him in a very big way.

She bustled about, automatically doing the things she did every evening: preparing cocktails, putting out canapés, getting dinner on the go, anything to keep herself occupied and to stop her mind from wandering to Charlie Pencombe and her desire to know whether or not he had been interested in her at all, or whether it had been all about the *Earth Star*. Had she been just a means to an end or had she been more than that? She longed to know.

Trying to keep her brain from imploding, she imagined him as a businessman in a suit. After all, he'd said something about being an accountant, and how dull was that? Which brought her back to money and millions. You'd need to be good with figures just to read the bank statements – all those noughts!

From her cabin next to the galley she heard the tinny warble of Rod Stewart's 'Sailing'. She wondered who could be phoning her as she dashed to grab her mobile before she missed the call. Flipping it open, she checked the caller ID.

'Hi, Mum,' she said. 'How's things?'

There was a pause which Poppy put down to the distance of the connection. Then she heard her mum sob.

'It's your dad. He's terribly ill. You must come home.'

Poppy sank on to her bed. 'Wh-what?' Her insides went into freefall. Her dad, her lovely, hearty, healthy dad, was ill.

'He's had a stroke. He's really bad.'

'Oh my God,' said Poppy, feeling giddy with the shock. 'Of course I'll come home. I'll get on to it right away. I'm sure something can be fixed. Is he in hospital?'

'In intensive care. He was rushed in this morning. Oh, Poppy, I found him collapsed in the cellar. It was awful. I thought he was dead but then I found a pulse.' Poppy could hear from the wobble in her mother's voice that she was still terribly shocked at what had happened. 'I've just got back from the hospital now but only to grab some things. The staff here are being wonderful and Dan is going to run me back into Truro in a minute.'

No surprise that Dan was being a rock for her mother, thought Poppy. Dan had worked at the pub for as long as she could remember and was a friend as much as an employee. He'd make sure her mum was okay and that she didn't have to worry about the business. Which was a comfort to Poppy stuck, as she was, miles away. 'Look, it may take a little while to sort things at this end but I'll do everything I can to be home as soon as humanly possible.'

'Okay, love, I know you will. I just think it's important that you should be here in case . . .'

Poppy blinked back tears. She knew what her mother didn't dare say. 'You'll give Dad my love, won't you? I'll be there to do it myself just as soon as I can. And phone me if . . .'

'I will. I've got to go now, Dan's waiting.'

In a daze Poppy closed her phone and went up on deck. Instantly Jake could see something was wrong.

'What is it, Poppy? You're as white as a sheet.'

'I've just had my mum on the phone. My dad's had a stroke.' Voicing the awfulness of the news unleashed her emotions. She couldn't hold back her tears any longer and they spilt down her face as huge sobs convulsed her.

Ronnie looked up from the book she was reading in the evening sun. 'Oh my Gawd, Poppy. How terrible. How is he?' She dropped her book and got up to put an arm round Poppy.

Poppy could barely speak, so she just shook her head.

'He's not . . . ?' said Jake.

'He's in h-h-hospital,' Poppy got out through her sobs. 'I have to get home.'

'Too bleedin' right you do,' said Ronnie. 'Jake, get on the blower to head office and if they say Poppy can't go till she gets replaced you tell them that the Garvies are perfectly happy right here and I can cook if needs be.'

'But—' Poppy started.

'No bleedin' buts. You're needed at home.'

12

The biggest problem, it seemed, was not relieving Poppy of her duties but getting her to Preveza airport. Jake was all for setting sail and trying to take her there as quickly as he could on the *Earth Star* but Sally at the shore base told him to sit tight while they sorted out travel arrangements for Poppy from their end. Meanwhile Poppy was left in limbo, beside herself with anxiety and fraught and frustrated about going nowhere.

Ronnie insisted that Poppy mustn't worry about supper that evening and took all her tribe off the boat to a nearby taverna to eat, leaving Poppy and Jake alone. The trouble was that having nothing to do only made things worse in some ways as she had no distractions to take her mind off her worry. She tried ringing her mum's mobile to get an update and to tell her that she probably wouldn't make it back till the next day but either it was switched off or there was no reception. She rang the pub at Polzeal to see if Dan had heard anything but he didn't know any more than she did.

'Your mum said she'd let me know if anything changes, me 'andsome, so as she hasn't rung . . . Everyone in the pub is wishing him well. And the medics can work miracles these days.'

'Can you tell Mum that I'm having problems getting back? I'm doing my best but I'm stuck on an island and I don't know how I'm going to get to the airport.'

'Don't you worry, just get here when you can. Your mum will understand and there's nothing you can do.'

'Yes, but I want to be there. Supposing . . .'

'Suppose nothing, me flower. Your dad is going to pull through this, you see. He's as strong as an ox.'

But Poppy wasn't convinced by Dan's reassurances and the sick feeling of dread lay leaden in her stomach. She hugged her arms around herself and stared blankly at the bulkhead.

Jake sat despondently on the other side of the saloon table wondering whether he should be doing more to help her. Her despair was palpable and he felt useless and impotent.

'Would you like me to radio the shore base again?'

Poppy shook her head. 'They said they'd be in touch as soon as they heard anything,' she said dully. 'Maybe I should shove some stuff in a bag so I'm ready to go when I get the word.'

Jake nodded. 'That would be a good idea. Do you want a hand?'

Poppy shook her head again and got up listlessly. As she made her way to her cabin Jake slumped in his chair and wondered if Poppy's dreadful situation was something to do with his Medusa touch with women he encountered. Was it his fault that she was now so bitterly upset? Logic told him it was nothing to do with him but he still couldn't shake the feeling that somehow he was responsible.

He went up on deck and stood at the bow of the yacht and stared across the harbour. He could see the occasional flash of phosphorescence, and above the weird purplish gleams and sparks the reflected lights of the village twinkled and glistened on the black, calm sea. The smells and sounds of a holiday resort in full swing drifted over the water. All those happy carefree people had no idea of the private tragedy that was affecting poor Poppy, and yet until that dreadful phone call earlier that evening she'd been as happy and carefree as anyone. How life could turn on a sixpence, he thought. His mobile trilled and he pulled it from his pocket and flipped it open.

'Jake,' said a woman's voice without any greeting. He recognised Sally from the shore base.

'Hi, Sally,' he said.

'Right,' she said. 'I think it's all fixed.' Jake felt a rush of relief. 'There's a launch coming to pick Poppy up. It's the boss's son who's authorised it; he's holidaying in the area. It's on its way but I don't have an ETA, so any time in the next couple of hours. Make sure she's ready and waiting for it. I can't think Mr Pencombe will want to be kept hanging around, especially considering what a huge favour he's doing her. He says he'll take her straight to Preveza airport. A seat on a flight has been arranged for her and I'm told a car has been organised at the other end to get her to the hospital.'

'Good heavens,' said Jake, genuinely stunned. 'That's fantastic.'

'I know,' said Sally shortly. 'Make sure she's got her passport with her, won't you. If everything goes according to plan she'll be back with her family tomorrow morning.'

'I'll go and tell her. She's packing right now.'

'Jake,' said Sally. 'If things are . . . you know . . . tell her we'll send the rest of her kit back. I doubt if she'll want to complete the season. I'll send a replacement out for Poppy as soon as I can. You said the Garvies are being really reasonable about all this.'

'They're being fantastic,' affirmed Jake. 'And I can sort out a couple of meals tomorrow. I'm not completely useless in the kitchen,' he added. Looking after his mother had given him plenty of practice in that department, but Sally didn't need to know that.

After he rang off he went to break the news to Poppy.

'And it's Mr Pencombe's son who has organised all this. You're bloody lucky he's in the area and could pull such fantastic strings. Maybe this is a sign that things are going to be all right after all.'

But Poppy, sitting on her bunk twisting a pair of socks in her hand, barely looked at him. Jake didn't think she'd done much in the way of putting anything in her bag so he took the socks out of her hand and stuffed them in the open holdall.

'Come on, Pops,' he said gently. 'It won't be long before that boat is here. You need to be ready; you can't keep Mr Pencombe waiting. What do you need?'

'Jake.'

'Yes?'

'Mr Pencombe . . .'

'Is being fantastic. You don't expect that sort of treatment from the boss's son, not down at our level.'

'Mr Pencombe . . .'

'Yes?'

'It's Charlie.'

'Charlie?'

Poppy nodded her head. 'I found out earlier today.

Read it in a magazine of Jade's. They had a picture of him along with the *Wet Dream*.'

Jake sat down on the bunk next to Poppy. 'Bloody hell, Pops.'

'I know. It's my day for shocks, isn't it?' She tried to smile bravely but tears sprang to her eyes instead.

Jake put his arm round her and gave her a cuddle, trying to be supportive while he too came to terms with this bombshell. Well, that explained the interest Charlie'd had in the *Earth Star*, although as far as Jake was concerned he was still a slimy git. A rich, slimy git, but a slimy git none the less. But whatever he was, they couldn't keep him waiting.

'Come on, Pops, we've got to get your packing done. What do you need?' he said gently.

'I don't know.'

'Well, enough for a week I would have thought. So – jeans, sweaters, T-shirts, undies. Maybe some stuff in case it's hot in the UK. Unlikely I know in July but still . . .' He smiled weakly at her, willing her to show some sort of animation. The Poppy he had got to know wasn't this shadow, this wraith.

Poppy roused herself enough to drag open a few drawers and start stuffing things in the bag.

'Where's your passport?' said Jake. 'You're going to need that.' Poppy found it wordlessly and shoved it in a side pocket. Jake unhooked a lightweight yellow waterproof jacket off the back of her door and handed it to her. 'And you'll probably need this.' He flashed her a grin but it elicited no response from her. She looked so completely down and drained his heart went out to her.

Despite all his promises to himself about ever getting

close to anyone again he couldn't help himself. He reached his arms out and drew her to him to comfort her. Poppy leant against his chest as if she might draw strength from him while Jake rested his cheek against her hair and willed it to be possible that she could. They stood like that, in silence, the comforter and the comforted, for what seemed an age. Then Poppy drew back.

'Well,' she said, 'I'd better get on. My packing won't finish itself, and you're right, I can't keep Charlie waiting.'

Jake nodded. Holding Poppy had made him feel strong and capable and for those few moments he'd forgotten his vow to keep women out of his life. Cradling Poppy he'd felt needed and . . . useful. And she'd felt so right nestled there. And maybe it had been a good thing. Maybe she had drawn something from him, as she seemed to have recovered a minute flicker of energy and life.

He put the idea out of his mind. What was he thinking of? The poor kid didn't need him; she needed her mum, and her dad to get well. Jake was an irrelevance in her life.

'How about a cup of tea,' he offered, to keep his mind off the feeling of holding her – a feeling that lingered because of its sheer rightness. A feeling he hadn't experienced since Julie had died. A feeling that he now realised he had missed dreadfully.

'Any chance of anything stronger?' Poppy asked with a sad smile that made him want to enfold her again.

'Sure. Gin?'

She nodded. 'That would be lovely. I'll finish here and join you on deck.'

She appeared a few minutes later in the cockpit, in her own clothes and dragging her holdall, still looking pale and sad but less withdrawn.

Jake handed her the drink. She took it and swallowed a large gulp.

'I know drink doesn't solve anything but right now I need something.' She took another sip. 'I left my uniform in my cabin. I thought I may not be able to get back for a while, so . . .'

'You'll be back before the Garvies have to go home. I bet you'll get to the hospital and find your dad sitting up in bed tucking into bacon and eggs.'

Poppy regarded Jake over the rim of her glass. 'Maybe,' she said. 'You'll have to get more salad stuff tomorrow, and we're low on yogurt and orange juice.'

'Don't worry about a thing. I'll cope. You may not believe it, but I'm quite a good cook. I can hold the fort until shore base can find us someone to replace you.'

Poppy shrugged. 'I'm sure you'll be fine.' She sipped at her drink and stared sightlessly at the harbour as tears slipped silently down her cheeks once more.

The throb of a powerful engine made the air vibrate. Poppy looked across the harbour. A large, sleek speedboat was nosing in past the mole. The throaty roar lessened as the skipper throttled back and steered the vessel towards the *Earth Star*.

'I think this may be your lift,' said Jake.

'Ahoy there,' called Charlie as the engine was killed. He picked up the painter from the deck and cast it expertly across to Jake, who caught it neatly and wound it round a cleat before hauling in the speedboat so it rested against the fenders. 'You ready, Poppy? I asked Sally to radio ahead to tell you about the arrangements. Also I thought it only fair that she told you it was going to be me coming to get you.'

'Well, she told us Mr Pencombe's son was going to pitch up,' said Jake. 'Luckily, Poppy had seen something about you in a glossy magazine this afternoon and already knew exactly who you were. I think we'd be in a state of shock if she hadn't.' He tried to keep the animosity out of his voice but he wasn't sure he'd succeeded.

'Oh well, that's all right then,' responded Charlie easily, as if Jake had just found out that he was keen on tennis or kept goldfish and not that he was their boss's son and heir to a fortune that beggared belief. 'As long as you know I'm legit when I say I can get Poppy back to her dad. Do you want to pass me the luggage? The sooner we get Poppy to the airport the sooner we can get her home.'

Jake swung Poppy's holdall across to him. 'It's good of you to do this for Poppy. You can imagine how worried she is.'

Charlie nodded. 'I was on the radio to head office when the call came in from the shore base here. I got hold of my father and asked him if he could spare the tender from the yacht. Max' – he gestured to the helmsman – 'picked me up from where I was moored.' He held his hand out to Poppy to help her across to the speedboat. 'And hey presto. This baby has a couple of really powerful inboard engines – she can put up enough speed for Dad's guests to waterski behind her. We'll have you at Preveza in no time.'

Poppy turned to Jake. 'Thanks,' she said, 'for being there for me today.' She leant forward and kissed him gently on the cheek.

'Goodbye then,' said Jake. 'Time you got going.'

Poppy stepped across to the speedboat and sat down on the bench seat at the back of the cockpit.

'Look after her,' Jake exhorted Charlie as he untied the painter.

Charlie waved goodbye as the engines throbbed into life and the boat roared back out of the little port.

Jake stared after it. He still couldn't bring himself to like Charlie, but there was no denying that what he was doing was kind; there was no reason on earth why the company's owner's son should help out a lowly minion like Poppy. Jake just had to hope that Charlie didn't have any ulterior motives for making Poppy beholden to him.

Jake shook his head – now he was being melodramatic. That was the sort of thing that happened between masters and servants in Victorian gothic novels and not in the real, modern world.

He hoped.

13

Conversation was almost impossible as the speedboat thundered across the dark sea, leaving a broad, creamy wake that shone in the moonlight and trailed behind them like a path to the horizon. And it wasn't just noisy, it was also deeply uncomfortable as the waves caused it to smack down hard every few seconds. Poppy clung to the side to stop herself from being flung about on the slippery leather seat as the jolts made her teeth and head ache. Her hair was whipped across her eyes and with the speed that the wind ripped through her thin clothes she found herself shivering.

'Come here,' shouted Charlie over the racket. She moved across to him and he put his arm round her and held her close. 'Warmer?' Poppy nodded and although her teeth were still chattering she could feel the heat of his body through her shirt. She melted against him. Her head was telling her he was just being kind, just looking out for her because she was an employee; it was nothing personal, he was just doing his duty as her boss . . . but her heart was in freefall. Maybe it was because she was vulnerable, maybe it was because she was scared, but she nestled against him and allowed herself to feel cherished. She could feel his left hand rubbing against her upper arm, little strokes, up and down. Was he doing that to comfort her or because he liked the feel of her body under her thin clothing? She wished she knew. She wished it didn't feel so right.

Max, the helmsman, steered the boat between Ithaca and Kefalonia and Poppy watched the lights of the harbours, villages and towns drift past. She tried to work out exactly where they were to keep her mind off her worry about her dad, but it proved impossible. She shut her eyes instead. When she opened them again the land was behind them.

'It'll probably take us a couple of hours to get there,' said Charlie into her ear.

Poppy glanced at her watch. 'What about the flight?' she hollered back.

'No worries there.'

Poppy had no idea what flight WorldFleet had managed to get her on but obviously it was one that was going to be going out first thing the next morning; by the time they reached the little provincial airport operations would have stopped for the night. And it was more than likely she was going to be in a jump seat. Most charter flights went out chock-a-block at this time of year so it was unlikely they'd been able to get a proper seat for her. God alone knew where she was going to land. Knowing her luck she'd find herself in Glasgow or Gatwick or somewhere miles from bloody Cornwall. And getting into the county in the summer months was a mission in itself with the A30 crammed with cars and caravans and the trains packed to bursting point. Still, she shouldn't complain. She was on her way, thanks to the kindness of Charlie and his dad and the efforts of the WorldFleet team.

She felt a huge surge of gratitude and smiled at him.

'What's that for?' he asked, shouting into her ear.

'For sorting all this out for me. For making sure I get home as soon as possible,' Poppy shouted back.

'You know, there's a lot to be said for being loaded, but one of the main advantages is that there are precious few problems that can't be solved if you throw enough money at them.'

Poppy nodded. In the main he was right, of course. Sadly, she thought that her dad's situation was one where it wouldn't matter how much money was chucked at him right now. His recovery was down to the skill of the medical team and probably a dose of luck.

Worry, combined with the acute discomfort of the journey, conspired to make her feel exhausted. She shut her eyes again.

It was a change of engine note that roused her. She jerked awake in a flash as the situation crashed into her consciousness. She sat up so suddenly that she nearly slipped off the seat.

'Steady,' said Charlie in an almost normal voice as the engine note lessened to a veritable purr.

'Where are we?' she asked as she rubbed sleep from her eyes.

'Lefkada town. If the plan works there should be a taxi at the jetty to take us to the airport.'

Poppy yawned and glanced at her watch. No wonder she felt knackered – one in the morning. 'What's the rush? There won't be a flight at this time of night.'

'Not necessarily,' said Charlie.

Maybe he knew about flights other than the charter ones she dealt with. It was likely that carriers other than

British tour operators used the little airport. If she was honest with herself, whenever she went to collect passengers at the start of their holidays she didn't pay any attention to the other flights arriving and leaving, just checked out the flight numbers she was after. Besides, they always changed over on a Sunday – Lord alone knew what the flight schedules were for weekdays.

The speed boat's bow sank down in the water as Max throttled back until they were nosing into the little harbour east of the main town on Lefkas. It was only a couple of minutes later that Max had sprung ashore with Charlie and the pair had the boat tied up. Poppy shoved her holdall on to the quay and then scrambled after it. Charlie swung it over his shoulder and set off along the harbour, Poppy trotting at his heels.

'If it's all working the car should be just along here.'

The car park at the top end of the harbour was almost deserted, the sightseers and the day-trippers having long since gone home, but under one of the streetlamps lurked a large black Merc.

'Jolly good,' said Charlie, heading for it.

'Some taxi,' muttered Poppy.

'Well,' said Charlie with a disingenuous grin, 'perhaps chauffeur-driven limo might be nearer the mark.'

'Something else that you can have if you throw enough money around,' said Poppy wryly.

'Absolutely,' replied Charlie easily. The driver leapt out of the car as they approached and opened the rear door. Charlie handed Poppy's bag to him and then helped Poppy into the car before nipping round to the other side and climbing in himself. 'We should be at the airport in no time now.'

Poppy didn't like to point out that she'd probably have a hideously long wait once she got there so she just sank back into the opulent comfort of the leather seats on the principle that she might as well enjoy the squashy softness on offer now, as once she got to the airport she'd be stuck with vile hard plastic seating.

The driver dropped them outside the main terminal and Poppy was amazed to find a reception committee waiting for them. She was even more amazed when she realised that the airport was empty but for them and the welcome party.

'What . . .'

'As I said, money has its uses,' said Charlie, stepping forward to greet a middle-aged man in rapid and fluent Greek. He then turned back to Poppy. 'Passport?'

Dumbly she handed it over. The middle-aged man took her and Charlie's passports, gave them a perfunctory inspection and passed them back with a small bow. Poppy had to stifle a giggle. This was getting surreal!

'Right, that's the formalities over and done with,' said Charlie. 'Follow me.'

'But . . .'

But Charlie was already striding across the deserted concourse and Poppy had almost to run to catch up.

'But where are we going?' she demanded as she drew level.

'You'll see,' was all Charlie said as they sped through the departure lounge to a glass door that stood open giving access directly on to the apron outside the terminal.

Poppy's curiosity was answered when she saw the little executive jet, steps lowered, waiting just outside.

'Oh my God,' she said. 'Is that yours?'

'My father's, but he's not using it at the moment so I thought I would.'

'And the reception committee?'

'You can't just take off and land on a whim – not even with the sort of money my dad's got. Things have to be legal and above board. For all they know you might not be a damsel in distress but an international drug smuggler or arms dealer. So passport, immigration, customs – to say nothing of air traffic control and ground staff – all have to be here.'

'But that must cost shitloads.'

'It doesn't come cheap. And dragging them all up here at this sort of time – well, let's just say I had to make it worth their while.'

'But why are you doing this? I mean, I could have waited till morning.'

'And have you worry all night? I'm doing this because I care about you. I do, Poppy, I really do.'

Poppy felt her jaw go slack. She knew she'd fallen for him, but blokes like him – no, *millionaires* like him – didn't go for girls like her. Not really. They just didn't.

14

Charlie led a stunned Poppy across the concrete to the waiting plane. She climbed the steps and ducked her head to enter the cabin. She barely noticed the grey leather upholstery, the deep carpet or the walnut trim. She plonked herself down in one of the seats as she tried to get her head round what Charlie had just said.

She wasn't the sort of girl that millionaires cared about. She was so ordinary as to be almost invisible and, although she knew she wasn't hideous, she thought that her looks were like everything else about her – pretty unremarkable.

Charlie sat down opposite her, reached across the walnut table and took her hand. 'We'll have you back home in two shakes of a lamb's tail,' he said. He flicked a switch by his seat. 'Okay,' he said into a concealed mike, 'let's rock and roll.'

A man came out of the cockpit and introduced himself to Poppy. 'Hi. I'm Rick, Mr Pencombe's pilot. Well, one of them. As you can imagine, Wing employ quite a few.' Poppy gave him a weak smile. 'Anyway, I just thought you'd like to know we've filed a flight plan direct to

Newquay and so we should have you home for breakfast.'

'Newquay!'

'That's the closest airport to your home, isn't it?' said Rick, sounding a little worried.

'It's perfect. Better than perfect.' To her embarrassment Poppy found her eyes welling up. 'You are so kind,' she said to both Charlie and Rick.

Rick reached out of the cabin door and hauled it up into place, then disappeared back into the cockpit. A couple of minutes later there was a clunk followed by the distinctive whine of a jet engine starting.

'Seat belt on,' said Charlie gently. 'And as soon as we get in the air I'll see what's been shoved in the fridge for our delectation. You must be famished.'

Poppy realised with a shock that she was completely starving. Her last meal had been lunch but it had been a pretty scratch affair. She smiled in gratitude at Charlie as the plane began to taxi towards the end of the runway.

'And after you've eaten, I suggest you get some sleep.'

Poppy nodded. That was a no-brainer: she was knackered. As soon as they were airborne Charlie rummaged in the fridge and brought out quiche and salad. He served the pair of them and then drew the cork of a bottle of Chablis and poured them both large glasses. Poppy ate and drank mechanically, hardly tasting the food, while her brain jumped from worry about her father to bewilderment at what Charlie had said. As she finished her last mouthful and drained the last of her wine she suddenly became overwhelmed with exhaustion. She barely noticed Charlie clear the table or tuck a pillow under her head as she slid into a deep sleep.

*

They touched down shortly after dawn. Poppy had been woken up about thirty minutes before when Charlie had gently shaken her and asked if she'd like some breakfast. As she came to, she had vague memories of a dream that involved herself and Charlie, but as she became aware that she wasn't on the *Earth Star* but semi-reclined on a fabulously comfortable seat on an executive jet, her dream disappeared beyond any hope of recapture. The reason for the private jet catapulted itself into its place. She was wide awake in an instant.

To cover her angst she stared out of the window at the grey void of the near-dawn sky and the silvery layer of cloud thousands of feet below while Charlie, at the back of the cabin, ferreted about in the fridge. As the plane began to descend he offered her fresh coffee, orange juice and smoked salmon bagels.

'You'll have to eat up quickly so I can get everything stowed before we land,' he informed her, 'but I thought I'd leave you to sleep for as long as I could.'

Poppy was touched by his thoughtfulness. 'I could get used to this,' she mumbled as she munched, feeling horribly self-conscious under his concerned gaze. His attentiveness seemed to lend credence to what he'd told her the night before but she still couldn't get her head round it. 'There's a lot to be said for executive travel,' she added to try to move Charlie's focus away from her.

Charlie raised an eyebrow. 'This'll spoil going cattle class for a long time.'

'Hey,' said Poppy. 'What's to spoil? The experience is already as dire as it can get. Well, not Wing's, obviously.'

'Wing's cattle class is as bad as anyone else's and you know it,' said Charlie. 'Now stop yakking and eat.

I don't want your parents to think I didn't look after their precious daughter properly.' He fussed about her, offering her more coffee and orange; the sort of thing that Poppy had always done for her guests on the *Earth Star*. It was funny having the tables turned on her quite so suddenly.

'You know, seeing as how I work for Wing and you are my boss, shouldn't I be waiting on you?'

Charlie shook his head. 'Don't be silly. You're on this plane as my guest.'

'I have to say the service on this flight is a cut above that on most of the planes I've flown on.'

Charlie gave her a mock bow. 'One good thing about knowing a lot about the travel industry is that you have a complete understanding about how it *should* be done, and a nice breakfast is always a winning touch.'

Poppy didn't tell him that it wasn't just the breakfast that was so exceptional. She'd never come across a steward so easy on the eye before either. Or so wealthy, or attentive . . . Him, waiting on her because he cared about her. And how did she feel about him? She tried not to let her eyes stray to him as she thought about it. She knew how her body reacted whenever he was close, whenever she thought about him, whenever she heard his voice. There were no two ways about it – he set her heart racing and it wasn't just because he was rich. She remembered how they'd flirted and laughed at the Blue Dolphin, how he'd tracked her down to the beach where she'd picnicked with Ronnie Garvie, how they'd chatted and shared a beer on his little sailing boat, how he'd held her in the speedboat. He filled her thoughts and her dreams and the fact that he was behaving now like a knight in shining armour made him even more special.

'Done?' asked Charlie, hovering to take her cup and plate.

She smiled at him and nodded. As she handed them to him their fingers touched and a thrill squeezed her chest, making her skin prickle with delicious goosebumps.

Her ears popped and she could tell from a glance out of the window that while she'd been eating breakfast the little plane had been heading rapidly earthwards, towards Cornwall and her dad. Dad. A shot of panic made her insides lurch and scattered her thoughts about Charlie to the far recesses of her mind. Supposing if, even with all Charlie's kindness and help, she was still too late to get to her dad in time? It just didn't bear thinking about. Not that there was anything she could do to alter the situation, but she desperately wanted to know just what that situation was. If the worst had happened . . .

Charlie returned to his seat and buckled up just a couple of minutes before the plane touched down. It was light enough to see the shapes of the buildings as they hurtled along the runway, but although Poppy was looking out of the window she was so wrapped up in her thoughts that she saw nothing.

'There! I said I'd have you back in time for breakfast – only you've already had some.' Poppy didn't respond. She'd hardly registered that Charlie had spoken. He took her hand. 'What's the matter?' he asked, seeing the look on her face.

Poppy shrugged. 'I was just wondering how my dad is. I don't think I could bear it for my mum if she had to tell me . . .' Her voice trailed off. She couldn't bring herself to vocalise the thought that her dad might be dead.

'Then we'll find out.'

'But how? Mum's phone was switched off when I last tried and anyway, if she's getting some sleep it would be mean to wake her at this hour.'

'We'll ring the hospital.'

'I haven't got the number,' Poppy admitted sadly.

'We'll find it,' said Charlie. 'I'd better just wait till Rick gets us to our stand. Then give me a couple of minutes.'

The plane slowed and then turned off the runway. It seemed to take an interminable time to taxi up to the main building before Rick shut down the engines. As soon as the whine of the twin jets began to descend in pitch Charlie reached into his trouser pocket and brought out a mobile phone. 'It's scary how reliant we've all become on technology and the Internet.' He pressed a few keys. 'So which hospital is it?' Poppy told him. Charlie pressed a few more keys then handed her the phone. 'It's ringing,' he said.

'Hello,' she said to the operator on the switchboard. 'My dad was brought in with a stroke yesterday. I don't know what ward he's on but I'd like to find out how he is.'

'Name?'

'Bill Sanders.'

'One moment.' Banal music filled the silence. After a few seconds it was interrupted. 'Putting you through now.'

A click, and another phone, somewhere else in the hospital, rang. Poppy waited impatiently, aware of her dry mouth and thudding heart. Please God, she prayed silently, let him still be alive.

The phone was picked up and Poppy was so fraught she could barely speak.

'Hi,' she stammered. 'My dad's had a stroke. B-Bill Sanders. How . . . how is he?'

'He's poorly but stable.'

A little sob of relief escaped her. Charlie looked horrified but Poppy shot him a reassuring smile and a little shake of her head. 'Is it too early for me to come and visit?' she asked. Charlie looked relieved.

'Where are you?' said the nurse. 'Last night your mum said you didn't know when you'd get here.'

'I'm back now.' She smiled gratefully at Charlie. 'Thanks to a very kind friend.'

'Well, we allow visitors at any time so come along when you want.'

'Thanks.' Poppy ended the call and handed the phone back to Charlie.

'Right.' Charlie unbuckled his seat belt. 'Let's find a taxi and get you to your father.'

'Do you want me to come in with you?' asked Charlie as they drew up outside the large modern building. The car park was almost empty; it was too early for outpatients and other visitors. A solitary ambulance waited outside A & E. The place had a strangely deserted air although Poppy knew that inside nurses would be rousing patients and the bustle of a new day would be going on.

She considered the question. Could she prey on Charlie's goodwill and patience any longer? Hadn't he already done more than enough for her? Could she really ask any more of him?

'I won't be offended if you say no, you know.'

'I was worried I've already asked too much of you.'

Charlie shook his head. 'You couldn't do that. I'd go to

the end of the earth for you. I would, Poppy, really. I want you to know that.'

Poppy shook her head as if by doing so she might shake some sense into his words. He was doing it again, telling her that she really mattered to him. But how could she? She was . . . a nobody.

She heard the wail of an ambulance siren. It brought her back to the reason for her visit. Her dad was what mattered. Charlie would have to wait.

'No,' she said, making up her mind. 'No, you go off. I can manage from now on. If I can just have my bag. I'll see Dad and then I can get a taxi back to the village or get Dan to come and get me, or maybe even get a lift home with my mum.'

Charlie asked the driver to get Poppy's bag out of the boot and handed it to her. 'Now, you are sure you'll be all right?'

Poppy nodded. 'Yes, honestly. I'm near home, I have loads of friends around who can help. You've done more than enough.'

'Okay. If you're sure.' Charlie paused. 'Right. Now don't forget, you've got indefinite leave and you will be welcome back with WorldFleet any time, I promise.'

Poppy nodded again. 'Thank you. It may be a while.'

'It can be as long as it takes.' Charlie gazed at her. 'I'll be off then.'

Poppy swung her bag on to her shoulder. 'Goodbye, Charlie. And thanks for everything. I don't know what I'd have done without you.' Awkwardly, not quite sure how to say farewell properly, she stuck out her free hand.

'Come here.' Charlie took her in his arms and kissed her gently. 'Make sure you stay in touch,' he said. 'I want to see you again, but when circumstances aren't quite so fraught.'

Confused and speechless, Poppy pulled herself from his arms and hurried into the hospital.

15

Still shaking, Poppy went over to the reception desk and asked how to find the ward where her father was being cared for. She was given directions and made her way along the endless, soulless corridors that smelt of cleaning fluid and polish, too distracted to notice the neutral colours of the paintwork or the bland 'corporate' pictures on the walls. Eventually she arrived at her destination. The door had a bell beside it, which she rang. A tinny voice asked her who she was.

'Bill Sanders's daughter,' she replied. There was a quiet buzz and she pushed the door open.

Instantly she was assailed by myriad bleeps and blips, bright lights and quiet bustle. She was standing in a lobby with an office and a nurses' station nearby.

'You must be Poppy,' a nurse said, coming towards her as she stood unsure of what to do next.

Poppy nodded.

'Let's put your bag down over here, and then I must ask you to use the handwash before you go any further. Your mum went home last night to get some rest, but I expect she'll be back in a few hours.'

Bemused, Poppy let herself be guided by the nurse

and relieved of her holdall.

'How's Dad?' she asked as she squirted clear gel on to her hands from a dispenser on the wall.

'Poorly but stable. I imagine you want to see him?'

Poppy nodded. She could feel her eyes pricking with tears at the thought of quite how ill her father had to be to be on a ward like this.

'He's over here.'

Poppy followed the nurse to a corner of the room. She passed a couple of other beds with patients wired to and monitored by banks of gizmos and machines. It all looked terrifyingly complex and serious. Every now and again it seemed as if alarms went off but no one seemed to rush about. Everything took place with quiet efficiency.

Her father was lying perfectly still on the bed, covered by a sheet, with wires and tubes connected all over him. He looked worse than Poppy had imagined and the shock of seeing her vibrant, bouncy, jovial dad reduced to this state made tears well up in her eyes.

The nurse squeezed her shoulder sympathetically. 'It looks worse than it is, you know. And he's in safe hands. He was quite fit for a man of his age so we have high hopes he'll make a full recovery.' Poppy nodded, not daring to speak. The nurse pulled a chair out for her to sit on. 'Talk to him, tell him about your work abroad.'

'But . . .' She didn't want to say the word 'coma'. It sounded so desperate.

'The stimulation of your voice may help. I'm sure you've lots to tell him. I'll get you a cup of tea. Or would you prefer coffee?'

Poppy plumped for tea and then sat down and began, hugely self-consciously, to talk to her father. She told him about the *Earth Star* and the Garvies and teaching Ronnie to swim, and by the time she got on to telling him about her trip home in a private jet she was on to her second cup.

A movement nearby interrupted her flow and she looked up.

'Mum!' Poppy leapt to her feet and spun round, the dregs of her tea slopping dangerously in her mug.

'Poppy! When did you get back? How . . .'

But Poppy was laughing and crying all at once and unable to speak. It was all quite inappropriate for the ward and guiltily they shushed each other.

'There's a relatives' room over here,' said Anne Sanders. 'We can chat in there. Oh, it's so good to see you.' She put her arm round her daughter's waist and gave her a big squeeze.

Once in the relatives' room and settled in one of the tatty, saggy armchairs, Anne insisted Poppy told her everything. Her eyes widened in amazement at the details of her daughter's trip back.

'My oh my. How the rich live.'

'I know. Gobsmacking. But it came in handy for me.'

'And you say you had no idea about this bloke until just before he came to your rescue.'

'Not a clue. He just seemed to be bumming around the Med. When I saw him on his dad's yacht I thought he was just ferrying it from its winter berth. He was so scruffy . . . and then when he pitched up again he was on this really ordinary sailing boat – the sort of thing that isn't expensive to charter for a few days. And then I saw his picture in a glossy magazine. Well, I was so amazed.'

'My, my.'

'Incredible, huh?'

Anne nodded. 'So how's Dad?'

Poppy shrugged. 'I can't judge. The nurses are all upbeat but he looks so ill, Mum.'

'I know. It's been dreadful. And I can't help wondering . . . what if . . .'

'Shh,' said Poppy. 'We must stay positive. Dad wouldn't want us to get all downhearted. He's getting great treatment and I'm sure everything that can be done is being done.'

Anne nodded. 'Come on, let's go and sit by him for a bit. I promised Dan I'd be back for lunchtime.'

They walked back towards Bill's bed. 'How's it going?' Poppy asked.

'Well, everyone's rallying round but I can't deny that we're short-staffed without your dad. And at this time of year, everyone who wants a job has got one.'

'I'm back now. And I've got indefinite leave. I can help out for a while. At least till we know what's what.'

Anne and Poppy got back to the pub just as the lunchtime rush was building to a climax. Poppy barely had time to put her bag upstairs and roll her sleeves up before she was back behind the bar pulling pints and taking orders.

'It's great you're back,' said Dan. 'We've been struggling.'

Poppy rang up a bill and dealt with the change before she answered. 'It's a shame I had to come for this reason, though.'

'Terrible,' said Dan as he hauled out several packets of crisps, took the tops off four mixers and topped up a pint of Guinness.

Very few in the pub were regulars. They tended to

keep away in the height of the holiday season when the village was heaving with grockles, as the locals were wont to call the visitors. The one or two who knew Poppy gave her sympathetic smiles from across the mass of tourists clamouring for pints and pasties. Part of Poppy wished they wouldn't. While she was working she managed to push the awfulness of her dad's situation to the back of her mind, but these well-meant gestures of kindness made her worry about being at the pub not the hospital.

By three o'clock the rush had all but gone and Poppy, stressed about her dad, short on sleep and out of the habit of bar work, was done in.

'You must go and have a lie-down,' said her mother, seeing Poppy's exhausted face and the dark circles under her eyes. Poppy began to protest but her mother pointed out she'd be more of a hindrance than a help if she made herself ill. 'I've got enough on my plate with your dad.'

'But I want to go back to the hospital with you.'

'You can do the visiting tomorrow. Today you need to sleep. How much did you get last night?' Poppy muttered something about three or four hours. Anne sighed. 'My point exactly. If you get a couple of hours now you'll be more use this evening.'

Poppy gave in; she was too knackered to argue further.

'It's an hour earlier in England,' said Ronnie, as she joined Jake in the cockpit.

Jake looked up at her, startled. 'I didn't hear you come back on board,' he said.

'Didn't go,' said Ronnie flatly. 'I was that pooped after today I decided to 'ave a lie on my bed with a book instead. I sent Mick off with the kids. Just because I can't take the pace don't mean he shouldn't have some fun.'

'I'm sorry,' said Jake. 'If I'd known we were going to get a replacement for Poppy so soon I would have said we should stay put on Ithaca. But I was worried about getting you back up the coast in time for your transfer to Preveza.'

'Don't you worry about nuffink. We had a great time helping you sail the boat. Just all that running about on deck. I don't do running. Anyway,' said Ronnie, staring at Jake, 'this doesn't alter the fact that it's still early in the evening in England.'

'You've lost me.'

'You're not fooling no one, Jake,' said Ronnie. 'I was watching you for a good five minutes before I came along to join you. You've been staring at your mobile like my daughters do when they're waiting for a call from the latest man in their lives. They don't want to be the one to phone him – that would look way too keen and uncool – but they think that if they wish hard enough for him to call them, by some magic he'll get the message and put them out of their misery. Not that there's a bloke in existence,' added Ronnie, with a chuckle, 'who is that tuned in to a woman's mind, but my girls 'aven't learnt that yet.'

'So what are you saying?' said Jake.

Ronnie leant forward a little and put her hand on Jake's. 'You're missing Poppy like buggery. So phone her. Find out how her dad is. Ask if she's okay.'

Jake shook his head and shrugged. 'There's nothing . . . I'm not . . .' He sighed. 'I'm just worried she might not have got back in time.'

Ronnie looked him in the eye for a second or two before she said, 'Yes, of course. Still,' she added, 'a call from a friend wouldn't do no harm, would it?'

'But supposing,' said Jake. 'Supposing she *didn't* get there in time.'

'Then a call from you ain't going to make things any worse for her, and hearing a friendly voice, a caring voice, might be a big help. And, even if she doesn't feel up to talking, what's the worst she can say to you? *Not now, Jake. I want to be left alone?*'

Jake stared at Ronnie and then reached out for his mobile which lay on the cockpit table. Ronnie nodded encouragingly as he picked it up.

'I'll think about it. Maybe I'll call her tomorrow.' He slipped his phone into the pocket of his shorts. 'I think I'll go for a stroll round the harbour before I turn in.'

Ronnie watched him lope off down the gangplank. 'Who are you kidding, Jake?' she said quietly to his back view. 'You're potty about that girl or my name ain't Ronnie Garvie.'

16

The noise coming from the bar roused her. Guiltily she started up and checked her watch. Shit – half past eight. She should have been downstairs helping Dan and her mum ages ago. There were always a few part-timers working in the bar in the summer but they were never as efficient as the full-timers and without Bill to help Dan keep an eye on them it was going to be tricky. Her mum would be up to her eyes in the kitchen so she had to get her arse downstairs now. She dragged a comb through her hair with one hand and rubbed the sleep out of her eyes with the other. She grimaced at herself in the mirror. That'd have to do, so she just hoped the punters weren't too easily frightened.

She thundered down the stairs behind the bar and cautiously opened the door, not wanting to jolt drinks out of the hand of some passing worker who was probably already stressed enough without Poppy adding to the chaos.

The muted roar she could already hear crescendoed to a cacophony of overloud voices, laughter and the occasional shout; a typical Thursday night at the Polzeal Arms in high season. (Thursday night in the winter was a whole different issue. Then there'd be only half a dozen locals in – if they were lucky.)

'Poppy, me 'andsome,' Dan called from the far end of the bar. 'Sleep well?'

'You should have woken me,' Poppy yelled back.

'No way. You looked all in. Besides,' added Dan, pulling a pint as he spoke, 'me and Glad are managing fine. Although it wouldn't half be good to have another pair of hands.'

Poppy rolled up her sleeves and got stuck in, and after less than thirty minutes she was so deep in the old routine she almost felt as if her fifteen months in the Med had just been some interlude she'd imagined. By the time she and Dan were throwing out the last of the stragglers while her mother, who had stopped cooking bar snacks and dinners a couple of hours previously, bottled up ready for the next day's onslaught, she felt as though she had never been away at all.

At around eleven thirty, when she was just about to turn the lights off in the saloon bar, she felt her mobile phone vibrate in her pocket. Her heart stopped for a second. A call at this hour? No one rang this late unless it was urgent – like news from the hospital. In a panic she pulled the phone out of her pocket to check the caller ID.

Jake? The relief was almost overwhelming. She stared stupidly at the screen while Rod Stewart continued sailing, far away, across the sea. Then she pulled herself together. What on earth did Jake want at this time of night? She was stressed, she was knackered, she was worried sick about her dad and now Jake was ringing her because he couldn't find something in the kitchen or he didn't know how to work the dishwasher. Angrily she hit the answer button.

'Yes.'

'Poppy?'

'And who else might be answering my phone?'

'I . . . I was just ringing to find out how you are.'

Poppy could hear the concern in Jake's voice despite the fifteen hundred miles between them. Instantly she was contrite; she shouldn't have snapped.

'Oh. I'm fine. Well, tired, obviously. It was a bit of a journey.'

'When did you get home?'

'This morning.'

'This morning?' His incredulity travelled the distance really clearly too.

'Charlie borrowed his dad's private jet.'

'Oh. And your dad?'

Poppy paused and took a breath. 'He's . . . he's still alive. And the hospital is hopeful.'

'Well, that's good. Isn't it?'

'Hmm. I suppose. It's just . . .' Poppy swallowed. She didn't trust herself to speak and the silence reached across the miles.

'Poppy?' said Jake. 'Hello, hello?'

'I'm still here. Lousy connection, probably.' She cleared her throat. 'I was just saying he's very ill still.'

'I'm sorry. Really. How's your mother?'

'Stressed. Trying to do too much. At least I can take some of the load off her now. I think it's a help having another pair of hands here. Although I wasn't much good today – too tired.'

'In which case you ought to get to bed. Sorry I'm

ringing so late. It's just . . . well, you know how it is. I've been quite busy.'

'Got a replacement yet?' Poppy was glad for the excuse to change the subject.

'Someone called Sophie. Do you know her?'

'No. Perhaps she's new this season.'

'Dunno. At least I'll have a hand for the changeover.'

'I hope she knows what she's doing. You don't want all that hassle and have to teach someone what's what as well. Say goodbye to the Garvies for me.' Poppy yawned. 'Sorry, Jake. I've got to go. I'm dead on my feet.'

'Of course.'

'Thanks for ringing.'

'No problem. Let me know how things go,' said Jake gently.

'Yeah. Bye, Jake.' She severed the connection. There were only two ways things could go: either her dad would make a recovery or he wouldn't, and with those options Poppy didn't want to think about it.

She flicked the switch and the saloon bar went pitch black, but Poppy knew exactly where the latch was on the old wooden door that led to the stairs. Her hand felt along the planking until she found it and pulled it open. The glow from the landing light enabled her to see the stairs. As she climbed them she heard her mother call out.

'Poppy?'

'Yes, Mum?'

'Who was that on the phone?'

'It's all right, Mum.' She knew why her mother wanted to know. Anne had thought the same as she had when her phone rang. 'It was only a friend. Just someone ringing up to make sure I got back safely.'

'That's good. I was worried it was the hospital.'

'I know. Sleep well,' she said softly as she went towards her own room.

'You too. Night, sweetheart.'

But Poppy knew that 'sleep' would be a mission for both of them. 'Rest' was probably the best they could hope for. As for her, she knew she had too much whirling around in her brain for sleep to be likely: her dad, Charlie, the future . . .

'Did you ring 'er?' said Ronnie without any preamble when she came up on deck the next morning.

'Morning, Ronnie,' replied Jake.

'You're not answering the question. Did you?'

Jake nodded. 'Yeah, I did.'

'An' how is she, and more's the point, how's 'er dad?'

'Poppy's fine and her dad's, well, still alive,' Jake said bleakly.

Ronnie sighed. 'Don't sound too good.'

'I wouldn't know. I mean, a stroke is really serious, isn't it? If he's hanging on I suppose it gives the medics a better chance.'

Ronnie shrugged. 'Dunno. Poor Poppy. She didn't deserve a tough break like this, nice kid like her. You'll keep in touch with her, won't you?' she shot at Jake, a steely look in her eye.

Jake was taken aback. 'Yes, of course.'

'Only she'll need all her friends. Especially if . . .'

'I'm not really a friend,' protested Jake.

Ronnie raised her eyebrows. 'Don't give me that.'

'We just work together. Besides, I think it's Charlie she's interested in.'

'Money isn't everything,' said Ronnie.

'Yeah, but it's quite a big deal when you're skint.'

'You're not, are you? I mean, I know you're not paid a fortune to do this' – she paused as Jake laughed out loud – 'but you get a living wage and precious few overheads.'

'True, but when you're saving up for your own boat, to run your own charter, it's just not enough.'

'So how much would "enough" be?'

'There's a twenty-metre yacht I've got my eye on, four double berths and a crew cabin. The owner wants seven hundred thou.'

'Fuck me!'

'But if I was lucky I could take enough in bookings to service a bank loan. Well, more than enough in the high season. The low season would be a struggle but it depends where I based it.'

Ronnie whistled. 'It's still one helluva risk.'

'I think it's doable,' said Jake. 'But I'd have to find the deposit, and the insurance would be expensive. If I went for somewhere with all-year-round appeal it might be prohibitive because of hurricanes. The Med would be cheaper but then it's seasonal.' Jake shrugged. 'But the initial outlay is putting the whole venture out of my league at the mo so I don't know why I'm worrying about it.' He spotted a buxom blonde, toting a large holdall and sporting the WorldFleet uniform, approaching along the quayside. 'Looks like Poppy's replacement is here.'

Ronnie turned to look, shielding her eyes from the bright morning sun. 'Is she old enough to have left school?'

'Just as long as she can cook and sail I don't care,' said Jake. And even if she could do both as well as Poppy, he realised that Sophie had a hard act to follow. Sophie might be filling an employment vacancy but she wasn't going to fill the hole that Jake now realised had opened up in his life.

For Poppy, the weekend passed in a blur of grafting behind the bar, hospital visits and sleep. There was little time for anything else, least of all thinking about the *Earth Star* or Jake or wondering how the new girl was doing or whether the Garvies got away all right or what the new guests were like.

Or Charlie.

Even Charlie and his unlikely protestation of his feelings for her had to go to the back of her consciousness. Every now and again the memory of that kiss outside the hospital muscled into her brain but she shoved it right back out again. She didn't have time to think about it or him. The only things which she allowed to occupy her waking thoughts were the health of her father, who remained 'stable but poorly', and work.

The hospital was unwilling to tell them if 'stability' was good or bad. Even a direct question was answered with ifs and buts and maybes. The only thing Anne and Poppy could cling to was the fact that Bill Sanders was still alive. To take their mind off their worries the pair of them threw themselves into their work, which, given the time of year, was easy. From opening time at ten thirty in the morning to closing at eleven at night, the pub was packed with holidaymakers and day-trippers. Dan and Glad and the three part-time girls covered the less busy hours, when Anne and Poppy were at the hospital, but other than that the two women were on the go in the pub from waking to sleeping.

Over the weekend Poppy found a moment of quiet amid the frenetic business of serving hot and thirsty customers and did what she'd been meaning to do since she got home: phone her best friend from school, Amy.

'Hi, Ames,' she said when she heard the mobile being answered.

'Poppy!' squealed the familiar voice. 'How are you? Whatcha doing? How's the Med?'

'I'm back,' said Poppy, halting her friend's chirpy but envious outburst.

'Back? But you should be swanning around on some swanky yacht and getting paid for it. Don't tell me you got fired?'

Poppy laughed at the glamorous view Amy had of her job. 'No, I didn't get fired. I had to come home. Dad's ill.'

'Oh, Poppy. Nothing serious . . . What am I saying? Of course it's serious. You had to come home.' Amy's voice sobered up. 'I am *so* sorry, Pops. How bad is he?'

'He's had a stroke.' Poppy told Amy the bare details.

'Oh my God. How awful. How are you – and your mum?'

'We're coping. It's tricky with the pub and finding time to visit but everyone is being wonderful.'

'Does this mean you haven't got time to have a proper catch-up? Over a drink? Not at your pub, obviously.' Amy knew as well as anyone that if Poppy wanted to go for a drink the last place she would choose was the Polzeal Arms.

'I'm off on Tuesday, but I can't promise anything. It all rather depends on Dad. And what Mum wants to do. I'm back to give her enough free time to visit Dad – and visit him myself – not to go out on the lash.'

'But you could come out for an hour, couldn't you?' wheedled Amy. 'Tell you what, suppose I come over on Tuesday evening and we hit the bright lights of St Austell?' Poppy guffawed. 'Yeah, I know it's a dump but it's handy and there are a couple of decent pubs there. What do you say?'

'I say yes, but I'll have to make sure it's okay with Mum. I'll call you nearer the time and let you know.'

'Great,' said Amy. 'I can't wait; I've missed you. You going left a big hole in my life. Give my love to your mum and tell her I'm thinking about your dad. I'll cross everything that he'll pull through.'

Poppy rang off. Amy was right about the big hole in their relationship. For best friends they'd hardly exchanged more than a few sentences since the previous Easter when Poppy had gone off to the Med. Luckily it seemed as though time and distance hadn't wrecked the friendship – and given the events of the last couple of weeks, Poppy needed a friend to talk to right now.

Things eased off as the British summer – three fine days and a thunderstorm – ran true to form when Monday dawned with a sudden drop in temperature and overcast skies. Weather like that inevitably meant the tourists would find activities away from the seaside.

'Just as well, as it's Dan and Glad's day off,' said Anne

as she bit into her toast and marmalade. 'I've booked a taxi
to take me over to the hospital at ten.'

'But I can drive you,' protested Poppy.

'I think one of us should be here for the start of the
lunch rush. I should be back when it really begins to kick
off, and you can go and visit your dad in the afternoon. If
that's okay with you?'

Poppy nodded. 'Tomorrow, though . . .'

'Yes?'

'Can I go to the hospital first thing? It's just that as it's
our day off, I thought I might go to the sailing club in the
afternoon. But only,' she added hastily, not wanting to
seem selfish, 'if you haven't any plans that involve me. And
I wouldn't mind if I could go out with Amy too.'

'Amy! You haven't seen her for an age. Of course you
two must have some time together. I'll be fine. I've a load
of little jobs I need to catch up on. You go out and have
some fun. You've been on the go ever since you got back
and I don't suppose you were having a holiday while you
were in Greece, despite what some of the locals here
thought.'

Poppy shook her head. 'It wasn't all work. The guy I
worked with was nice.'

Annie lowered her toast to her plate. 'Nice?'

'No, Mum, just *nice*. We worked well together. We
were a good team. I knew when he needed me to pitch in
on deck and he knew when to help me with the guests.'

'Okay. It would be good, though, to see you, you know,
settled.'

'Mum, I'm twenty-two. I'm not on the shelf, and I don't
need a bloke in my life right now.'

Her mother raised an eyebrow. 'When I was your age

I'd been married to your dad for a year.'

'Yes, and the wheel was still a new invention. Honestly, Mum, I've got a great life, I've got a great job and I'm very happy just as I am. And all I need is for Dad to get better for everything to be perfect. And he will,' she added defiantly, as if her determination alone would make all the difference.

So Poppy made arrangements with Amy, trying to shove aside the guilt she felt about going out and enjoying herself.

'But your dad would be livid if he knew you were just moping around at home,' said her mum. And Poppy knew it was the truth; her dad, more than anyone, always liked to see everyone about him enjoying themselves.

She set out for the sailing club straight after lunch the next afternoon, glad that the weather had perked up again after the day before. Although the cove and the village shared the same name, there was, in fact, a fair distance between the two. The village nestled in a fold in the hills safe from the winter battering of Atlantic storms and, in past times, the marauding attentions of pirates, brigands and other attackers, while the cove had provided safe shelter for the little fishing boats which had supplemented the local economy with pilchards when stocks had been high and pilchard oil had been a valuable commodity. Now the only boats that sailed in and out of the cove did so purely for pleasure.

Poppy strolled along the narrow lane that wound between the picturesque cottages, some of natural stone, some washed with sugar-almond colours, but all with slate roofs, tiny windows and picture-book front gardens stuffed with hollyhocks and petunias, roses and geraniums, making every tiny patch a rainbow.

Ahead she could see a typical summer traffic jam of several cars trying to enter the village coming up against the brewery lorry, which had just made a delivery to the pub and was now bent on leaving. It would be tricky for the lorry to reverse given the width of the road and the sharp corner it had just negotiated but the cars didn't seem to be disposed to give way. Poppy squeezed past and left them to it. It was an almost daily occurrence at this time of year. If it wasn't the brewery lorry blocking the road it was the local bus or the Tesco van making home deliveries or the ice-cream man touting for business or even just locals trying to get out of their own driveways. Why the car drivers didn't park, as a large notice advised, in the field at the top of the lane and walk defeated her. What wasn't there to understand about the sign that said that the road through the village was unsuitable for vehicles and was a dead end? As she rounded the corner at the end of the village and began climbing the steep hill that led to the turning down to the cove, she heard the hooting begin.

At the top of the hill she came to the turn and in the gap between the high banks on either side she could see the glistening blue of the bay. Her spirits lifted, as they always did at the sight of the sea. It wasn't visible from anywhere in the village and their daily travelling to the hospital and back hardly afforded a glimpse of it, despite the fact that they were so close.

Opposite the lane and facing the sea through the gap was a big, late-Georgian or early-Victorian manor house that had, some years back, been broken up into holiday flats. However, with the rise in popularity of foreign holidays and the dire summers of the past few years, she knew it had suffered from quite serious under-occupation. It wasn't much of a surprise to see a 'For Sale' sign hammered into the hedge next to the big gravel drive that swept up to the old grey mansion. It wasn't a spectacular place; it probably wasn't a house that the National Trust coveted, even before its conversion into apartments, but it was solid and large and its position meant it commanded great views over the bay. What's more, it had a fair bit of land attached so the last time it had changed hands there had been some speculation about developers moving in and building a load of holiday cottages or a theme park or some other carbuncle that threatened to spoil the village. There had been a collective sigh of relief when the worst that had happened was the internal alterations to make half a dozen separate holiday lets. But now it was for sale again.

Poppy stood between the big gateposts and studied the house; it had certainly seen better days and there was a distinct air of dilapidation about it now. The front door, once a glossy black, looked dull, the windows were all grimy, there were weeds growing up through the gravel, the lawn was spotted with the gold and white of dandelions and daisies and there were tufts of grass sprouting from the gutter under the weathered slates. It certainly didn't look like an enticing proposition for anyone with the sort of millions that were probably needed to buy it.

The thought of someone with millions made Charlie pop into her mind. She wondered what he was up to now. Back in the Med, she supposed, finishing off his holiday. After all, he had Daddy's jet to get him back there, and besides, he had that lovely little Contessa to muck about in. She thought about his kiss and the times they had spent in each other's company and once again she wondered whether their meetings had been coincidental. As the boss's son he could certainly have planned them – but it didn't explain why he wanted to.

Poppy tried to tell herself that the attraction had been the *Earth Star* and how she and Jake had been running it, but he could easily have found out those details by contacting the guests or reading the feedback forms. For the umpteenth time Poppy told herself that guys like him didn't fancy girls like her; not when he could have the pick of all the totty in places like Monaco or Capri or any of the resorts where the *über*-rich hung out.

But, unlikely as it was, it seemed he had fancied her, and she knew that she had found him deeply attractive in return. Unsurprisingly, she wanted to believe that it might be a fairy tale with her as the real-life Cinderella, the girl who filled the rags-to-riches role. With life being as shitty as it was at the moment it was a wonderful fantasy to hang on to and the very thought of it made Poppy feel warm and fuzzy inside.

The trouble was, she was stuck here, in the back of beyond, while he was out playing around in the big wide world. How long would it be before he forgot all about her? Sadly, Poppy thought it might be quite soon.

Of course, she thought wistfully, hankering after a relationship that had never really had a chance to get going, there was always the possibility that he, with his connection to WorldFleet, might cross her path again. But realistically she had to face up to the fact that she'd had her chance, circumstances had blown it, and it wasn't going to come round again.

S he returned her attention to the house and wondered
how long it had been on the market and who was
likely to buy it. She didn't know much about property but
she would have had to have been on the moon, not just in
the Med, to know that things were in a bad way and this
was no time for investors to be taking a risk on bricks and
mortar. She hoped it got sorted out soon – another half-
dozen families holidaying in the area would be good for
trade and a little village like this needed all the help it
could get in the short summer season to keep the bank
balances topped up for the winter months – but she also
hoped that nothing would happen to the place that might
wreck Polzeal. There were a number of horror stories in
Cornwall of villages that had been trashed by greedy
investors and weak-willed local councils.

She turned down the lane, her stride lengthening as
she dropped down towards the sailing club and the beach
at the bottom of it. She passed the field where the club
members parked their cars and was gratified to see about
a dozen vehicles there. She'd been a bit worried that, this
being a weekday and so many of the members being
seasonal workers and thus unable to take much time off in

the summer, she'd find that she was all alone when she got there. Sailing a boat single-handed would be no problem for her but hauling it back up the steep road from the beach to the club at the end of the day would be a nightmare without another pair of hands.

She stopped at the gate and admired the view. The air was as clear as gin and she could see all the way to Gribbin Head across the bay, while between her and the horizon the sea sparkled in the bright sunshine. Just as it should be in July, she thought with satisfaction, although she'd seen it wild, covered in white horses and a threatening gun-metal grey, in every month of the year. Today, however, the weather was perfect; there was just enough breeze to make sailing interesting but not enough to make it challenging and uncomfortable. Lush, she thought as she strolled down to the little clubhouse perched just above the beach.

'Hi, stranger,' called Rob, as she walked into the club's lounge to see who was about. 'I was sorry to hear about your dad. How is he?'

Rob, who had been a member of the sailing club since before Poppy was born and was the man who had taught her to sail, had a soft spot for her and Poppy knew it. And, although he lived several miles away and wasn't a regular at their pub, preferring to drink at the club, she wasn't the least bit surprised that he knew about her dad's stroke. It was probably common knowledge the length of the coast. She filled him in with the little information she had.

'And Mum and I feel so helpless. We go and see him as much as we can and we talk to him, tell him what's going on, but it's tough keeping going and sounding cheerful when he doesn't respond at all. The nurses say that hearing our voices probably helps him but . . .' She swallowed and paused. She didn't want to break down in front of her friend.

'So you're having a tough time.' Rob draped an avuncular arm over Poppy's shoulder.

'It's not easy. But my old job said I could take as long as I need. At least I don't have to worry about losing it because of taking too much time off.'

Rob gave her a comforting squeeze. 'I was thinking of taking the Kestrel out. I don't suppose you fancy crewing for me? The tide's right for a beer at the Smuggler if you fancy one. My treat. And it's a lovely day,' he added, gazing out over the sea through the huge picture windows, shielding his eyes from the sun.

Beer was a clincher. 'Like I need encouragement,' said Poppy. 'I'd love to.'

'Come on then. You can help me with the trailer.'

The pair of them went outside and got the boat ready, tugging off the protective tarpaulin and checking the sheets, the halyards and the sails. When all was done they went off to the changing rooms and squeezed themselves into wet suits. After fifteen months in the Med Poppy had almost forgotten just how tricky it was to shoehorn herself into tight neoprene. However, the Med wasn't freezing like the English Channel, and if the worst happened and she took a ducking, a wet suit would mean that she wouldn't die of hypothermia in less time than it took to say 'Bugger me, that's cold!' As she walked back out of the girls' changing room she caught sight of herself in the mirror and grimaced. Even with her slim figure, now she was clad in the suit and a life jacket she bore an uncanny resemblance to Mr Blobby.

'All set?' asked Rob.

Poppy nodded and together they began the business of manoeuvring the little craft out of the sailing club's premises and on to the lane. As they kept it under control going down the hill Rob said, 'There was a guy here the other day asking about you.'

'Really? Who?'

'Scruffy bugger.'

'Well, that narrows it down. Like people round here in the holiday season dress in business suits. Did he say why he wanted me?'

'No. He just asked if you were a member here. He hung around for a bit and then moseyed off.'

'Not a local?'

'Not one I've ever seen. Might be an incomer. Maybe someone said you might be able to tell him about the sailing club. Or maybe he wanted to ask you about sailing holidays.'

That seemed a likely answer, Poppy thought, since if he'd wanted any gen on the club he'd have asked one of the others hanging around. However, if he'd been in the village and mentioned something about a sailing holiday – well, he would have been instantly told to 'talk to Poppy'. She wasn't going anywhere for the foreseeable future so if he still wanted to find her it could be easily done.

Rob and Poppy shoved the trailer across the shingle of the beach to the shoreline and then floated the dinghy off. Rob dragged the trailer back above the high water mark while Poppy held the boat, head to wind. She was glad of the suit; despite the fact that it was July and sunny, the sea was perishing. She watched some young kids playing at the edge of the surf and wondered why they weren't blue.

By September the temperature wouldn't be too bad and she might consider swimming herself, but until then she would rather muck about on it than in it.

Rob came back and together they hauled themselves over the side. Then they set the sails and lowered the centreboard and rudder and the Kestrel came alive.

'This is more like it,' said Poppy with feeling as the boat heeled over and sliced through the waves and the breeze whipped her hair across her face. 'The yacht I was on in Greece was beautiful but it never seemed to be proper sailing. We pottered around while the guests posed on deck.'

'And you were head galley slave.'

'I was the *only* galley slave. Jake did the sailing and I did the cooking and cleaning.'

'Sounds a bit chauvinistic.'

'Not really. I got the job I applied for. Besides, I took the helm occasionally.'

'And you had a good time.'

'Mostly. Cleaning up after seasick guests wasn't a load of laughs but luckily it didn't happen too often.'

'So you haven't done much proper sailing for a while?'

Poppy shook her head. 'But this is making up for it.'

'Want to take the tiller?'

'I'd love to. But aren't I supposed to be crewing for you?'

'My treat.'

Poppy carefully changed places with Rob and grasped the tiller. She checked their heading and their proximity to the shore and made the decision to go about.

'Lee-ho,' she called as she pushed the tiller over and loosened the main sheet, and the pair of them slid under the boom as it snapped across and sat again on the other side of the boat as the little craft heeled over on to its starboard side. 'A promise of beer *and* giving me the helm. I'm going to owe you big time.'

'No more than you deserve,' said Rob.

'Tell me,' she said when she was happy with the way she'd trimmed the sails, 'when did Polzeal House go on the market?'

'Easter, I think. From what I've heard the current owners didn't get anyone at all booking for the summer season so they decided to throw in the towel. Why are you asking? Are you interested?' said Rob with a laugh.

'I wish. What are they asking for it? A million? Two?'

'I've no idea, but I know I can't afford it either. Someone at the club said that while they were at the dentist they'd seen it advertised in *Country Life* and all it said was "price on application".'

'My granny always used to say that if you had to ask what something cost, it meant you couldn't afford it.'

'Probably very true. Anyway, with things as they are I can't see it selling soon.'

They sailed across the bay, towards Fowey, chatting about people at the club, trivial matters of local interest, and sailing in general. Sometimes they lapsed into companionable silence and on other occasions they pointed things out to each other: a seal that popped up a few metres away to have a look at them, and then a shoal of fish, probably being chased by some predator, maybe the seal, which suddenly began leaping into the air around them. As they got further out to sea the wind picked up slightly and the boat zipped over the water, the hull just kissing the surface and the craft so neatly balanced that she barely made a sound. Behind them their wake gave an indication of their speed and Poppy felt utterly alive and completely relaxed for the first time in days.

Just as they were arriving at their destination, Poppy slackened the sails and brought the bow of the Kestrel round into the wind to slow her down ready for Rob to jump out on to the little jetty that projected from the tiny beach and tie them up. As she did so she realised that she hadn't thought about her dad for over an hour. Although she felt a twinge of guilt she also reasoned that it might be exactly what she needed: some time to herself to allow her to wind down completely.

With the sails lowered and the painter securing the boat, the pair crossed the beach and walked up the steps to the terrace of the Smuggler. A few holidaymakers gave their wet suits a curious stare but many of the drinkers looked more envious than anything, having seen them come flying across the bay.

They only stopped for the one pint before heading back. On the return Rob took the helm and Poppy crewed, the pair working well as a team.

'Just like old times,' said Rob.

Poppy thought back to the days when she and Rob had taken part in the sailing club races together; the days when her only worries were what to wear or how she was going to persuade her mother to let her go clubbing in St Austell with her school chums, or whether or not the spot on her chin was going to ruin her chances with the fit bloke in the year above that she fancied the pants off. She couldn't have imagined, back then, that one day she would think those problems so completely trivial, nor that the time would come when her wonderful and energetic father would be fighting for his life.

It was getting towards supper time when they finally headed back to Polzeal. As they approached the shingle, Poppy hauled up the centreboard to allow them to get as close in as possible while Rob leapt over the side and went to fetch the trailer. Poppy jumped overboard too, to hold the dinghy steady till he reappeared.

By the time they had the Kestrel back on the trailer and had hauled it back to the club behind Rob's car it was time for Poppy to race home if she was going to grab a bite to eat before she went out again with Amy.

'Sure you can't stay for a drink?' said Rob as they sorted the Kestrel out and hauled the protective tarpaulin back over it.

Poppy looked wistfully at the clubhouse, which showed signs of livening up as the social members joined their sailing partners and friends for drinks at a venue which wasn't knee-deep in trippers and holidaymakers – like the Polzeal Arms. Poppy could fancy an evening catching up on the gossip with old friends and chatting about local matters, but she had an arrangement with Amy and she couldn't do both. The club would have to wait till her next day off. She shook her head.

'See you around then,' said Rob as he gave the tarp over the dinghy a final tweak into place.

Poppy waved goodbye and strolled back towards the village. Once again she stopped at the manor and studied it. It was, she decided, a lovely house; beautifully proportioned, and with a comfortable air. It deserved a caring owner. She hoped someone with the house's best interests at heart would come forward, rather than someone with an eye to making money.

Poppy let herself in at the side door of the pub rather than run the gauntlet of the main bar, which already sounded as if it was doing a brisk trade. If she showed herself and the bar staff were under pressure she knew from experience that she'd find herself helping out for a few minutes despite the fact that it was her day off. And 'helping out for a few minutes' had a nasty habit of morphing into 'helping out for the whole evening'.

'Hi, Mum,' she called as she ran up the stairs.

'Poppy! Thank God you're back!'

Poppy froze. That wasn't the response she'd been expecting. Dear God, did it mean something had happened to her father? She raced into their tiny sitting room and skidded to a halt when she saw her mother's face. It was obvious she'd been crying. Poppy's high spirits from her exhilarating sail plunged and she felt her legs weaken.

'Mum,' she almost whispered. 'What is it?'

'Your father . . .'

Poppy's heart stopped. She dreaded what her mother was going to say next.

'Your father . . . he's come round.'

It wasn't the news that Poppy had nerved herself for and for a second she couldn't take it in. 'He's what?' she said stupidly.

'He's come round,' repeated her mother.

Poppy shut her eyes and leant back against the door. 'Oh, Mum!' Then she felt her eyes well up. 'But why didn't you call me?'

'I tried, but I went straight to voicemail.'

Poppy plunged her hand into her pocket and pulled out her phone, then raised her eyes to the ceiling. 'Duh – I forgot to charge it. Flat as a pancake.' She chucked it on to the armchair beside her and went over to hug her mother. 'You could have left a message at the club.'

'But I wanted you to be the first to know. If I'd done that everyone from here to Penzance would have heard before you did.'

Poppy nodded. Wasn't that just the truth? 'So how is he?'

'It's a bit early to tell,' said her mum gently. 'I mean, it's great news that he's on the mend, but he's not out of the woods yet.'

'Yes, but . . .'

'His left side is quite bad. It'll be a while before they can tell how much movement he'll get back. And he can't speak.'

'But he will.'

Her mum shrugged. 'Poppy, no one knows,' she said quietly.

Poppy sat down on the sofa. 'They can work wonders though, can't they?'

'Sometimes. Poppy, the consultant saw me while I was there. Just because Dad's got his eyes open doesn't mean he's back as we remember him. There's a long row to hoe yet. We've still got to be brave – and strong.'

'Okay,' said Poppy. 'I'll try.' But with this news to cheer her up she went off to change for her evening out with a lighter heart than she had known for nearly a week.

'So tell me all about Greece,' said Amy, her blue eyes smiling in encouragement as she took a large sip of her WKD through the bendy straw.

'Honest, Ames, there isn't that much. I sailed, I cooked—'

'You got lucky,' suggested Amy hopefully.

'Fat chance. Who with?'

'That skipper you were telling me about. Jack?'

'Jake.'

'Jack, Jake, the important thing is he's fit.'

'How do you know? I never mentioned anything about him being fit.'

Amy snorted. 'Oh, come on. Let me guess. Suntanned, blue-eyed, lean . . .'

Poppy held her hand up. 'Enough! Yes he was, but absolutely *not* interested in me.'

'Oh, gay. Shame.'

'No, not gay. At least I don't think so, just . . . I didn't do it for him.'

Amy spluttered. 'Oh, Poppy, I find that so hard to believe.'

'It's true. When I first met him I thought now here's a bloke I wouldn't kick out of bed.'

'As you do.'

'As you do,' agreed Poppy. 'But dragging him into it in the first place just wasn't going to happen.'

'You're losing your touch, Pops.'

'That's what I thought, until . . .' She paused. Did she really want to tell Amy about Charlie? Would Amy rip the piss out of her for her fantasy that a multi-millionaire fancied her?

'Until?'

'Now look, you've got to promise me you won't laugh.'

Amy nodded eagerly.

Poppy told her about Charlie, the boating accident, the meeting on the beach, the third rendezvous and the flight back in his private jet.

Amy's eyes grew wider and wider. 'You're joking me,' she said as Poppy finished.

Poppy shook her head. 'Honest.'

'But – and I don't want to sound mean here, Pops – but why you?'

Poppy nodded. 'I know. I keep asking myself that too. Maybe it's because when we met I had no idea who he was and didn't fawn or anything. You know, just treated him like a normal bloke.'

Amy thought about this. 'Maybe. Who knows? So when are you going to see him again?'

Poppy shook her head and shrugged. 'I don't know, Ames. I doubt whether our paths will cross again. I can't see Polzeal becoming the new millionaires' playground, can you? Cannes, St Tropez, Monaco, Polzeal.'

Amy giggled. 'Put like that?' She shook her head. 'Well, stuff it then. Let's drink to other fish in the sea.'

She clinked her bottle against Poppy's and they both took a hefty slurp.

'But he was nice.'

'You fancy him?'

'Of course. He was lovely to me and then he kissed me.'

Amy looked disgusted. 'Is that all? You *are* losing your touch. I bet you hope to see him again so you can go a bit further.'

Poppy tried to look annoyed but splorted with laughter instead.

Poppy swayed up to her room as quietly as she could, giggling as she cannoned off the walls of the staircase.

'Oops,' she told herself, as she tripped on the top step. Then 'Shh' as she dropped her handbag.

'Poppy, is that you?' came her mother's voice from the main bedroom.

'Yesh,' slurred Poppy, none too clearly. 'Go back to shleep. It'sh late.'

'Shall I bring you tea in the morning? Remember we're going to visit Dad, early.'

Poppy had completely forgotten. 'Tea would be great,' she lied, making a huge effort to enunciate clearly. She leant against the doorjamb of her bedroom and forced her brain to come to terms with the impending early call. Water would be good. She zigzagged across the landing to the bathroom and slurped handfuls straight from the tap, then stood up too fast and had to hang on tight to the washbasin as the room spun around her. She had just enough sense to take a couple of aspirin before she tacked her way back to her bedroom and collapsed, fully dressed, into her bed.

'You had a good time, I take it,' said her mother, plonking a mug of tea noisily on her bedside table and flinging open the curtains, allowing brilliant sunshine to stream into the room.

Poppy groaned and blearily opened one eye. She tried to moisten her lips with her tongue but her mouth felt as if a prankster had poured some vile concoction into it and then superglued it shut.

'What time is it?' she croaked.

'Half past six,' responded her mother breezily. 'I want to be away before seven thirty to miss the traffic. I told you we would be leaving early this morning.' She gave Poppy a steely and reproving stare. 'Don't you want to see how Dad is now he has come round?'

'Of course,' replied Poppy groggily.

'Cooked breakfast?'

Poppy swallowed the bile rising in her throat. 'The tea's just fine.'

Her mother swept out of her room, closing the door, Poppy thought, with a little more enthusiasm than was strictly necessary. She levered herself gingerly up on to one elbow to get her tea. She noticed that under the duvet she was still wearing the previous night's clothes.

She gave up on the effort and flopped back. Blearily she recalled coming home, drinking water, and then . . . Shit, she must have been pissed. However, even through her throbbing headache she could remember the fun she and Amy had had – well, some of it. The last hour was a trifle hazy.

With a supreme effort she threw back her covers, crawled out of bed and headed for the bathroom where she stripped off and got under the shower. Normally the blast of warm water would leave her feeling invigorated but this morning all it did was make her feel marginally less dreadful. Wrapped in a towel she returned to her room and her now lukewarm tea. She was just about to take a life-saving sip when her mobile rang. Groaning, she grabbed it with her free hand and flipped it open.

'Hello. Whoops,' she added as her towel fell off.

'Hi, Poppy.'

'Jake! How are you? Hang on a mo.' She put her tea and mobile down and wrapped herself up again.

'Sorry, have I caught you at a bad moment?'

Poppy grimaced through the pain of the sudden moves she'd just made. 'Not really. I just lost my towel and was standing here in the buff.'

There was a pause down the line. 'That's an unsettling image,' said Jake after a second or two. He cleared his throat. 'I was just ringing up to find out how things are.'

Poppy put him in the picture, then added, 'I'll know more in about an hour when we get to the hospital. I'll ring you then. How's Sophie doing?'

Jake lowered his voice. 'Not a patch on you. I mean,

you can't fault her cooking and the guests seem to like her but she's no fun. Absolutely no sense of humour. To be honest, we're not the happiest crew in the fleet. In fact . . . No, forget it.' He sighed.

Poppy wasn't stupid. She could tell from his sigh that there was obviously a problem between him and Sophie. And if they weren't gelling as a team, in the confined space of a yacht, it wasn't going to make for a happy relationship. They might be able to front it out for the guests but underneath it would be a nightmare. She felt really sorry for him, but what could she do?

'I really miss you, Pops. Any chance you'll be able to make it back out here before the end of the season?'

'I don't know. It depends how Dad gets on. The trouble isn't so much him as the pub. I'm hoping Mum can get some help soon, and now Dad seems to be on the mend it isn't out of the question that I could come back to work with WorldFleet. Maybe I'll be back out before the end of the month and working on the *Earth Star* again.'

'That'd be good,' said Jake. 'That would be *so* good.'

'Yeah, well, there are a lot of ifs and maybes going on here.'

'I'll cross everything.'

'Did the Garvies get away okay?'

'Fine, and they left a fat tip. There's a cheque in the post on its way to you.'

'Goody.' Her pleasure at the thought of getting an unexpected bonus temporarily masked her hangover. 'Seen anything of Charlie? I mean, he just dropped me at the hospital and took off. I was wondering if he went back out to Greece.'

'Not a sausage. As you were the attraction and you're back in the UK there's no reason for him to come sniffing round here again.'

'He didn't sniff.' Poppy heard a snort down the line.

'Anyway,' said Jake, 'that gin palace has upped anchor and left so he's probably gone with it.'

Poppy didn't remind Jake that Charlie had been sailing a little Contessa, and apart from ferrying the big motor yacht over to the Ionian Sea for his father he didn't seem to have anything to do with it. Maybe it wasn't politic to talk about Charlie to Jake. 'Look, Jake, I've got to go. Mum wants to leave for the hospital shortly. I'll give you a ring later when I've got a better idea about Dad.'

'I hope he gets better really quickly. I miss you, Poppy.'

Poppy rang off. He missed her? As she dressed she wondered if he missed her because Sophie sounded like hard work as a colleague or for a more personal reason. If she was being honest with herself, she missed him: his laid-back attitude, the way they worked as a team, his unflappability, his competence as a skipper. If she was going to get cast adrift with someone, she reckoned she could do a lot worse than Jake.

The thing was, she *had* fancied the pants off him when they'd first met. Her off the cuff remark to Amy about not kicking him out of bed had been completely true – but there's only so long a girl can be kept at arm's length before she loses interest. At first she'd been bemused, and then hurt. But, as she had to face a whole season of working with him, she'd decided that he probably hated blondes, or cooks, or maybe just women in general. So she'd given up, moved on and knuckled down to the business of looking after the guests.

Maybe, she thought as she brushed her hair very gingerly and slicked on some lip gloss, maybe her reaction to Charlie, the fact that she'd invited him for that first drink, had shown an interest in him, had even gone so far as to flirt with him, had been a kick-back at her lack of success with Jake.

She returned to the bathroom to snarf a couple more aspirin to try to clear her aching head, then took her empty mug and made her way carefully down the stairs to where her mother was working in the bar, emptying a glass washer.

'There's some toast for you in the kitchen.'

Poppy forced a smile. 'Lovely.' She tottered across the hall and into the industrial-sized kitchen at the back of the pub. There on the stainless steel counter was a plate of now cold toast, slathered in butter and marmalade. Poppy swallowed. Dry toast might have been manageable but this . . . all that grease . . . She swallowed again and glanced at the kitchen door. Swiftly she flipped open the lid of a bin and shoved the plateful in with a shudder. She gave it a couple of minutes, long enough to pretend to have eaten it, and then re-joined her mother in the bar. She slapped on a smile.

'Right,' she said breezily, 'I'm ready if you are.' She grabbed the car keys off a hook and prayed that the Devon and Cornwall Constabulary were well up to speed with their quotas for drink-drive and weren't out on patrol looking for easy pickings to make up the numbers for the month. Poppy was pretty certain that, given the amount of alcohol she'd shipped the night before, she might not be quite under the limit this morning. But she felt her mother already had too many reasons to be mad at her to allow her to admit that maybe she oughtn't to drive. It would only precipitate a row. Under the circumstances Poppy decided she'd rather risk her driving licence than her mother's wrath – especially with her headache.

Jake slipped his mobile into his shirt pocket and stared across the startling blue sea to the green hills of Paxos rising through the crystal clear early-morning air into an azure sky. Around him the turquoise water was mirror calm in the little bay where the *Earth Star* had been anchored overnight and he could see down through the limpid water to the white sand some fathoms below. When he'd got up he'd rigged an awning over the boom to shield the cockpit from the early-morning sun and he was now dickering with the idea of going for a refreshing dip in the sea before the guests put in an appearance. He was lost in his thoughts about a swim, interspersed with happy memories of working with Poppy on the yacht, when he became aware of movement behind him.

'Who was that you were talking to?' said Sophie, brushing her thick blond fringe off her forehead.

He wondered briefly if she'd been eavesdropping. Even on a boat this size it was incredibly easy, with skylights, hatches and portholes all open, allowing conversations on deck to be easily discernible below. If she had she might have heard his comments about her. Tough, he thought. It would serve her right.

'A friend,' he said, hoping she'd get the hint that he didn't want to share his personal life with her.

Sophie narrowed her eyes. 'Who? Poppy?'

'Yes,' said Jake brusquely.

Sophie made a moue of disapproval. 'For God's sake, Jake. What is it with you and her? She's gone. I doubt if she'll be coming back this season. Get over her.'

Jake took a deep breath and said, remarkably calmly he thought, given the provocation, 'For a start, there's nothing for me to "get over". Poppy and I were friends, nothing more, nothing less. Secondly, she may well be coming back this season, as her dad seems to be a whole lot better. And thirdly, may I suggest you stop interfering in my personal life and start doing what you are being paid to do – namely, look after the guests.'

Sophie tossed her heavy ponytail off her shoulder, sent Jake a look of pure venom and swept off to the galley.

Jeez, thought Jake, another few months of this. Through one of the skylights he could hear her clattering about below decks. Poppy, he recalled, had always been careful to be as quiet as possible when preparing breakfast so as not to disturb the guests. Sophie just wasn't in the same league as Poppy. Still, the racket emanating from the galley decided him. He tugged off his shirt and walked to the stern. If Sophie was going to upset the guests by waking them up early, she could take the flak.

Maybe he oughtn't to have harped on about Poppy's great way with the guests when Sophie had first arrived on board, and probably shouldn't have suggested that Poppy's way of carrying out a couple of tasks was better than Sophie's – but, hell, he'd only been trying to help.

Jake sighed and admitted to himself that maybe it had been more than a couple of times. But Sophie had been crap for the first forty-eight hours and had needed licking into shape. He'd been doing her a favour, he thought angrily. If she couldn't take the heat she ought to get out of the kitchen.

He dived off the stern and into the sharp chill of the sea, the noise of the water rushing and bubbling past his ears replacing the gentle creaking of the yacht and the crash of saucepans. He surfaced five metres from the boat and flipped over so he was floating on his back. The sun was warm on his face and his body quickly adjusted to the temperature of the water. He let himself drift, the buoyant water supporting him as he bobbed on the surface. The sensation soothed his annoyance and his problems with Sophie drifted away, to be replaced by thoughts of Poppy.

He missed her more than he liked to think about. It wasn't just her competence as a yacht hand and steward; she'd been fun to have about with her easy sense of humour and her amiable character. If he ever got the money together to go into the charter business himself he would do his very best to poach her away from WorldFleet. He could think of worse people to spend his life with for the foreseeable future.

God! The phrase 'spend his life with for the foreseeable future' shot him from relaxed daydream mode to fully alert in a nano-second, so much so that he relaxed his body and sank under the water. He came up spluttering and snorting.

Where had *that* come from, he asked himself? He tried to tell himself that he meant his *professional* life, but on board a yacht, in close proximity with another crew member, keeping professional and personal lives in separate compartments was easier said than done. He knew Poppy had fancied him rotten when she'd first arrived on board; her body language, the way she looked at him, the way she'd brushed past him in the confines of the galley, had left him in no doubt. And he'd been flattered, of course he had – he was a red-blooded male, for God's sake. But he'd shut her out deliberately. He hadn't risen to the bait. He'd done his best to ignore her, despite the hurt he knew he'd caused her, because he hadn't dared to let himself have feelings for another woman. He knew it would only end in disaster.

'Look at that,' said Anne.

'What?' Poppy was concentrating on keeping the car going in a straight line. Her hangover seemed to lend the high banks on either side of the narrow lane a magnetic appeal and it was taking an immense effort to stop the car from thudding into them. She prayed she didn't meet anything coming the other way that would demand any sort of manoeuvring, and she certainly wasn't going to risk looking at whatever her mother was pointing out.

'The manor's got a "Sold" sign up.'

'Really?' Wow, someone must have been out early to fix that in place. It hadn't been there the day before.

'It was on the market for ages. Mind you, I heard the last owners wanted squillions for it.'

'Hmm,' said Poppy. 'Rob at the yacht club said something similar.'

'Did he know anything more? I heard a rumour there's been a planning application submitted to turn it back into one house. Perhaps it's been accepted and that's why the sale is going ahead.'

'Maybe,' said Poppy, changing down to negotiate a sharp bend on a steep hill and crashing the gears as she did so.

'It'd be nice to see the place lived in properly again.'

But Poppy was far too busy concentrating on her driving to listen to her mother.

When they got to the hospital they were met by the familiar smell of polish and disinfectant. As they walked along the corridors they stripped off their jackets and wished that someone would turn the heating down a degree or two.

'No wonder the NHS has a cash crisis if they keep it running all year round,' Anne grumbled as they approached the ward. Bill had been moved from intensive care to one they hoped might have fewer machines and less noise; one which might be less scary. They made their way in through the big swing doors, Poppy feeling rather apprehensive about how her dad would be.

Bill Sanders was propped up in bed. His eyes were open but his face looked as if it were made of wax which someone had held too close to a heat source. The left side was drooping as if it had melted, to the extent that for a second Poppy didn't quite recognise him. Although her mother had done her best to prepare her and she was pleased that her dad was conscious, she wasn't expecting . . . this.

'Hello, Dad,' she said, finding it hard to keep her voice under control. This wasn't the big, bluff, hail-fellow-well-met man that had been her father. He blinked at her. 'You're looking great,' she lied.

He blinked twice, rapidly.

'Does that mean you disagree with me? Once for yes, twice for no.'

One blink.

'You look a whole lot better than you did last week.' She smiled at him.

Anne joined in. 'Hello, darling.' Bill switched his gaze slowly to his wife. Even in his frozen state, the way his eyes softened when he saw her spoke more than words. 'Poppy's right. It's great to see you looking so much better.'

Another blink.

'See, I was telling the truth,' said Poppy. She and her mother settled themselves in the chairs on either side of the bed. 'Would you like me to tell you about the sail I did yesterday?'

One blink.

She described her afternoon on the water, then went on to tell him an expurgated version of her night out with Amy. She could tell by the look in her dad's eyes that she'd cheered him up. 'But now I expect you and Mum would like to be on your own. I'll go and get a cup of tea, shall I?' One blink. 'Thought so. I don't want to play gooseberry.' She tried to sound upbeat and light-hearted but it was tough. Her dad looked so dreadful, and so vulnerable; it was difficult to believe he was ever going to be restored to full health. It was heartbreaking.

Poppy gave her mum's arm a squeeze as she left the bedside. Anne smiled back at her daughter, grateful for her thoughtfulness. Poppy went off to the canteen, got her tea and settled down as comfortably as she could on a plastic chair at a formica table. Across the table was a folded copy of *The Cornishman* – the local rag. With nothing better to do to pass the time she pulled it towards her, flipped it flat and scanned the front page. There was the usual parochial stuff – outrage over a planned wind farm, a compensation award for a man injured by a cow, a new book by a local author. Nothing likely to shock the natives there, thought Poppy as she turned the page.

The picture on the inside held her attention, though: it was the manor at Polzeal. MANOR EARMARKED FOR CORPORATE TRAINING HQ blared the headline. Poppy read the paragraph under the picture. It seemed that a London-based company had bought the old manor to turn into some sort of college for team building exercises and management training courses. The paper reported that it was likely to bring jobs and money to the area. Poppy thought it could be a good thing for Polzeal, as the trainees might fancy the odd drink in the pub and buy the occasional paper or bar of chocolate at the shop. Of course, when it had been holiday flats the tenants had done that too, but out of season the manor had tended to stand more or less empty. It sounded as though these courses would run throughout the year. And what was more, with a need for kitchen staff and cleaners and maybe a gardener or two, it should provide half a dozen full-time jobs that weren't dependent on the season, which would be a huge bonus for the area.

Poppy finished her tea, bought another cup to take back to her mother and returned to her dad's bedside, where she passed on the good news that she'd gleaned from the local rag.

'Well, that explains how anyone could afford the huge

price tag,' said Anne on the journey home. 'Did the paper say what the business is that's bought it?'

Poppy shook her head. She noticed, with relief, that her hangover must be wearing off as it didn't feel as though she had a lead weight clanging around inside it any more. 'No, just some lot from London.'

'Well, I suppose their money is as good as anyone's. Besides, if their employees like it down here they might come back for a holiday.'

Well, they might, thought Poppy, but she didn't think that Polzeal would have much appeal for the sort of young executive these training courses were likely to be aimed at. They were much more likely to head off for the dubious delights of Faliraki or Kavos – pasties, pixies and clotted cream probably weren't going to cut it.

Still, whoever it was who was moving their business down here, they could be assured of a warm welcome.

21

Towards the end of that week Poppy knew that her dad's condition wasn't going to change dramatically any time soon. The physio was hopeful but it was obvious that progress was going to be desperately slow and that Bill Sanders was going to be in hospital for some weeks before being moved to a specialist home for the foreseeable future. She also knew that she was going to have to decide about her own future, although she felt that the decision had been pretty much made for her. Her mum couldn't run the pub single-handed, and until she found a full-time assistant, which probably wouldn't be till after the summer rush, she was going to need Poppy.

It was time to ring HR at WorldFleet and find out where she stood. Would they consider allowing her to extend her compassionate leave indefinitely – possibly without pay – or would they expect her to throw in the towel and hand in her notice? Poppy was pretty sure it was going to be the latter. Charlie had told her to take as long as she wanted, but she couldn't see WorldFleet continuing to pay her when there was no chance of her returning to work that season. Why should they? She was missing the high season, they'd found a replacement for her on the *Earth Star*, so why would they want her back? She knew that the chances were she was going to be effectively unemployed – well, apart from bar work in her mum's pub – from the end of the week.

Poppy sighed deeply as she picked up the phone in the sitting room above the pub and dialled the WorldFleet head office.

'Which department?' she heard the receptionist say.

Poppy asked for the human resources co-ordinator, waited to be put through and then gave her name.

'Good. I've been waiting for a call from you. I'm Monica, by the way.'

Poppy, who had had her spiel all planned out, was a bit thrown. 'Oh . . . Monica. Hello.' She hadn't expected them to be waiting to hear from her, nor, given the number of employees that must be on their books, to have her name recognised.

'Now, first, how is your father?'

Poppy, who spent most evenings telling various friends, regulars and well-wishers the latest news on her dad's condition, was able to trot out a short, concise summary of the facts.

'So he's out of danger. That's really good,' said Monica. 'So would it be okay if I asked you to pop up to London to see us? Perhaps tomorrow?'

'London? Tomorrow!'

'We'll reimburse your train fare, of course.'

Poppy, who knew what a return to London was likely to cost if not booked some weeks in advance, had been about to make a snaky comment about not being able to afford the journey on her pay, but bit it back. The silence, as she took in the suddenness of the request and wondered if the implications were sinister, worried Monica.

'Hello, Poppy? Are you still there?'

'Yes.'

'So could you make it? You know how to find us, don't you?'

'Unless you've moved from South Ken, yes.'

'Yes, we're still in the same place. So is that okay then?'

'Yeah.' Poppy still felt dazed.

'What time can you be here?'

'It's a long journey – after lunch, maybe.'

'Shall we say two thirty?'

'Fine.'

'That's settled then. Two thirty tomorrow. Looking forward to meeting you.'

'Fine.' Poppy said goodbye, and hung up feeling as though she'd been ambushed. Surely she ought to have asked the reason for the meeting, or why she couldn't be told of her position over the phone, but instead she'd agreed to trek up to London. What a waste of time and money, she thought disconsolately. She made her way downstairs and told her mum.

'Of course you must go. I can manage without you. Dan and I will cope just fine. Shall I ask Dan to run you to the station, or would you like to take the car and leave it there?'

Poppy shrugged. 'I don't know, I haven't thought. Taking the car would be easier; then I've got wheels when I get back. If I don't meet Monica till two thirty I won't get a train till late afternoon and I'll be *very* late home.'

'That sounds sensible. I'll get hold of the hospital and tell your Dad I may not be able to get over tomorrow.'

'Mum! That's awful. Of course you should go. Poor Dad.'

'Your job is more important, and if you've got the car I can't keep running up taxi bills to get to the hospital and back.'

'But couldn't Dan—'

'Dan's been doing more than enough for over a fortnight now. I can't keep prevailing on him. Your dad will cope without a visitor for a day.'

Poppy sighed. She knew what her mum said made sense. The cost of a taxi from their village into Truro was prohibitive and Dan had been an absolute rock where lifts and helping out had been concerned. And he hadn't taken a bean off them for his petrol or extra time. But she still felt guilty that her dad was going to be abandoned because of her.

Poppy crawled out of bed when her alarm went off and blearily checked the time. Yup, six thirty; that was when she'd set it to go off. So why did it feel as though she'd barely been to sleep? Probably because by the time she and her mum had finished in the bar the night before it had been after midnight. Then she'd lain awake in bed wondering why on earth WorldFleet wanted to see her in person in London and had come to the inevitable conclusion that they were going to fire her – or 'let her go' as they would no doubt phrase it. She supposed it would be better to be told in person than by letter or in a text, but it seemed like a dreadful waste of a day and a train fare. She had no idea when exactly she'd fallen asleep, but it felt as if it had been only moments before her alarm had rung.

She rubbed her eyes and stretched, and then stumbled to the bathroom to grab a quick shower. She needed to be away by seven fifteen to get to Truro in time to catch the train to Paddington. The shower had revived her a little, and by the time she was driving along the main road towards the station she was beginning to feel as though she was waking up properly; a cup of espresso in the buffet on the platform completed the job.

Which was a shame, because the tedium of the journey to London beggared belief and a snooze to pass the time would have been good, but she was jangling with caffeine. But on the positive side it did give her time, something which had been in precious short supply for days now, to think about her, Jake and Charlie and what she would do with the rest of her life if her job went to the wall. By the time she got to Plymouth she'd made up her mind that neither of her relationships had been anything more than transitory holiday romances – probably not even that – and that distance and her current circumstances wouldn't allow either to survive. There might be some residual friendship with Jake; she and Jake had spent an awful lot of time in each other's company when all was said and done. And she'd really liked him, still did for that matter, although it was all a bit one-sided.

But Charlie . . . What was going on there? At the start he'd been fun, but then he kept cropping up in random places. What had that been all about? Had he been stalking her? But he'd shown such amazing kindness getting her back to her dad. And then That Kiss. What did that signify? Wake up, she told herself. It probably meant nothing to him. He was wealthy and good looking; he kissed girls all the time because he could. She was nothing special and she was reading far too much into it. She had allowed herself to fall for him and to fantasise that she meant something to him, but it was time to face reality: he'd just been kind, had used his resources to help her out. So now that she was, fairly comprehensively, out of his life, what were the chances of his taking any further interest in her? None, that was what, she told herself firmly. As soon as someone better, different, richer or prettier came along she would be history. Actually, realistically, she probably was already.

She would be left with some nice memories; memories of the way he'd made her heart beat faster and that frisson of excitement and desire when he'd pitched up out of the blue. And he'd made her laugh. And they'd had fun. Hardly enough to justify hopes that she had a chance of being his life partner or significant other, now was it?

And if Charlie hadn't been around, would she have got closer to Jake? Poppy thought probably not. She wouldn't have minded closing the gap, but she didn't think Jake was interested in anything but a sound working partnership and an efficiently run yacht. Or maybe he was from the 'treat 'em mean, keep 'em keen' school of relationships, which Poppy had never subscribed to. Life was too short to have to jump through hoops to get a bloke to give you the time of day.

So, circumstances had shoved a bloody great divide between her and Charlie, and Jake had put one of his own devising up between her and him. Well, that was life for you.

Now that she didn't have to worry about blokes, she could turn her thoughts to her future. And all she could see was helping her mother out with the pub for the immediate part of it. Not what she had planned for herself, but what else could she do? She could hardly abandon her mother, and if and when her father got better then maybe she might be able to make a second attempt to escape back into the wide world again. She tried to be positive: Cornwall was beautiful and the work wasn't so bad. The only trouble was she'd tasted freedom and it was going to be difficult to climb back into the cage Polzeal represented and slam the door shut behind her.

She gazed at the countryside flashing past the train windows, at the hedges, fields, streams and hills, and wondered when, once she went back to the village, she'd get away again. Not that there was any way of knowing, but it was certainly going to be a while. If her dad's improvement continued at the snail's pace it was currently showing it was going to be months, if not years. Drearily she considered the fate of some of her acquaintances and old school chums: married to a local lad, living in a council house, and having kids, just for something to do; being reliant on seasonal work and having no spare cash. She sighed. That was so far away from what she wanted for herself, and yet it just might be her future. Pretty countryside and warm summers – sometimes – weren't going to compensate for the mundaneness of it all.

And what was the likelihood of her ever meeting blokes like Charlie and Jake again: good looking, bags of get up and go, out-doorsy, sharing her passion for sailing? She'd blown her chances with both of them. She pulled herself up short. Who was she kidding – what chances? She'd established that. No, they were out of her life for good, not that they'd ever really been in it. Although if either made a reappearance she wouldn't be sorry. Feeling fed up, she watched the view change from mostly farmland to mostly urban sprawl and realised that finally they were out of the South West and entering the much more crowded South East. She leant back in her seat and shut her eyes. The caffeine had finally worn off and she dozed, lulled by the rhythm of the train, and dreamt of Charlie and Jake and sailing in the Med.

They were still in her thoughts as she walked to the tube at Paddington station, and now she was nearly at her destination the thought struck her that there was a real possibility that she might run into Charlie at head office, and the thought made her heart beat faster.

'I'm Poppy Sanders, here to see Monica,' she said to the girl on reception.

'Sign here, please.' The girl fiddled with a pen as Poppy filled in a visitor's docket. The receptionist took the sheet, tore off a portion of it, stuffed it into a plastic wallet and handed it to Poppy to pin on her jacket.

Poppy thanked her and headed towards the stairs.

'Actually,' said the receptionist, 'you need to take the lift.'

Poppy was confused. The last time she'd visited head office HR had been on the first floor, and one flight of stairs was quite within her physical capabilities.

'Okay,' she said.

The receptionist spun round in her swivel chair and then clacked her way across the lobby to a lift door that Poppy had never noticed before, tucked, as it was, behind a large potted palm. The girl pressed a couple of buttons on the keypad on the wall beside it and the stainless steel door slid open. She stood back to allow Poppy to enter then leant in and pressed another button. Poppy watched her glossy smile disappear as the door slid shut again and the lift began its upward journey with the faintest of lurches. She glanced around to find an indicator of which floor they were going to and saw nothing. Not that it mattered what floor she was heading for. She imagined there would be a sign telling her how to find Monica's office when she reached her destination.

Another slight bounce signalled the lift had stopped and the door slid open again. Poppy was surprised to see that she wasn't confronted with a bland corridor or an open plan office with half a dozen work stations but by an airy open space, at the far end of which was a huge bank of windows giving a stunning view out over a roof garden and then across the rooftops to a distant London Eye and Big Ben.

A movement to her right caught her eye. She turned to look at the person seated behind a solitary desk.

'Charlie?'

'Surprise,' he greeted her cheerily.

Poppy rocked back on her heels. Oh my God – surprise indeed! She'd hoped . . . she'd wondered . . . she hadn't really thought it would happen, but here he was. She was suddenly aware that her pulse rate had soared and her temperature felt as if she'd developed some sudden fever. Charlie! How bizarre. Only it wasn't bizarre at all. This was where he worked, so naturally there had been a chance that she might see him, but she'd expected to get a glimpse of him through an office door or maybe catch sight of him in a corridor. But to see him like this – face to face! In his office. And he'd arranged it.

She felt almost dizzy with the emotions that surged through her. She gazed at him, taking in his golden hair and blue eyes and thinking once again how gorgeous he was. She took in the business Charlie in a neat suit, plain shirt and subdued tie, and mentally compared him to the holiday Charlie in his stained T-shirt, shorts and deck shoes. She noticed too that his pearl grey shirt emphasised his terrific tan and the cut of his suit made his shoulders look wonderfully broad . . . Enough!

'It certainly is,' said Poppy, gathering her wits and trying to sound calm.

'So . . .' Charlie stood up and walked round the desk. He took her hand and clasped it warmly. A tingle shot up her arm. My God, she thought, did he know the effect he was having on her? She gazed at him, wondering if he remembered that last kiss before they parted at the hospital, the way he'd told her he cared about her. But she couldn't see a flicker of emotion. Zilch. Sadly she realised that her thoughts on the train were being borne out; she'd been a phase, a fling, nothing more.

Charlie gestured at a pair of comfortable chairs near the window and indicated they should both sit down. 'How are things? In particular, how is your dad?' he asked when they were settled.

Poppy swallowed down her disappointment at his apparent coolness. His question was exactly what she would have expected from an employer to an employee who had been absent on compassionate leave. She might have hoped that he wanted to know about her, had a genuine concern for how she'd been coping, but instead his question was designed to find out what use she was going to be to the company in the future. She updated him. 'Out of danger but not out of the woods,' she finished. 'Not by a long chalk.'

'And your mother?'

'Coping. Business is mad – it always is this time of year, and we're a bit short-staffed, but we're coping. Once we get to September it'll be fine, but it's quite a few weeks of hard slog before we get there.'

'And you rely on the summer business to tide you over the winter months.'

Poppy nodded.

'So you can't see that you'll be making it back out to the Med. Not this season at any rate.'

Poppy shook her head. She could see where this was going. Why, she wondered, had WorldFleet spent a shedload of money dragging her up to London just to tell her they didn't want her any more? Their money, she supposed, but if they were going to throw it around she would rather they threw it in her direction than at First Great Western. She wouldn't have minded getting the news by letter if it had meant that the money they'd saved had come her way.

Or maybe there was another agenda. Maybe he wanted to see how she reacted to meeting him again. Maybe, if he had moved on, he wanted to be sure she wasn't a bunny-boiler who couldn't accept that she was history. Well, she could. And although it was a bitter pill, wasn't this just the confirmation of what she'd known in her heart – that guys like him, *millionaires* like him, weren't really interested in girls like her.

Act cool, she told herself, act cool. You knew what the score was probably going to be.

'Tea? Coffee?' he asked.

'Er, tea, please,' she stuttered, wrong-footed.

Charlie got up and went over to the intercom on the desk and ordered it. 'And you? How are you?' he said, taking his seat again.

Did he really care or was this a professional enquiry, like the other one? 'Okay. Short on sleep, rushed, stressed. Like I always am this time of year.' Poppy was getting fed up. She wanted the axe to fall so she could get out and get home. Why refreshments if she was going to be sacked? Time to cut to the chase. 'Look, Charlie . . . this is all very nice, and I appreciate the fact that you're not being brutal about this, but I do realise why I'm here.'

'Really?'

'I'm not stupid, you know.'

'I never said you were.'

Poppy fixed Charlie with a hard stare, quite forgetting just how important the man was in the company. 'Look, why don't you just get this over and done with?'

'What?' Infuriatingly, Charlie grinned at her.

The door opened and an efficient-looking woman with glasses came into the room bearing the tea things. She dumped the tray and left.

'Shall I be Mother?' said Charlie.

Poppy was beginning to feel sulky and impatient. Charlie was annoying her. She didn't really want tea and she certainly didn't want the sack, but she was pretty certain she was going to get handed the latter along with her cuppa. And Charlie's light-hearted treatment of her at such a time really, *really* wasn't helping. Besides, as her train wasn't leaving for a few hours, if she escaped from here soon she'd have time for a quick trawl round the shops before she had to be at Paddington.

'Whatever.'

Charlie dispensed the tea in silence and pushed milk, sugar and biscuits in Poppy's direction, indicating that she should help herself. Holding his cup and saucer, Charlie leant back in his seat.

'I've got a proposition to put to you,' he said.

Poppy felt suddenly wary. Slowly she rested her cup back on the table. 'What sort of proposition?'

Charlie laughed. 'Nothing sleazy, I promise. I think you'll like it.'

I'll be the judge of that, she thought, but she said, 'Okay, shoot.'

'You may have heard WorldFleet had problems and that we thought of selling it. Well, instead of doing that I have decided to expand the charter business and to do that we need to train our own staff to our specifications. We have some great cooks and some really good, highly qualified skippers, but most of the skippers can't cook and some of the cooks really don't have enough sailing experience. If I expand the charter side of the operation I need more personnel who can do both. The thing is, it's a whole different ball game being a charter host from being a flotilla holiday host.'

Poppy was confused. Was he throwing her a lifeline; saying that if she did the course she might be kept on? 'So you want me to retrain?'

'You!' Charlie let out a bark of laughter. 'For heaven's sake, Poppy, you're the last person who needs training.'

Ah yes, that would be because she was about to be given the sack. What a fool she was. But she was still at a loss to know quite where this conversation was leading. Why tell her about his plans for the future if she wasn't going to play any part in them at all? He was still talking.

'You are the perfect WorldFleet employee: a fantastic cook and a skilled yachtswoman.'

Okay, now she'd really lost the plot. 'I don't get this. You've lost me.'

'So I want you to help me run the training college.'

Well, it was a flattering offer, but what bit of her predicament – the fact that she had a mother who needed her help to run the family business because her father was desperately ill – did he not get? Her circumstances hadn't changed; if she couldn't go back out to the Med there was no way she could up sticks and run some sort of school. 'But I can't. I can't leave Mum, not with Dad the way he is.'

'But this is the beauty of it: you won't have to leave your mother.'

'Okay, you've *completely* lost me now.'

'The training college . . .'

'Yes.'

'It's in Polzeal.'

Thunk. The penny dropped with an almost audible thud. 'Shit. The manor.'

'Exactly,' said Charlie.

'But . . . how come . . . I mean, you'd never even heard of Polzeal a month ago.'

'Well no, but do you believe in fate, Poppy?'

Poppy shrugged. Did she? 'Er, no, not really.'

'Well I do. After I dropped you at the hospital I decided to have a mooch around. Rick was out of flying hours and couldn't ferry me back to the Med till the next day so I was stuck in Cornwall. I got the taxi to take me to Polzeal. I had a look at the village, your old sailing club . . .'

'You were the scruffy bugger.'

'What?'

'Nothing. Go on.'

'And I saw this house up for sale.'

'Polzeal Manor.'

'I'd been looking for a suitable place for an age but the instant I clapped eyes on the manor I knew it was perfect – the size, the location, everything. I got my people to find out from the council if there were likely to be any objections to a planning application for a change of use and, as they couldn't see that there would be, I put in an offer. I heard on Monday it had been accepted, so the planning application is now going ahead as fast as we can push it through. I've been assured it'll go through on the nod.'

'That wouldn't surprise me. Not if WorldFleet is going to provide some year-round local employment opportunities.'

'God, yes. Cleaners, kitchen staff, a couple of gardeners – to say nothing of the workmen and builders we'll need when we convert it back from flats into one huge house. It'll be more like a hotel than a college, and if we ever decide to get rid of the property that's what we'll market it as. I imagine it wouldn't do Polzeal any harm to have a decent hotel in the village.'

Poppy shook her head. 'But I still don't see what on earth this has to do with me.'

'You understand the hospitality business, you understand sailing, you've worked with WorldFleet so you understand our ethos, so I want you to be the housekeeper of the training college. I want you to meet and greet the trainees; to be in control of the budget for the college; to hire and fire the cooks, cleaners, handymen, gardeners; to organise the transfers for the students from the nearest station to Polzeal; and to be in general charge.'

Poppy felt completely confused. 'So you're not sacking me,' she said, a frown puckering her forehead.

'Sacking you? You thought I'd brought you all this way to tell you that you were sacked?'

Poppy nodded.

'You thought I'd spend all that money just to tell you some news you could have had in a letter at the cost of a stamp?' Charlie shook his head. 'I know I'm a great employer, but I draw the line at that sort of waste.'

He got up from his chair and went over to the intercom again. He buzzed it. 'Monica, I've got Poppy Sanders with me. Can you come to my office for a moment?'

'Certainly, Mr Pencombe.'

Charlie lifted his finger off the button. 'While we're waiting, would you like more tea?'

As Poppy had barely touched her first cup she declined.

'So what do you say? Will you take the job?'

Poppy chewed her lip as she considered the offer. This was her dream come true, she knew it. And furthermore, Charlie had shown that she meant more to him than just a friend. He valued her as an employee as well, which was somehow almost more important to her. It meant that he didn't just like her, he respected her. Wow. But even so, he was asking her to make a big commitment to Wing Travel and at a time when things were still incredibly tricky in her life.

Part of her wanted to grab the offer with both hands, but she knew that in fairness to Charlie maybe she oughtn't. She had to level with him. 'I'm not sure, Charlie. I mean, Mum still needs a lot of help at the pub, Dad's still ill, we're up to our necks in trippers . . . It's a great offer and I'd like to do it, but if I did I'd want to give it my all and I just don't see how I could.'

'But that's the beauty of it. It's going to take months to convert the manor. There's no way we're going to be able to run a course till after Christmas. By that time the tourists will have all gone, your dad might be a whole lot better, your mother will have been able to sort out some staff to help her . . .'

Poppy held her hand up to stop his flow. 'But staff don't come cheap. The pub works because Mum and Dad don't have to employ that many other people – well, Dan and Glad all year and a few part-timers in the summer. Employing another full-timer will play havoc with the profit margin. And there's no guarantee about Dad. No one knows how he'll be in a month, or even six months. This isn't an exact science.'

'Yeah, well anyway,' said Charlie, glossing over these problems, 'I'd make it worth your while to work for me.'

The lift opened and a woman entered the office.

'Ah, Monica.' Charlie made the introductions and Monica handed over a wodge of papers to Charlie.

'This is the contract you wanted drawn up,' she said.

Charlie passed it over to Poppy. 'Cast your eye over this and see how you feel about the terms and conditions WorldFleet have put on the table,' he said. 'You might find page two especially interesting.'

Poppy began to read the contract. She swallowed. Should she admit that it made almost no sense at all to her? All that legalese and long words: paragraphs, subparagraphs, clauses and subclauses, the party of the first part, heretofore ... ? Shit, why couldn't they just write in English? She flicked the page over and had a look at the second one. *Fifty thousand pounds per annum.* Hell's teeth. She could understand that bit all right. *Fifty thousand pounds!*

She glanced up. 'This must be a mistake,' she said, her shaking finger pointing to the figure.

'No, I don't think so. Monica?'

'That's the sum you instructed me to insert in the contract, Mr Pencombe. No mistake.'

'So what do you say, Poppy?'

She gulped. 'And you say I won't be needed till after the summer rush?'

'By the time we get planning permission, get the plans drawn up properly, get the contractors on board . . . No, I can't see building work getting started before mid-August. Probably later. Once we get the project really off the ground I'd like you to oversee the finishing touches, so I'd want you available for the latter stages of the conversion and renovation, but I can't see you'd be needed before October at the earliest.'

Poppy knew there had to be a catch. She wasn't qualified for that part of the job, no way. At a pinch she might be able to run the admin side of the college; that would just be organising things like minibuses and menus, making sure the cleaners did their jobs and the bedlinen got changed. But conversion? Renovation? She didn't have a clue. She said so, then added, 'I don't know anything about property development. I've never even held a paintbrush.'

'Oh, you won't have to do that. What I want is someone to come up with colour schemes for the rooms, buy soft furnishings, that sort of stuff. I've got an architect and a project manager on board for the big stuff. You'll be given a budget, naturally. I'm sure it'd be quite within your capabilities.'

Would it? Well, it might be. Supposing it wasn't?

'So what do you say?'

Poppy was glad she was sitting down. She felt quite shaky, she realised. Fifty thousand pounds as an annual salary was an enormous amount, but then he did seem to want a fair bit in return for his money. Could she deliver?

She thought about it. Probably. It would be a bit like running a yacht but on a bigger scale, and she would have to learn to delegate a lot of the jobs rather than doing them herself.

With that sort of salary she could make a real contribution to the family finances; she'd be able to pay her mother for her food and rent, save some against a rainy day and still have loads left over.

'By the way, I'd prefer it if you lived at the manor – rent free, of course. I think if you're the administrator you ought to be on hand.'

'Oh.' Fifty grand *and* all found? Incredible.

'Is that a problem?'

'Not really.' Maybe her mum would understand the sense of accepting money from her if it kept the pub going till her dad was fit enough to work again – assuming he ever got to that stage.

Charlie handed her a pen. 'Happy to sign?'

Poppy felt as though she was being railroaded, but so what? Fifty thousand pounds and all found. He was taking the risk on her rather than the other way round. She gave a cursory glance at the rest of the four-page document and took the pen. She signed her name with a flourish, Charlie signed his and Monica witnessed both signatures. The other copies were dealt with in the same way.

Monica gathered up the paperwork, welcomed Poppy back into the company, 'not that you really ever left it', and departed.

'Time to celebrate,' said Charlie. He went over to a bank of cupboards on the wall by the lift and opened a door. A fully stocked bar was revealed. 'Champagne, I think.'

'Lovely,' agreed Poppy, still feeling dazed. What a turnaround the day had proved to be: not sacked but a new job and a huge pay rise.

He got out a bottle of Cristal and a couple of flutes, then deftly removed the foil and the cage. He popped the cork with the minimum of fuss; it left the neck of the bottle with an almost imperceptible hiss.

'No point in behaving like a grand prix driver with this stuff – far too good to waste by spraying it around, even though I say it myself.'

Poppy had been brought up in the licensed-victualling trade. She knew about Cristal and the sort of money a bottle would cost, and agreed with him.

Charlie handed her the glass of golden, bubbling wine and raised his own. 'To new ventures,' he toasted.

'New ventures,' repeated Poppy.

He sat in the chair beside her, moved it even closer, and stared at her. 'So, now we've got the sordid business stuff over we can relax.' He gazed at her. 'You look tired, Poppy. Are you overdoing things?'

'I'm busy. You know, hospital visits, helping run a pub, not enough hours in the day really, trips to London.' She flashed a smile at Charlie. 'So short on sleep, stressed but getting on with things, trying to make life easier for my mum, you know, like you do.'

'You're a wonder, Poppy.'

She shook her head. 'No I'm not. I'm a very ordinary person.'

Charlie leant forward in his chair. 'I don't think so.' He took her free hand in his.

Poppy took another sip of her wine. Oh, God, her heartbeat was going berserk, and her insides felt all gooey.

If she let herself she could fall for him hook, line and sinker in a second. But only a few hours ago she'd convinced herself that she and Charlie were never going to be an item; they'd just had a bit of fun together and she was never, realistically, going to be in a serious relationship with him. She'd made up her mind that she'd just been a bit of a distraction in his life, but now, here he was, changing everything again. Talk about a roller-coaster ride.

She put her half-finished drink on the table, next to her half-finished cup of tea. 'Goodness, Charlie,' she said. 'I just don't know what to say. This,' she pointed at her glass of bubbly, 'the job offer, the pay rise and now this.' She looked at his hand covering hers. Tentatively she closed her other hand over his. God, this was all so unbelievable – her and Charlie Pencombe. 'It's all a bit of a shock.'

'A nice one, I hope.'

Poppy nodded and then gave a shy laugh. 'I came expecting the sack and instead got the opposite. It's been quite a day really.' She let go of Charlie's hand and took another sip of champagne. 'I'm just a bit worried about meeting your expectations. You seem to think I'm capable of an awful lot.'

'I'm sure you're going to fulfil my expectations. *All* of them.'

There was something in his tone of voice that caused a sudden change in the temperature and Poppy felt a bolt of apprehension course through her. She glanced up at Charlie and saw a look of naked lust on his face which made her feel deeply uneasy. Things seemed to be hurtling in a direction she wasn't sure she wanted to go in. One second he'd been all concerned, sympathetic and friendly and now . . . now he looked like a wolf. She knew she was no Little Red Riding Hood but she didn't think her imagination was playing up that much.

'Well,' she began, 'you know I'll do my best.' Keep it light, keep it general, take the situation back to where it was a few seconds ago.

'I'd like that.' Charlie's eyes roamed over her body.

Poppy felt even more threatened. She wanted out and she had a plausible excuse to hand. She drained her champagne glass. 'I expect you've a lot to do and I've got a train to catch, so I'll get out of your hair now.' She hoped it came out sounding casual.

She got to her feet and Charlie leapt to his, standing a little too close for her liking. She was reminded of the time she'd first met him on the *Wet Dream* when he'd invaded her space, as Americans would phrase it.

'Don't go, Poppy. I've invested a lot of time and effort in you. I think I'm entitled to see a bit of a return, don't you? In fact I think I'm entitled to see a big return.' Then he leant forward and kissed her. Not the gentle kiss she'd received outside the hospital, but much more urgent, insistent. This wasn't just a kiss, this was something far more invasive. He was pushing her back towards the wall, his hands all over her chest, and there was nothing seductive about the mauling she was getting.

She pushed back at him, suddenly aware that no one was likely to come barging into his office. If he decided to play rough, or dirty, she was on her own. This wasn't tenderness, this was a bloke who expected sex because he felt he'd paid for it. Well, he could dream on. She might have fancied him when she thought he cared for her, but now it seemed all he cared about was getting his leg over.

She made a huge effort, gave him an enormous shove and tore her mouth away from his. 'Stop it. Stop it,' she panted. She glared at him.

'Come on, Poppy, you know you want me.'

No. Not like this she didn't. And what made matters worse was that he was her boss. Suddenly she felt as if she had been 'groomed' for a purpose and she felt hideously grubby.

Charlie advanced towards her again.

'Get off,' she said, using all her strength to push him back.

Charlie stopped and stared at her. 'Oh, come on, Poppy.'

What didn't he understand? Was he some sort of saddo who thought girls who said no really meant yes? Was that how he got his kicks? Forcing himself on women? Jeez.

The pair faced each other across a couple of feet of expensive carpet while Poppy felt her fantasy about dating a millionaire crumble into ashes. In the fantasy there had been mutual respect and mutual desire. But this . . . this wham, bam and not much of a thank you ma'am was the action of a spoilt, selfish bastard who was used to getting his own way regardless of how others felt or reacted. His way wasn't her way and he could shove it. She had standards even if he didn't.

Breathing heavily from the exertion of fighting him off she moved towards the lift. 'I've a train to catch.'

'Don't be ridiculous. You can't go straight back to Cornwall today. Besides, I've booked us a table for dinner.'

Didn't he get it? Didn't he understand that what he'd just done was completely unacceptable? It seemed not. Maybe other girls were happy to end up as notches on his

bedpost for some fancy fizz and a classy dinner. There had
been that line in the mag about 'charmer' and 'playboy'.
Was that code for letch and womaniser? A bloke who
expected girls to roll over and open their legs in return for
a bit of attention and a nice meal? Well she wasn't going to
and she wasn't going to put herself in a position where
she'd be even more beholden to him. She shook her head.
'I'm sorry. I promised my mum I'd be home tonight and I
can't let her down.'

'Ring her, say you've been delayed.'

'Can't. The car's at the station.' She knew that if she
phoned her mother she'd be told not to worry, to take as
long as she needed, and the car wouldn't be a problem.

'So?'

'If I don't get it back to my mum tonight she won't be
able to visit Dad tomorrow.'

Charlie looked annoyed. 'Can't she take a taxi?'

'Have you any idea how much a taxi costs?'

'Oh, come on, Poppy, I'm sure your mother could
afford one.'

'That's not the point.'

'What about me, Poppy? What about me? I'm giving
you this fantastic opportunity; I've stuck my neck out for
you. Christ, think what I did for you to get you home.'

Poppy had wondered when he'd mention that, use it as
a bargaining chip, make her feel she owed him.

'All I want in return is for you to have a meal with me.
Is that so much to ask?'

His tone of voice seemed to have returned to normal
and for a second Poppy thought it might be her who was
being unreasonable. Maybe a meal was all that he
intended. Maybe the other event – that revolting kiss –

had been an aberration. Maybe he was just a crap kisser and needed some tuition. But somehow Poppy wasn't willing to take the risk. She still sensed he was after more than her company and there was something about his manner that made her definitely uneasy. 'If I'd known, if you'd told me in advance, I would have made other arrangements,' she lied.

'I wanted to surprise you.'

'I think we've established that you did that, but, Charlie, I really am sorry. I would like to stay but I can't.'

He glared at her. 'I could change my mind about your job, you know.'

Poppy couldn't believe her ears. Now he really was behaving like a spoilt brat. That kiss hadn't been an aberration. These were his true colours. Why hadn't she noticed before? She quickly scrolled through their other encounters and realised that she'd never been put in a position where she'd had to say no before. Nor had she been entirely alone with him except when they'd gone below decks in the *Wet Dream*, and she'd sensed danger then. She should have paid attention to that gut instinct. Well, now they were in private again and she was seeing a distinctly unpleasant side of Charlie Pencombe. And if this was his real personality, maybe she'd be better off without the hassle of keeping him sweet, even if it meant giving up on fifty thousand quid. She'd managed without it so far; she reckoned she could cope for a bit longer.

'Go on then.' She glared right back.

A sullen silence descended. Poppy decided she'd had enough. If he wanted to play mind games he could play them with someone else. She grabbed her handbag from beside the chair and headed for the lift. She pressed the button and waited for it to arrive.

'Where are you going?' Charlie demanded, suddenly beside her.

'I told you, the station.' The door slid open.

He grabbed her arm. 'No.'

Poppy stared at him, then shook his hand off.

'There's a name for girls like you,' he sneered.

Head held high, she got in and pressed the button for the ground floor. As the door closed she wondered what the repercussions might be of denying Charlie Pencombe something. She had a nasty feeling that Charlie wasn't a man who took being thwarted lightly.

'Prick-tease,' he threw at her just before the stainless steel plates met.

Had she blown her job? But if she had, she might be better off without it.

'So that's it then,' said Jake. He turned to look at the *Earth Star*, her masts bare, her hatches battened down, her decks cleared, moored alongside the harbour below WorldFleet's shore base. Above their heads the sky was still a deep sapphire blue but now a few clouds skated across it, propelled by a breeze that had an edge of coolness to it.

'That's it,' agreed Sophie, pulling her zippered sweatshirt on and doing it up. 'Guests gone, season finished, time to bugger off home.'

'But it was . . .' Jake paused. 'Fun', which was what he had been going to say, wasn't the right word at all. He and Sophie had never had fun, but ultimately they'd learnt to rub along okay – most of the time – even if only for the sake of their guests.

Sophie looked at him with a raised eyebrow. 'It was . . . ?' she prompted him.

'A good season,' finished Jake lamely.

'It was. We didn't poison anyone, lose a punter overboard, sink the boat or upset head office. All in all it could have been a lot worse.'

'And I'm sorry we got off to a rocky start.'

'Poppy was a hard act to follow,' admitted Sophie grudgingly.

Jake shrugged. 'Yeah, well . . . Maybe I banged on about her a bit much to start with,'

It was Sophie's turn to shrug. 'A bit. It did seem to be quite a lot of Poppy this, Poppy that and Poppy the other.' She stared at Jake. 'And I know it's absolutely none of my business, but was there any?'

'What?'

'A bit of the other – with Poppy. Did you and she . . . ?'

Jake gave her a hard stare. 'You're absolutely right that it's none of your business but no, there wasn't.'

'Oh. I thought . . .' Sophie tailed off.

'Yes?' His tone was icy.

'Oh, never mind. I just assumed that you and she were an item. You seemed to miss her so much when she went.'

'I did, and I'm sorry I made it so obvious.' But he didn't sound it. 'She was a good colleague and a friend,' he added pointedly.

'So why didn't you and she . . . ? Because it was against company regs?'

Jake snorted. 'Like that has ever stopped anyone.' He stopped and gazed at the horizon. 'I just . . . it wasn't . . .' He paused. 'It didn't happen.' He said that with such finality that even Sophie wasn't tempted to pry further. Jake bent down and picked up his holdall. 'Right, we'd better report to base and find out what they have planned for our flights out of here. Want a hand?'

Sophie shook her head and grabbed her own holdall by the handles. 'I can manage.'

Jake took her at her word. 'Good.' He strode off along the jetty and left Sophie behind him looking bemused and more than a tad annoyed at being so comprehensively dismissed. Whatever rapport they'd managed to find just moments earlier was lost again.

When he reached the local office of WorldFleet he dumped his bag outside the door and strode in.

'Hi, Sally,' he greeted the girl at the desk. 'How's tricks?'

'Same old same old. The *Earth Star* all shipshape and Bristol fashion?'

'Yup.'

'Good. We'll do the inventory and the checks as soon as we can.'

Sophie crashed through the door. 'Thanks for waiting,' she mumbled sourly.

Jake stared at her. She'd said she could manage, so why was she upset that he'd left her to cope? Women! He turned his attention back to Sally. 'When's that likely to be?'

'It'll be tomorrow at the earliest. I've got my hands full with the staff barbecue tonight. And the boss has decided he's going to fly out and make sure everything is in order. I can't possibly get you and the *Earth Star* sorted out today. I don't know if I'm coming or going.'

'Oh joy,' said Jake. 'The staff barbecue. My cup runneth over.'

'And you *will* be there and you *will* enjoy yourself,' said Sally. 'Mr Pencombe may well be there himself if he arrives ahead of schedule – which I've been told is a distinct possibility.'

Jake sighed heavily. 'Message received and understood. I suppose if I don't pitch up I'll find myself on the very last available flight home.'

'It might happen like that, yes. But actually . . .'

'Yes?'

'You're going as soon as I can fix it, probably tomorrow, as soon as we've dealt with the *Earth Star*. I had an email from head office. They want to see you in South Ken next week and they thought you mightn't appreciate going straight from the airport to them without a few days off.'

'Why do they want me?'

'They probably want to send you to charm school,' said Sophie, still sulking.

'Very possibly,' said Jake coolly. He returned his attention to Sally.

'They didn't say,' she told him. 'It can't be anything disciplinary and the yacht's all in one piece – those are the usual reasons for a summons. Maybe they want to talk about your prospects.'

Jake shrugged. 'Maybe.'

'Prospects? A lonely old age beckons, if you ask me,' said Sophie.

'Well I didn't,' shot back Jake. 'And who rattled your cage?'

'Children, children,' said Sally. 'I hope to God you two didn't behave like this in front of the guests – and that you don't in front of Mr Pencombe.'

Jake sighed. 'As if.' He glared at Sophie, who was raising her eyebrows and looking disbelieving.

It was Sally's turn to sigh. 'Then I take back what I said about your interview not being disciplinary. You both look like you need a good talking to. If you want to carry on fighting I suggest you go outside. I've got work to do.'

'Before I go,' said Jake, 'can I have the key to my room?'

'Sure.' Sally pushed her chair back and opened up the key press at the back of the office. 'You're in apartment thirty-four, sharing with a couple of the flotilla skippers.' She consulted a list. 'And you, Sophie, are in twenty-eight.' She picked out the keys and handed them over, together with the forms for the two employees to sign to say they promised not to damage the now empty holiday apartments and to leave them clean and tidy. 'And try not to lose the keys. Head office is beginning to get shirty about it and it's me they're taking it out on. Besides, I'll dock your pay if you do.'

Jake took his key and moseyed off to find his new accommodation. It would be odd sleeping on dry land after all those months at sea.

Sophie watched him go and shook her head. 'God, that man can be so . . .' she narrowed her eyes and pursed her lips as she scrabbled for the word she wanted, 'irritating.'

'But he's a fantastic skipper. The punters always rave about his itineraries.'

Sophie snorted. 'Well, maybe they wouldn't rave about him if he treated them the way he treated me.'

'He's grumpy with everyone. It's nothing personal.'

'Huh. I bet he wasn't with the blessed Poppy.'

'I've no idea, but he's been with WorldFleet for quite a few seasons and as far as I know he's never really made friends with any of his colleagues. Always the loner is our Jake.'

'But why?'

'Tragic past. I don't know the details but a girlfriend of his drowned.'

'Wow. His fault?'

'I don't think so. It happened during the Sail Fast, the

year there was that terrible storm and quite a few people died and no end of the yachts got damaged or worse.'

Sophie nodded, remembering. 'Still, there's no reason for him to take it out on other people.'

Sally shook her head in total disagreement. 'Personally, I should think it would give him every reason.' Sophie muttered something about 'moving on' which riled Sally yet further. 'Maybe if people were a little more sympathetic he'd be less grumpy.'

'Whatever.'

Sally bit back her retort of choice and instead said, 'I mustn't keep you. No doubt you want to get ready for the fun and games tonight.' She pulled some papers towards her and began to work, thus indicating the conversation was over. Sophie, dismissed, jangled her keys and left the office.

A vat of punch sat on the long trestle table and the WorldFleet staff gathered around that or the barbecue, depending on whether they preferred booze or warmth as a focal point. Jake had chosen the barbecue and sipped slowly at the lethal concoction, knowing that it had been specifically designed to make the drinker relax. The trouble was he also knew it could make the drinker so relaxed that he or she would wind up horizontal. Unlike his chattering co-workers, he was silent as he stared at the glow from the charcoal and watched the sparks float up into the night sky. Beside him, the sea lapped quietly at the pale sand, which shone in the light of a nearly full moon. The cool air was heavy with the smell of cooking burgers and sausages and the sizzle and spit of hot fat melded into the susurration of the sea. Occasionally a burst of laughter echoed round the little bay as one or other of the skippers or hostesses recounted something one of their punters had done that summer.

He pondered about his summons to head office. Realistically he knew that it couldn't be anything bad. If a guest had accused him of some misdemeanour earlier in the season it would have been dealt with by now, and he couldn't believe that there had been a complaint from their last party – a group of retired captains of industry and their wives. So it really had to be something positive, but what? He wondered if, maybe, they wanted him to move from the Med to another location, but surely that could be done over the phone or by letter. They couldn't have decided he was too old or expensive to be retained. At thirty and with only the standard wage for a charter skipper he couldn't possibly fall into either category. Maybe Poppy had said something to Charlie on her trip home which had got him into trouble, but he didn't think that was likely. And surely if she had, the company wouldn't have waited till the end of the season to confront him about it. Nope, he was stumped.

He drained his glass and changed his musings to weighing up the arguments for and against getting a refill. He knew he was probably about the only person on the beach who was taking it steady. Everyone else around him was knocking back the booze as if it were water. But it wasn't often that the company gave the employees something for nothing, and consequently, when they did, the workers took full advantage of it and as quickly as possible – just to make sure they got the full benefit. And to judge by the noise level and the general jollity, this evening was no exception.

As he watched he saw a silhouette detach itself from the group by the booze and head determinedly but erratically towards him. Sophie.

'Here you are,' she said with a giggle. 'Mr Happy.' She stumbled slightly on the uneven sand. 'Whoops-a-daisy.' She peered at Jake's glass. 'You haven't got a drink. You must have a drink. It's company regs that everyone should have a drink.'

'Is it? Bully for the company regs.'

'Oh, lighten up, Jake,' said Sophie, trying to land a playful punch on his shoulder and almost falling over in the process. Jake caught and steadied her.

Behind him a call went up from the team tending the barbecue that the food was ready.

'You need to eat,' he said to her. 'I think you could do with some blotting paper.'

'Could I? Tell you what, I'll get both of us another drink and you get both of us some food. Deal?'

'You don't need a drink, just food.'

'Don't be such a killjoy. I'm going to get a drink.' She turned round to leave, tripped over her own bare feet and fell heavily on to the sand. She didn't move.

Fuck, thought Jake. Maybe she'd hurt herself. He put his own glass down and crouched down beside her. 'You all right, Soph?'

'No. Help me up, Jake.' She put her arms up and as he reached out to take her hands she grabbed him, catching him off balance, and he toppled over, landing beside her.

'Don't be a prat, Sophie. Do you want a hand up or don't you?' Jake righted himself but stayed crouching beside her.

'Oh,' she said, 'you are masterful.'

Jake straightened and stood up. 'Forget it, Sophie. Sort yourself out. I'm going to get some food. And if you take my advice you'll get some too.'

Jake stamped off to join the back of the queue. At least, he thought, he'd soon be on a flight home and away from this lot. Of course, going home presented a whole other set of hassles – not least of which was where he was going to live and how he was going to earn the rent money. Between the last couple of seasons he'd stayed over at the shore base, helping repair and refit the boats and doing endless odd jobs around the place to bring everything up to the required standard before the season had started again at Easter. But this year his application to stay on had been turned down. He had a couple of mates at his old sailing club who would probably give him a bed for a few nights till he found somewhere to rent, but a job was going to be a whole other matter. The idea of being stuck indoors all day appalled him. He hoped he might be able to pick up something to do with boats – maybe some casual work at a marina. In the meantime he'd be able to sign on, but . . . Jake sighed. The prospects for winter and Christmas were hardly enticing. He hoped something would crop up.

'Sorry, Jake.' Sophie interrupted his thoughts.

'Forget it,' he replied. The queue for food edged forward a couple of feet.

'You're right. I'm pissed.'

'A statement of the bleeding obvious.'

'Will you get me some food?'

'If you promise to eat it and not muck me about any more.'

Sophie giggled, hiccoughed and crossed her heart. 'I'll sit on the sand and wait for you. And I'll be good. All right?'

Jake nodded.

'Actually,' she continued, before she moved away, 'I can be *sensational* if you ever want to find out.'

Jake narrowed his eyes as she drifted unsteadily off. No he didn't, thanks all the same. Nor was he sure that spending an evening propping up a drunken Sophie was entirely what he wanted, but there wasn't anything better on offer. Sophie tottered off and slumped on the sand a few yards away while Jake grabbed two plates and loaded them with meat, baked spuds and salad. Then, gathering some cutlery, he made his way over to her.

'Here you go,' he said. Carefully he placed the plates on the ground and settled himself beside her. 'Tuck in.'

Jake realised he was quite hungry and attacked his food with relish, but Sophie seemed to spend more time pushing hers around her plate than forking it into her mouth. Jake had nearly cleared his plate when he realised that she had hardly touched hers. And she ought to eat, if only to mop up the booze.

'Come on, Soph, eat up. It's not bad. I mean, I know it's not up to your standard and it isn't cordon blue, but it's hot and tasty.'

Sophie shovelled in some chicken and salad and chewed. After she'd swallowed she laid down her fork and shoved her plate off her lap. 'Actually, Jake, I don't think I feel all that bright.'

'What sort of not bright?' said Jake.

'Dizzy,' mumbled Sophie, leaning heavily against him.

Jake looked at her. Even in the moonlight the slick of sweat over her forehead was obvious and there was an unhealthy pallor to her tanned skin.

'You going to be sick?' he asked.

'Dunno. Don't think so.'

'Bloody hell, Soph. You really know how to show a guy a good time.' Jake pushed his own plate aside, stood up, pulled Sophie to her feet and then swung her up into his arms. 'Just don't hurl over me, that's all I ask,' he muttered grimly as he staggered off the beach and towards the apartments. 'Which one's yours, Sophie?' he panted as they approached the low blocks.

'Carn 'member,' she slurred, her head lolling against his shoulder.

'Where's the key then?'

'In bag . . . beach.'

'Fuck it, Sophie, you might have said.'

Jake made a decision and made towards his room. She'd have to lie down on his bed till she sobered up. He'd find somewhere else to sleep – the beach if necessary.

With a deal of juggling and fumbling he managed to extricate his key from his shorts pocket and not drop Sophie in the process. By now he was seriously short of breath and staggered thankfully into his flat, kicking the door shut behind him. By the time he dumped Sophie on to his bed his arms were agony in his shoulder sockets but he managed to restrain himself from dropping her and laid her down reasonably carefully.

Once he'd eased his aching back and torso, he rolled her on to her side and shoved a pillow behind her back to keep her in the recovery position.

'Okay, Sophie?'

'No,' she whimpered. 'I think . . .' She gulped. 'I think . . .' She began to heave.

'Oh, Christ,' said Jake, guessing what was coming next. He grabbed the plastic waste bin and got it under Sophie's head just in time. 'Marvellous, just fucking marvellous,' he said through gritted teeth as Sophie vomited long and noisily into his makeshift bucket. He sat beside her, held her head, kept her hair out of her face, reassured her and tried not to gag in sympathy, even though his own stomach was churning in disgust. When she'd finished he got a towel and sponged her face, gave her cool water to drink and rinsed out the bin.

The room smelt sour so he opened a window. Behind him Sophie groaned.

'Tell me I'm not going to die,' she whispered.

'Probably not. But in the morning you may wish you had.' Jake's sympathy stock was almost at rock bottom and he wasn't terribly inclined to mine it further for someone who had wantonly got herself into this state.

'I'm sorry, Jake. I am so sorry.' Sophie dissolved into noisy maudlin tears.

'Don't worry. It's no biggie.' Jake raised his eyebrows and shook his head. First she was sick, now she was unhappy. What a great evening this was turning out to be.

'Yes it is. I made a fool of myself, I feel crap, I spoilt your evening, it's all a mess.'

Jake sat beside her on the bed and patted her hand, wishing she'd shut up or pass out. Her sobs were doing his head in but he didn't feel he could just abandon her in this state. 'It's not that bad. There's no harm done.' But his ministrations did nothing to calm her and she continued to cry.

'I make such a mess of everything,' she wailed. 'No one likes me, I haven't got a boyfriend, my bum's too big . . .'

'Hang on, hang on,' said Jake. 'Of course people like you—'

'You don't,' Sophie interrupted.

'Don't be silly. Of course I like you.'

Sophie looked up blearily. 'Do you? Really?'

'Honestly,' he lied.

'B-but I thought you hated me,' she snuffled between sobs.

'I'm just not very . . .' Jake shrugged, 'touchy-feely.'

'Is that because of your girlfriend who drowned?'

Jake felt as if he'd received a physical blow. How the hell did she know about Julie? Or was it common knowledge amongst the WorldFleet staff? For a second or two he was speechless. 'What do you know about Julie?' he snarled, his voice sounding dangerous.

Even in her drunken state, Sophie knew she'd overstepped some sort of mark. Frantically she tried to backpedal. 'Nothing. I didn't mean . . .'

'Don't you ever talk about her.' Jake, furious, got up and strode across the room. Sophie cowered on the bed.

'I'm sorry, I'm sorry,' she whispered.

'Well you should be.' He leant on the windowsill and tried to regain some sort of control. He breathed deeply. The memory of Julie still hurt. There was rarely a day when something didn't make him remember something she had said, a mannerism, a kindness she'd shown. And to hear Sophie mention her so thoughtlessly had caught him completely off balance.

'I won't mention her again. Ever,' she whispered.

'Good.' Jake could still feel the blood pounding angrily round his veins but his breathing was back under control. And at least his anger had made her stop bawling. He turned round. 'I suggest you stay here and sober up. And as you've got my bed I'll go somewhere else tonight.' He grabbed his still-packed kitbag, stormed out of the room and slammed the door behind him.

He didn't know where he was going to sleep, but before he addressed that problem he decided to walk to calm down. Below him, at the bottom of the slight hill, down on the beach he could see the glow of lanterns and the red flicker of the barbecue, and the voices and laughter wafted up towards him on the gentle breeze. Behind the partygoers, the sea stretched inky dark to the horizon, the silver path laid by the moon glinting and twinkling. Above, the endless black was spattered with stars. Jake gazed about him, feeling the tranquillity of the scene seep into him, calmed by the sense of the infinity of space. He sighed. He'd flown off the handle at Sophie. Just because she was a fuckwit and a piss-head and had made an unfortunate remark about Julie didn't give him the right to be so mean. Plenty of the other kids who worked for WorldFleet behaved the same way off duty – they just hadn't upset him like Sophie had.

Poppy wouldn't have made such a thoughtless remark, though, even if she had known about Julie. And maybe she had. Maybe everyone in WorldFleet knew. It was a sobering thought, that his past might be common knowledge. Too late to worry about it now. Jake loped down the path, past the beach, keeping well in the shadows as he didn't want to be hauled back to join the revels – partying was the last thing he felt like doing right now. He carried on, past the company office, past the jetty and the *Earth Star*, past the harbour, crowded with the flotilla yachts and a number of local fishing boats, to the point at the other end of the bay. Here scrub and pine trees replaced the houses, tavernas and souvenir shops, and at this time of night the only sound to be heard was the constant, manic chirring of the cicadas.

Jake, his bag slung over his shoulder, wandered through the undergrowth to the water's edge and hunkered down, leaning against the trunk of a large pine. The smell of barbecued food was replaced by the smell of warm pine resin and ozone and the peace stole into him and replaced his anger.

He thought about Poppy; how kind she'd always been.

How she'd always gone the extra mile for the guests – and for him. She'd always got up first and brought him a cup of tea in his cabin; she'd always saved him lunch if he'd been busy at the helm – or made him something specially that he could snack on easily with one hand. She'd never complained at the long hours or about some of the more difficult guests. Paragon – that was the word that sprang to mind.

A bit like Julie.

That brought him up short. He'd never thought he'd get to the stage when he'd be able to compare anyone with Julie. Maybe he had moved on. Maybe it was time to put Julie behind him.

And his mother? What about her? Was it time for him to accept that he really wasn't to blame? That he'd done his best? Could he really put her behind him?

Maybe he could.

If he was honest he didn't want to spend the rest of his life keeping women at arm's length, apart from a few random and casual one-night stands which had been pretty unsatisfactory for both sides. And he had missed Poppy; *did* miss her. As he stared sightlessly out over the wine-dark sea he wondered if he'd see her again when he got back to England. It wouldn't be beyond him to take a trip down to Cornwall. He could look up Polzeal on the map and get a train or hitch down there. But would she want to see him? There was only one way to find out.

After a while he wandered back towards the main harbour. He had lost his bed for the night and still hadn't worked out where he might find another. Sleeping in the open was a definite possibility, although the beach didn't really appeal; too uncomfortable, too gritty, too exposed.

He thought about asking one of the others if they had a spare bunk in their accommodation but that meant returning to the party. However, there was one place he would feel right at home – the *Earth Star*. He might not be able to access the cabins any more – she was secured and the keys had been handed in – but the cockpit was relatively sheltered, and the cushions were still in place.

He strolled down the jetty and climbed on board. The *Earth Star* dipped and swayed gently under his weight as he moved around and made himself comfortable on the spacious banquettes in the cockpit. Then Jake lay on his back, positioned his kitbag as a pillow and gazed at the endless stars above, and let the yacht rock him to sleep while he thought about Poppy.

26

Jake cooled his heels on a pavement in South Ken waiting for his watch to tick round to the time of his appointment. More curious than nervous he was impatient to get the interview over and done with, to find out what the future held. Whatever it was it had to be better than his current prospects of dossing on a mate's sofa in Norwich and signing on for a fortnightly Giro.

Finally it was time for him to pass through the main door and announce himself.

'Go right up,' said a pleasant receptionist. 'Monica's office is on the first floor. Just follow the signs to HR as you go up the stairs. You can't miss it.'

Jake took his visitor's pass and headed for the stairs. Here goes, he thought, mentally crossing his fingers.

He knocked on Monica's door and was glad not to be kept waiting.

'Come in, come in,' she called cheerfully.

Jake entered and was relieved to find that not only did he feel welcome but he could tell from Monica's broad smile that this interview was going to be about something positive.

'Take a seat. Tea? Coffee?'

'Nothing, thanks.' Jake was already awash with coffee from killing a couple of hours since his arrival in London.

'Right, I'll get straight to the point. WorldFleet is setting up a new venture. We're having problems recruiting the skippers and crew for the high end of our business. The flotilla teams are fine; for that we just need enthusiastic and energetic young sailors who are happy to follow the same routine week in, week out, taking the punters to the same ports of call.' Jake nodded. He knew the form well enough. 'The trouble is the charter business; recruiting the likes of you and Poppy.'

'Poppy was a one-off,' agreed Jake.

'But that's exactly my problem. I can't run the HR side of WorldFleet on one-offs. What happens if I can't find enough Poppys – or Jakes for that matter?'

'You've got Sophie, and the other crews in the Med are pretty good from what I've heard. I never heard any complaints about the *Sea Star* or the *Sun Star*.'

Monica shook her head. 'Sophie was competent but she wasn't in Poppy's league and I think you must have recognised that. We promoted her from the flotilla because she was the best we could find at short notice.'

'Well . . .' Jake didn't want to spoil Sophie's chances of staying with the charter side of the business, but he knew that lying was useless. 'I expect she learnt a lot from this season.'

Monica didn't respond to that. Instead she continued, 'And the other crews are okay, but we have a lot of retention problems. The trouble is they get cherry-picked by private yacht owners who can offer them better terms and conditions and less work; year-round contracts for just a few weeks' real graft. We're finding it very hard to compete.'

'Well, you could always offer a winter retention package,' said Jake, thinking that it would be something he'd jump at.

'Yes, well, anyway . . .' Obviously WorldFleet didn't agree. 'As I was saying, we have problems with recruiting the right staff and we need to keep the people we do recruit working round the year.'

Oh well, thought Jake, *working* round the year. He ought to have known that the idea of being paid to loaf about for several months was a non-starter. Still, worth a try.

'So Mr Pencombe and his son Charlie are looking to expand the business. They were both out in the Med this summer—' Monica stopped. 'Oh, of course you know. Charlie was involved in getting Poppy back to England and you probably met them both at the end of season party.'

'I remember Poppy's departure very well,' said Jake, glad he could gloss over the fact that his participation at the staff barbecue had been minimal. He had certainly left by the time the top brass had pitched up.

'Anyway, to be honest, this is more Charlie's idea; he thinks that Wing ought to branch out to chartering yachts in the Caribbean and the Far East so that when the Mediterranean season closes he can move his top crews to other locations and keep them employed there.'

'That would suit me,' said Jake. It certainly would, and the idea of working in both the new locations appealed. In fact it appealed enough for him almost to be able to forgive Charlie for being a flash git who had made a move on Poppy.

'Yes, but it only exacerbates the problem of finding enough quality charter crews.'

Jake was lost now. He could see he was going to be offered more employment but he couldn't see why Monica was shovelling all her HR shit in his direction. He furrowed his brow, trying to work out just why he was there. Did she want him to do the recruiting or something?

'I want you, Jake, to help me train up people with potential. I've interviewed a lot of great kids to fill the chef and steward posts but they can't sail. Equally I've seen some fully qualified sailors with off-shore and masters' tickets who haven't a clue about the hospitality business. Charlie has spent the last few weeks acquiring and developing a property to turn into a college for exactly this purpose and we'd like you to help run the sailing courses there.'

'Cool,' said Jake.

'It's not ready yet. The developers are behind schedule – there are structural problems with the building – but we're getting ahead with working out a training programme. Charlie is recruiting a couple of skippers from Trinidad and Tobago to give us the low-down on great itineraries for yacht charters out there and we've got a chef on board to bring all our crews up to the highest possible culinary standard.'

'Great,' said Jake. 'But with all that talent I'm not entirely sure where I fit in.'

'Well, as I said, we want you to help run the sailing programme. Charlie thinks that we should recruit crew with a catering background and teach them how to sail. Similarly, we're going to find skippers who can't necessarily cook and teach them the basics – well, more than the basics, actually. You'll be teaching the sailing side to the cooks, and the chef will be working with the skippers in the kitchen. We also want you to liaise with the guys from the Caribbean to plan some eye-opening itineraries. So . . .' Monica paused and smiled at Jake. 'Do you think you can do it?'

Jake considered the question for a few seconds. Certainly the chance to be paid through the winter months was appealing, but what about next season? 'I could do it, certainly. Does it mean I wouldn't be dealing with charters any more?'

'Possibly not. We'd have to see how the training side of the venture goes. Maybe we could arrange for one of your protégés to succeed you in a year or two.'

A year or two? That wasn't quite what Jake had envisaged. The thing that he loved about being a charter skipper was the freedom it gave him: the ability just to up anchor and mosey off somewhere else, a new port every day. Okay, so he'd been sailing round the same bit of Greece for a couple of years now, but what with the changing weather and sea conditions, the turnover of guests, their different requirements, he'd never felt that there had been anything routine about his job. But to be stuck in a school . . .

'Have a think about it, Jake,' said Monica, sensing his qualms. 'Mull over the offer. It may help if I tell you where you'll be based – and what the salary we're offering is.'

'Shoot,' said Jake.

'Well, the school is in a tiny place in Cornwall – Polzeal . . .'

Jake had no idea what the salary was that Monica offered as he was too busy agreeing to take the post.

Poppy recognised Jake the instant he turned in to the drive: his casual, loping walk, the WorldFleet navy chinos and white windcheater that brought out his hunky tan, his hair just a touch too long – the same look she'd been so familiar with in Greece. Nothing about him had really changed since they'd parted so precipitately back in July. And she realised with a shock that the pleasure she was feeling at seeing him again was quite overwhelming. She knew that she still liked him as much as she always had; still wanted them to be friends and still wondered if there would ever be anything more between them, but this rush, this thrill at their reunion – that was unexpected.

Since she'd heard it was he who had been chosen to work with her she'd spent a lot of her free time mulling over their time together, thinking about their days on the *Earth Star* and how much she'd enjoyed his company. Okay, he could be a bit moody but he'd been a terrific boss and she knew he had cared about her. Look at the way he'd treated her when the news had come through about her dad.

And he'd been right about Charlie. She'd been swept along by his looks, his association with the huge yacht and his easy manners, but Jake hadn't been taken in by him at all; he'd never liked him, never trusted him, and he'd been right not to. Which put Jake even higher in her estimation.

Not that she was going to tell Jake that she'd been a fool. She wasn't going to mention the way Charlie'd made a grab for her in his office. It was too sleazy and horrid and . . . embarrassing. As far as she was concerned, Charlie and the summer were history and Jake was the present.

The present, almost winter, in Cornwall. Which was a long way from when they'd last worked together in Greece in July. No brilliant sunshine and blinding heat, no azure seas, scrub-covered hills and smell of thyme and pine resin hanging heavy in the air. Now it was sunken lanes, lush meadows full of dairy cattle, brown corduroy ploughed fields, copses atop rolling hills and outcrops of granite or moorland. It was a day of sudden squalls that had come and gone and clouds skittering across the pale blue sky bringing fat showers and fitful sunshine. The sea that Poppy could see from this upstairs window had a sullen grey look to it and there was a distinct chill in the air, even in the brief interludes of pale lemony sun. Greece and their time together on the *Earth Star* seemed years ago, not just a few months.

Poppy yelled his name through the unglazed window. Jake paused in his progress over the weed-strewn gravel and looked to see where the voice had come from.

'Up here,' shouted Poppy again, waving.

'Poppy,' he yelled back.

'I'll come down,' she hollered. She ran across the bare, dusty floorboards of the undecorated shell of a bedroom, dodging under the plasterer's scaffolding to get to the door, careered along a landing and then shot down the wide stairs, taking the shallow treads three at a time. Jake was almost on the doorstep by the time she reached the hall.

'Jake,' she shrieked. 'It's so good to see you again.' She raced over the grubby marble tiles and threw herself at him. Jake had to drop his baggage to catch her as she wrapped her arms round him, squeezing the air out of his lungs.

'Steady,' he said, embarrassed by the enthusiasm of her welcome.

'I'm so glad it's you,' she said, resting her chin on his chest and gazing up. 'I had nightmares about who head office were going to pick for this job. It never occurred to me it would be you.'

'Well, thanks a bundle,' said Jake, but his grin made a mockery of his words. 'Thanks for the vote of confidence, Poppy.'

'I didn't mean it like that.' She dropped her arms and Jake sucked in a deep breath. 'I mean, I knew you and Charlie didn't exactly hit it off, so I thought – well, never mind. I just didn't expect it to be you.' She slipped an arm through his. 'But I'm jolly glad it is. Come on, I'll show you your quarters. It's a bit basic still – no carpet yet, I'm afraid – but it's getting there.'

Jake hoisted his holdall over his shoulder again and followed Poppy up two flights of stairs to the top floor of the house.

'I've put the training staff up here. I thought it would be easier to keep ourselves to ourselves. I've got a feeling we might want to get away from our students in the evenings if we have to spend the rest of the day with them.' She opened a door. 'Besides, the view is better.'

Jake stepped over the threshold of a large room, freshly painted in sunny yellow and white, with a big dormer window. There was a row of built-in wardrobes along one wall and a cubicle in the corner which was obviously a tiny bathroom. A TV stood on a low unit under the window, and a desk, a large double bed and a squashy sofa completed the furnishings.

'Sorry about the lack of carpets. We've decided on a job lot for the whole of the upstairs and we can't get them fitted till the plasterers and decorators have finished. But I thought you'd be tough enough to manage without. At least you've got glass in your windows – not all the rooms have.'

'I reckon I can just about cope,' said Jake with a grin as he unhitched his holdall and slung it on to the bed.

'Good.' Poppy plonked herself down next to the bag. 'It's good to see you again, Jake. I didn't get a chance to say a proper goodbye.'

'It was a bit sudden, wasn't it? How is your dad?'

'Improved and improving but not back like he was. He's in a nursing home as he needs a lot of physio still. His memory is still a bit tricky but he's regained most of his motor skills and his speech is heaps better. But he gets tired and he's got a dreadful limp. It means Mum has to employ another part-time barman which bites into the profits. But hey,' Poppy said with a smile. 'It could be a whole lot worse and I've got a job in the village that pays serious money. Also, with my room vacant and the spare room to play with as well, Mum has branched out into doing B & Bs.'

'So all a lot better than when I last saw you haring off with Charlie in that swanky speedboat. And do I gather you're living in this place too, like me?'

'In the room next door. Just like old times. We can have fun together.'

Jake smiled at her, her good humour and her irrepressibility lifting his spirits yet further. The prospect of working with Poppy again was just great.

'Welcome, and good evening,' said Poppy from behind a lectern in the dining hall. She beamed at the twenty young men and women seated in a semicircle in front of her; the dining tables had been pushed against the wall to make space. To her right, under the windows, were the half-dozen people who would be the tutors in sailing and catering. She'd do a roll-call later and introduce them to the trainees. The students were all wearing name tags pinned to their best WorldFleet uniforms and clutching their folders, which contained their schedules, room keys, local information and WorldFleet corporate freebies: pens, notebooks and the like. Some of the assembled trainees smiled tentatively back. The tutors eyed them up, already assessing them.

The tutors had arrived the previous day and were already settled in on the top floor with Jake and Poppy. The students, however, had arrived, en masse, on a chartered coach from London, only about an hour earlier. Jake had been in charge of meeting and greeting them and had allocated rooms. Poppy had begged to be excused that bit as she'd been frantically rehearsing her opening presentation.

'I'll meet them all soon enough,' she'd said pleadingly. 'I *so* need to have another run through and you don't need me to help. It isn't as if they're proper paying guests and need cosseting and looking after.'

So now she was getting her first sight of them, and they

didn't look too scary. Some faces were even familiar. She relaxed slightly and smiled again. 'And a happy New Year. It's really great to welcome you all to the WorldFleet inaugural training course. As you know, some of you are here to improve your sailing skills, some of you are here to learn some galley skills and some of you are here to upgrade both. You are the first group through, which makes you all guinea pigs. We have aimed to create a training programme that you will find interesting, possibly a little challenging but certainly informative. However, it is in the nature of things that there is bound to be a shake-down period, sea trials as it were. We may have got things wrong, placed the wrong emphasis on some of the various sections, so I hope you will be patient and give us feedback when we ask for it.' She stopped and shrugged. 'Even if it's not very complimentary.' The group laughed.

'It's good to recognise some faces from WorldFleet and I see we have some new recruits, but whether you're an old hand or a newbie we hope you enjoy your stay here.' She smiled again. 'Now then, I've got a heap of boring admin stuff to run through but once I've done that I suggest we adjourn to the bar and get to know each other better before dinner in about an hour.' There was a rustle of anticipation and appreciation. 'However,' she continued, 'in the meantime I'd just like you to pay attention to some things I have to say about housekeeping, what we expect from all of you students, conduct while in uniform and the like. But first I want you to watch this short film about WorldFleet and our ethos, our operations and our hopes for this course.'

She pressed a remote and the curtains in the dining hall silently drew shut, the lights dimmed, a screen dropped down from the ceiling and the digital projector hummed to life. Jake took his cue to slip out quietly and check everything was ready in the bar.

'Hi, Dan. Ready for the charge?'

'Jake, if I can cope with the grockles in Anne's pub on a wet Saturday in August this lot will be a doddle. For pity's sake, there's only twenty or so and we're only offering wine, beer or soft drinks. I'm not having to cope with snack orders and cocktails and a brewery delivery all at the same time.'

Jake forced himself to take a deep breath. He was getting himself worked up over nothing. Dan was right and he said so.

'Besides,' continued Dan, 'I'd make sure I coped whatever. This job is a lifeline for the likes of me. I know I've got the job at the pub but the takings, the way they are in the winter, mean Glad and I only earn about half what we do in the summer, and with the cost of everything as it is we find it hard to make ends meet. There's no way I'm going to risk cocking things up and being sacked.'

'I know. And I have absolute faith in you. I'm just cacking myself that something will go wrong. We're expecting the big cheese from London sometime soon and I really, really don't want to let Poppy down. I hear Mr Pencombe can be a right stickler.'

'You'll be fine. And so will I, you can rest assured about that. How long is it before they get let loose from the dining room?'

'Another ten minutes or so, maybe less. Depends how many questions they ask. Then half an hour or so for drinks, then dinner. Piece of piss.'

Jake watched Dan polish glasses and uncork a couple

of bottles. He was dreading the next part of the evening –
when Poppy and Sophie would come face to face. He
didn't think Poppy had spotted that Sophie was here.
She'd been bunged on the course as a replacement for
another candidate who had broken her leg while skiing at
Christmas. The final list of students had only been
emailed through that morning from head office and Poppy
had been far too busy with last-minute arrangements to
worry about details like the actual names; all she'd been
interested in was numbers. He knew Poppy wouldn't
recognise Sophie, as their paths had never crossed, but he
wondered if she'd clock her name badge. And how would
the two girls react when they did finally meet? Poppy had
no reason to take against Sophie but he knew that Sophie
wasn't Poppy's number one fan. And he also knew full well
that Sophie could be a right shit-stirrer and he didn't trust
her not to antagonise Poppy. But please God she wouldn't.

A distant throbbing started to become a more obvious
clatter and a sudden light raked the uncurtained windows
of the bar. Jake looked out. This must be Philip
Pencombe's helicopter.

'The big cheese,' he said to Dan, raising his voice to be
heard above the increasing roar of the approaching
aircraft. 'I'd better get out there and meet him.'

He crossed the hall and opened the front door just as
the downdraught from the rotor blades caught the
remains of the last of the dead leaves lying on the now
weed-free gravel of the drive. Dust, dirt and leaf litter
spiralled into the air like a mini tornado as the helicopter
landed on the big circular lawn that the drive embraced.
Jake pulled the front door shut behind him to keep the
muck out of the hall and shielded his eyes against the

gritty onslaught. A second or so later he heard the engine note fall dramatically as the pilot killed the power. Jake ran forward to welcome Philip Pencombe.

The rotors were still spinning as he ducked under them and reached out to open the cabin door of the Squirrel, which was decked out in WorldFleet livery. He tugged at the handle with one hand, still covering his eyes with the other, and then stood back to allow the passenger to descend.

'Hi, Jake,' yelled a voice, barely audible over the whine of the cooling engine and the thwack-thwack of the slowing blades.

Jake looked up. 'Charlie!'

'Surprise!'

Shit.

28

The pair of them ran back across the gravel towards the house. Once inside with the door shut Charlie dumped his overnight bag and held his hand out to Jake. 'Sorry for the change of plan. My old man got held up at the last minute, so rather than cancel I offered to come. Hope you don't mind.'

'Of course not,' lied Jake, surprised that he still felt that spark of animosity towards Charlie that he'd felt back in Greece. 'Welcome to Polzeal Manor.'

Charlie looked around the grand entrance hall and whistled. 'Nice to see how the money was spent. What do you think of this place?'

'It's great. Great location, great facilities, so hopefully we'll get great results.'

'That's the plan.' Charlie cocked an ear. 'It's very quiet. Where is everyone?'

'Poppy's doing the welcome address and showing them the video you had produced to inspire them. They're all in the dining hall at the back. But as soon as she's finished we're having a drink in the bar to break the ice and to make sure everyone gets to know each other.' Jake checked his watch. 'Which should be in just a few minutes from now.' He looked at Charlie's bag. 'You're staying the night?' This wasn't in the plan. A flying visit was what Mr Pencombe senior had said.

'I hope to. Assuming you've got space?' Jake's hesitation answered his question. 'I know Dad planned on returning to London tonight but I wanted to get more of a feel for how everything is down here. If it's a problem I'll get a car organised and book into a hotel somewhere.'

'No, no,' said Jake. He knew by *get a car organised* Charlie really meant *get you or Poppy to organise a car for me, and book a hotel, and fix transport back here in the morning.* He took a breath. He really must try to put his antipathy to Charlie behind him. Be professional. That was what was required. 'No, no problem at all. Have my room.' He hoped to God his teeth didn't look as gritted as they felt. 'I can arrange to bunk up somewhere else.'

'That's ridiculous. I can't turf you out.'

Maybe his teeth hadn't done the decent thing. Jake was a bit taken aback. He'd thought that would be exactly what Charlie would do.

'Look, I don't need four stars, whatever you may think.' Which was pretty much what Jake *had* thought. 'Isn't there somewhere in the village?' continued Charlie smoothly. 'Surely a place like this has a B & B.'

'Oh. Well, actually . . .' Jake hesitated.

'Yes?'

'Poppy's mum might have a room.'

'And what about Rick?'

'Rick?'

Right on cue a draught carrying several dead leaves swept into the hall as the front door opened again and a man in a fleece with the WorldFleet logo stitched on the front came in with a small case.

'Jake, this is Rick, my pilot.'

'Hi, pleased to meet you,' said Jake.

'Jake and I were just discussing accommodation possibilities for you and me. Apparently there's no room here but there's a place in the village.'

'The local pub,' elaborated Jake. 'Poppy's mum runs it. Great food, and the beer's good. Not sure about the facilities. But knowing Poppy as I do, and knowing who she learnt her skills off, I should think it's terrific.'

'Hey, Rick and I are sold on the food and beer alone, aren't we?'

'I'll pass on the beer if I'm flying tomorrow, but as long as the bed is flat and the food is hot I'm happy,' said Rick.

'Can you fix it?' said Charlie.

'I'll ring and see if Anne's got vacancies. I should think so. This village is dead as far as tourists are concerned until Easter.'

Behind them came a burst of noise: a clatter and the hubbub of chattering voices.

'Poppy must have finished her session. Let's go and tell her you're here.'

Jake led the way to the bar. A crowd of trainees and staff were around the tables where Dan had laid out the drinks, helping themselves to the free glasses of wine and beer. Jake found an orange juice for Rick and got a couple of beers for himself and Charlie. He noticed that as he handed his boss his drink Charlie's eyes were darting past him, flicking round the room. He was searching for a face – and it had to be Poppy, Jake just knew it. Jake reckoned Charlie was the sort of guy who would always be checking a party for someone more important, looking over the shoulder of the person he was talking to for the next opportunity, the next celeb, the next person to network with, the old buddy who needed schmoozing. Here, with just WorldFleet staff on offer, it stood to reason he'd be after Poppy again.

The needle on Jake's mental antipathy meter flipped into the danger zone again. Deliberately he turned his attention to Rick and asked him about flying helicopters. Big mistake. To his annoyance, instead of antagonising Charlie, it gave him the perfect opportunity to slide off, while Rick was enthusing to Jake about the difference between handling a helicopter and piloting a small commercial jet.

And Jake was stuck talking to a flying bore while Charlie went off to stalk Poppy. Bugger, thought Jake as he tried to show an interest in the intrinsic difference between static and rotary wing aircraft. He alternated 'really' with 'hmm' and 'interesting' as he switched off from what Rick had to say and tried to see what was going on across the other side of the room.

He could see Sophie was chatting to – or more likely, knowing her, chatting *up* – a couple of the flotilla skippers and Poppy was in conversation with an earnest-looking girl with thick spectacles. Well, that was something. Thank God their paths hadn't crossed yet. Sophie saw him looking at her and flashed him a smile. Jake smiled back. She'd been genuinely pleased to see him when she'd arrived earlier that evening, which he'd found flattering considering the way he'd treated her, so there was no reason for him to be churlish now. Forgive and forget and all that. Besides, it had been months ago and their working relationship here at the manor was going to be totally different from the one they'd shared in Greece.

Charlie was working his way round the room, glad-handing his assembled employees, introducing himself and generally making sure everyone knew exactly who he was. However, it was obvious to Jake that his goal wasn't to meet as many as possible of his subordinates but to wind up with Poppy, despite the way his path was zigzagging through the assembled students.

'Don't you agree, Jake?'

'What?' Jake realised he didn't have a clue what Rick had been saying.

'That flying and sailing are both based on the same aerodynamic principles.'

'Absolutely.' Were they? Did he care? Jake could see that Rick was about to elaborate and felt that he really couldn't be doing with a lecture on sails, wings and air flow. 'Look, you'll have to excuse me but I think Dan needs a hand. Help yourself to anything you want.' He scooted off, leaving Rick looking rather lost. Tough. He dumped his beer on a nearby table and slid in beside Poppy, ousting the girl with thick glasses, just as Charlie pitched up too.

'Charlie,' said Poppy, ignoring Jake. He could see she was blushing and she looked really agitated. Dear God, she really is besotted with him still. He had honestly thought after a couple of months of working so closely with her on the manor, months in which Charlie's name had hardly been mentioned, that she had forgotten about him. But no, apparently not. Bugger.

'But I thought your dad was coming. Is he here too?' She looked about her.

'I'm his replacement,' Charlie explained. 'Hope I'm not too much of a disappointment.' He stared at her.

'Not at all,' said Poppy, looking even more fidgety, Jake noted disgustedly. 'We're delighted to welcome you here. Aren't we, Jake?' Luckily she didn't seem to want an answer. 'You will stay to supper, won't you?'

'I certainly plan to. Apart from anything else you owe me dinner, remember? Because I do.'

Did she? thought Jake. What was that about? He glanced from one to the other, hoping to glean a clue. Poppy, he noticed, went an even deeper shade of pink. His antipathy went off the scale.

'And since there's no room here, Jake was going to try to get rooms at your mother's pub for Rick and me. Weren't you, Jake?' he said pointedly.

'You're staying the night?' Poppy, Jake noticed, was looking completely stressed out now. Ants in her pants, he thought angrily, and wishing it was ants and not Charlie. Damn! 'Has Mum got a vacancy?'

Judging by the hectic flush on Poppy's cheeks there was a lot more going on between her and Charlie than just friendship. Jake didn't know much about body language but there was definitely something between them. He tried to shut the image of the pair of them together out of his mind. Disgustedly he turned away, feeling a sickening wrench of disappointment. What had happened to the rapport that had grown between him and Poppy? He knew he'd been taking things slowly but he'd really thought he and Poppy had got something going. But now Charlie was shoving his paddle in the mix. He was brought back to the present when he heard his own name.

Charlie repeated it. 'Jake?'

Oh shit, he'd been miles away. 'Yes, sorry.'

'You were going to find out. About the rooms.'

'Oh, I . . . um. Yes, of course.' Yes Charlie, no Charlie, three bags full, Charlie.

'Give Mum a call,' suggested Poppy helpfully. She reeled off the number of the pub.

'Right,' said Jake, feeling as though he'd been outmanoeuvred rather skilfully by his boss. Again.

As he made his way to the office Sophie greeted him again. 'Jakey-baby, we didn't have time to chat when I arrived. Maybe now . . .'

For God's sake, could things get worse? And *Jakey-baby*? Shit, so much for thinking everything had changed since Greece. Was he in for a whole fortnight of Sophie trying to cosy up to him? Jeez. It was one thing being pleased to see him, it was quite another thinking that he might want to be her bosom buddy while she was on the course.

'Can't stop. On a mission for the boss.' He turned and headed towards the door, but when he got there he saw that Sophie was hard on his heels.

'Come on, Jake, I just want to say hello properly. What's so urgent it can't wait?'

'I've got to find out if Charlie can stay at the pub in the village.'

'Is that all?'

Jake marched across the corridor and into the admin office. As he went round behind the desk to get to the phone he realised that Sophie had followed him and shut the door.

'Sophie,' said Jake, 'I haven't time for this right now.'

'Time for what?' she said provocatively. She leant over

the desk to give him the full benefit of her cleavage.

Jake ignored her and picked up the phone. He dialled the number of the pub, spoke briefly to Anne, got the answer he really didn't want to hear and replaced the receiver.

'So Charlie will be staying the night. That's nice,' said Sophie.

Jake didn't answer. He didn't agree but he wasn't going to let this little minx know that. She was a trouble-maker and he certainly wasn't going to give her any ammunition. If she got a hint that his relationship with Charlie was anything but friendly it wouldn't stay a secret for a nano-second.

'So where do you sleep, Jake? Here?'

He nodded. 'All the staff do.'

'That's cosy. What about Poppy?'

'*What* about Poppy?'

'It's common knowledge that this is her home village. Does she sleep here?'

'Yes,' answered Jake as curtly as he could. He began to move from behind the desk but Sophie barred his way. Jake stared down at her. He wasn't interested in playing her games.

Sophie took a step nearer and put a hand on his shoulder. It threw Jake for a second but he gathered his wits and was just about to tell her to bugger off and grow up when the door to the office swung open.

'Sorry if I'm interrupting,' said Poppy, suddenly ashen, her eyes wide with surprise. Sophie's hand stayed put, her impressive bust almost touching Jake's chest. Jake saw Poppy swallow and blink, then she said quietly, 'Charlie asked me to let you know that if Mum doesn't have two rooms he really doesn't want to share.'

'It's okay,' said Jake, feeling horribly guilty, although he knew there was no reason to. This wasn't a situation of his making. Crossly he shrugged Sophie off and moved away from her. 'It's fixed. A room each.'

Poppy glanced from him to Sophie and back as if she was trying to work out exactly what had been going on, her eyes suspiciously bright. Jake wanted to tell her that Sophie was a fast hussy, but before he could articulate the words Poppy said 'Good' and left hurriedly, without a backward glance.

'She didn't look happy,' said Sophie gleefully, fully aware of the damage she'd just caused.

'Piss off, Soph.' He'd catch Poppy and explain to her.

Sophie tossed her hair defiantly and smiled wickedly as Jake hurried out of the room after his colleague.

Poppy was feeling shell-shocked. She couldn't face returning to the bar and all the eager faces of the trainees and she certainly needed to get away from Charlie and Jake for a bit. She took herself off to the empty TV room and sat in an armchair while she got to grips with the last few minutes.

First she'd had to cope with the rush of embarrassment at seeing Charlie after that hideous last meeting in his office and then with the awfulness of catching Jake and Sophie together – had they just kissed, or were they about to? It didn't matter – the point was she'd certainly interrupted something. And which encounter had been the worst? Certainly Charlie's reappearance was going to be tough to cope with. She remembered vividly that vile final exchange when she'd turned down his offer of dinner. Prick-tease, that's what he'd called her.

She'd expected to be sacked after that but when the axe didn't fall she knew that if she continued to work for WorldFleet she was bound to come across Charlie again. Eventually the suspense of wondering when the moment would come got too much and she phoned Monica.

'Is Charlie – Mr Pencombe – coming to Cornwall any time soon?'

'Why? Is there a problem?'

'No, no, nothing like that,' said Poppy hastily.

'Good. I'm afraid I'm not really sure what Mr Pencombe's plans are. Can I put you through to his PA?'

'Actually, that would be great.' If she spoke to Charlie's PA, apart from finding out if Charlie planned on heading her way, the PA might put her through to him; she owed him an apology if nothing else. But when she asked if she could have a quick word she'd been told he was in a meeting. The PA had been perfectly polite both then and when she'd phoned back later. And the next day. And the next. Poppy got the hint. She might have the job but she was off his Christmas card list. She had the job because she was going to be good at it but she wasn't to expect anything else. She'd annoyed him and he was making sure she knew he wasn't pleased.

Of course this was always going to make the inevitable meeting even tougher, but until Poppy clapped eyes on him again she hadn't realised quite how bad it was going to be. She did now.

So when Charlie'd told her to tell Jake he wasn't prepared to share a room with his pilot it was with relief that she'd escaped from his presence to pass the message on. But then she'd barged in on Jake and some blonde getting up close and personal in the office. Just when she thought the evening had become about as bad as it could get it suddenly managed to drop to another level of hideousness. A quick glance at the name badge had told her all she needed to know. Sophie. So the buxom blonde she'd clocked at the intro meeting was Sophie. The Sophie who had replaced her on the *Earth Star*, the Sophie Jake had protested he didn't like. Yeah, well it really looked like it. Poppy was stunned at how much witnessing their moment of intimacy hurt.

A thought struck her. Sophie? What the hell was Sophie doing here? She hadn't been on the list of students she'd seen the day before. And why hadn't Jake told her there'd been a change – or had he deliberately concealed the fact from her? If so, why? Guilty conscience? What was going on here?

She'd obviously been a total fool as far as she and Jake were concerned, thinking that since Jake had been at the manor their relationship, while not getting intimate, had progressed from friendship to something deeper, more solid. Hah!

Except that until five minutes ago it had seemed as though it had. Working with Jake was fun, and in the evenings, when they'd finished for the day and the workmen had gone home, they'd taken it in turns to cook something in the partly finished kitchen or, if they were too knackered, wandered down the hill to Anne's pub for supper. They rubbed along incredibly easily, neither feeling the other was failing to pull their weight, often making each other laugh and frequently being able to brainstorm together and find solutions to seemingly impenetrable problems.

She'd realised that she was falling for Jake. One hint of encouragement and she'd be his, but there'd always been that barrier that he'd managed to erect between them, some invisible line that she knew he'd drawn to keep her at arm's length. It was obvious it wasn't because he didn't like her – she knew he did – but he didn't want her close. She could be his friend but that was it. Unrequited love.

What a mug's game that was. But love seemed only to be unrequited where she was concerned. Sophie didn't appear to have any such problems. So how come he'd let Sophie get close? What did Sophie have that she didn't? Poppy felt herself to be close to tears. Sod that. She wasn't going to give them the satisfaction.

She stood up and pushed her shoulders back. She couldn't, wouldn't, give in. She had too much to do and this was not the time to let personal relationships get in the way of professionalism. She couldn't let Charlie see that what had happened in London still embarrassed her. And Jake – well, she'd cope with that later. On her own.

Poppy opened the door of the TV room and, head held high, returned to the bar. She couldn't see Jake. So where was he, the bastard? At least he wasn't off somewhere private with Sophie because she had returned to the bar and was now in conversation with Charlie. Poppy sighed. She had to give Charlie the answer about his accommodation so she might as well put on a brave face, front it out and show him she wasn't bothered.

'All fixed,' she said lightly as she approached. 'A room each for you and Rick.'

'Good. I'm glad that means I can stay for dinner.' He grinned at Sophie before turning back to Poppy. 'So what's the food like here?'

Poppy was grateful for the banality of the conversational gambit. If Charlie had asked her anything verging on the personal she wasn't sure she would have been capable of a sensible or coherent reply. She could keep this on a professional basis, keep it cool, keep Charlie at arm's length. After all, that was where she wanted him.

'Fantastic. The chef Monica sent us is wonderful.'

'As he should be. He comes highly recommended.'

Poppy raised her eyebrows. 'Who by?'

'Dad. We pinched him off Dad's yacht.'

'Dad's yacht!' squealed Sophie. 'Now there are two words I like to hear a man say.'

Charlie laughed. 'Do you now?'

Bloody hell, woman, how obvious can you get, thought Poppy, smiling sweetly. Sophie turned her attention to her. 'And you're Poppy. So glad to meet you properly at last. I heard *so* much about you from Jake.'

'It's a surprise to see you here. I didn't spot your name on the list.'

'Last-minute replacement. Hannah was supposed to be coming but she had a skiing accident. Besides, I just couldn't pass up the chance of working with Jake again.'

'Could you not? Well, lucky you.'

'I know. I can't believe I got selected to come on the inaugural course,' she gushed. 'It's so exciting to be part of this. It's just so thrilling to be thought worthy to be here.' She simpered at Charlie. 'And meeting you, Charlie. Well, isn't that just the icing on my cake.'

Poppy had to restrain herself from slapping her. My God, she thought, has this woman no shame? If this was a course in sucking up to the boss, Sophie had just passed with distinction. 'It isn't so much the *worthy*,' she said, 'as those in need of training.'

Sophie looked like someone had just thrown a bucket of cold seawater over her. 'That's not what I was told,' she shot back, her mouth pursed and puckered like a cat's bum.

Poppy shrugged. Probably not, but she wasn't going to concede the point. 'Well, they wouldn't, would they?'

'Anyway, it's not so much training as upgrading,' interjected Charlie smoothly, smiling at Sophie.

Oh, for God's sake, thought Poppy.

'And I can tell you we're all terribly thrilled to have you here in person, Charlie. Such an honour for us all,' Sophie simpered.

Give me strength. Poppy saw Jake re-enter the room, and saw him clock the fact that she was standing next to Sophie. His eyes flickered from her to Sophie and back again and then a frown creased his brow. Well, if he was feeling uncomfortable it served him right. That's what guilt did to people.

Poppy watched him ease his way through the chatting groups of trainees, looking increasingly nervous as he approached her. Good. She might not be able to tackle him about Sophie right now – but she would.

'Thanks for sorting that out for me,' said Charlie as Jake reached them.

'What? Oh, that's fine.'

'It's a shame you're not staying with us at the manor tonight,' said Sophie with a pout. 'I'm sure someone wouldn't mind bunking up to make room.' She paused. 'Or sharing?'

Charlie raised an eyebrow and gave her a slow smile. 'Are we going to eat soon?' he said. 'I could do with something hot inside me.'

'Mmm, me too,' said Sophie with an arch giggle.

Poppy hoped that the surge of nausea that raced through her didn't show. Couldn't this woman keep her hands off anything in trousers? First Jake and now Charlie. Sheesh.

*

The food was sublime and an appreciative lull softened the general buzz of conversation as the students tucked in. Poppy barely noticed it as she was entirely consumed with her own thoughts about Sophie and Jake. Maybe Sophie was pitching for Charlie now, but it really rankled that something seemed to have gone on between her and Jake in Greece, otherwise why were they so lovey-dovey the instant they met up again? Dully she shovelled food into her mouth, barely tasting any of it.

'What do you think?' asked Charlie, indicating her plateful of food with his fork.

'Great.' Was it? Did she care? She just wanted to be left alone with her thoughts. In fact, the sooner she could get away from everyone the happier she'd be. Okay, so she wasn't being professional and she promised herself she'd sort herself out by the next day, but wasn't everyone allowed to let their standards slip just once in a while? It wasn't as if she didn't have a couple of bloody good reasons.

'And he can produce the same quality in a force nine gale.'

'Can he?' Bully for him. She assumed he was talking to her to show that one of them could be professional. Or maybe he was doing it to irritate her.

'Tell me about your father's yacht,' said Sophie, wheedling her way into the conversation.

'Well, it's pretty big. It's got a crew of twenty.'

'A crew of twenty! Wow,' said Sophie, leaning towards Charlie in a way that showed off her impressive cleavage. 'Your dad must be loaded.'

'He's not short of a bob or two,' conceded Charlie, staring straight down the chasm. He managed to drag his eyes away after a second or two. 'It's a big boat, isn't it, Poppy?'

'Very ostentatious.'

Charlie put down his knife and fork. 'Why not? If you've got it, flaunt it.'

Sophie put a proprietorial hand on Charlie's arm and smirked at Poppy. 'That's what I say too.' She giggled and wiggled her chest provocatively.

'Absolutely,' agreed Charlie, returning his gaze to Sophie's bosom.

Poppy found her depleted appetite waning even further despite the deliciousness of the food. She forced herself to plough through the braised guinea fowl, even though she barely tasted it and wanted it still less, and she had no idea what the dessert was when she'd eaten it. She went through the motions of being polite, of making small talk, of sipping her wine and trying to look normal. At last the meal ended. Coffee was to be served in the bar and Poppy had her chance to make her escape and retreat to her room.

Her flight was halted by Jake, who grabbed her arm as she stood up from the table. 'What the blazes is the matter with you?' he hissed into her ear.

'Nothing,' she snapped back. 'I'm fine. Apart from the fact that you obviously lied to me about how much you hated Sophie.' She shook his hand off and strode out of the dining room. Jake followed her.

'Oh, and why should that matter to you when you've obviously still got the hots for Charlie? Or are you in such a foul mood because he seems to prefer Sophie? And no wonder. At least she doesn't look like a wet weekend.'

'I haven't got the *hots* for him. In fact I couldn't give a stuff about him. He's a sleaze and a letch.'

'Really? You didn't think so in Greece.'

'Well I changed my mind.'

'Oh yeah? And is that why you blushed like a schoolgirl when you met him again just now?'

'I didn't.'

'Don't lie to me, Poppy, you went pillar-box red.'

'I'm not lying, Jake. I really don't like him.'

'Have it your way.'

'Besides, what about you and Sophie? Don't deny there was something going on in the office before dinner.'

'Me and Sophie?' Jake laughed. 'I couldn't give a fig about her.'

'It looked like it when I caught you red-handed.'

'She followed me in, and there wasn't anything going on. In fact I was about to tell her to sod off.'

'Says you.'

Jake snorted in exasperation. 'Believe what you like, but it's the truth.' Poppy felt herself wavering. Maybe Jake sensed it because he put his hand on her arm. 'You can't leave the party now. You're in charge here. If you disappear it would look completely unprofessional. What sort of signal would that send out to the students?'

'Look,' hissed Poppy, not giving a stuff about students or signals, 'I've had a long day, they've got Charlie as the duty management rep – although some bloody example he's setting the way he's behaving with Sophie – and I'm tired and fed up. If I spend any more time with Sophie I'm probably going to slap her, and for your information if I never see Mr Pencombe junior again it'll be far too soon.'

'Because you're jealous he's flirting with Sophie.'

'I am *not* jealous! How dare you? What don't you understand about the fact I think he's despicable? And Sophie is welcome to him.'

Jake said nothing for a moment or two, then: 'I don't know what her game is, whether she's trying to make me or you or Charlie jealous of each other, or maybe she's a nympho or maybe she just likes being a shit-stirrer, but whatever it is she's succeeding. You're as mad as hell with me, she's wound me up and it was never like this till she arrived.'

'I don't understand. Why would she want to cause trouble – because she is. It can't be anything I've done; I've never met her till today.'

Jake exhaled slowly. 'I think . . .' He paused. 'I think I may be at fault here.'

Poppy shook her head, even more confused now. 'She's causing trouble because she wants to get back at you?'

'Look, I may be wrong, but when she heard how Charlie had singled you out for special treatment she was pretty jealous. I think she felt that if she'd been on the *Earth Star* from the start she might have had a chance with him. I think it annoyed her when I kept telling her how you did things, how you treated the guests, how fabulous you were.'

'Oh.' That wasn't what she'd expected. And Jake thought she was fabulous? She knew they'd worked well as a team but he'd hardly even looked at her when they were on the *Earth Star*. But he'd really liked her. That wasn't something he'd admitted before. Wow.

'Sophie sort of guessed I'd fallen for you . . .'

'Fallen for me?' Double wow!

'Of course.'

'But you never . . . I mean, you were always a bit –

well, distant. In fact I thought you didn't even like me. You were pleasant enough, but,' Poppy shrugged, 'a bit cold.'

'I know, I'm sorry. It's complicated.' Jake put his hand on Poppy's shoulder. 'I wanted to tell you how I felt, I wanted to let you in . . . but it wasn't as simple as that.'

'There's someone else?'

'No. There was, but not now, not for years.'

Jake pulled Poppy towards him and kissed her. She felt tingles and sparks and the delicious softness of his mouth. She felt safe and protected and loved and she gave herself up to the feeling she was falling. She closed her eyes and relaxed against him, revelling in the feeling of his arms around her and his lips and tongue caressing her mouth.

'Now then,' said Jake softly as he drew back. 'We ought to get back. And don't worry about Sophie. I think she and Charlie deserve each other.'

Jake was right and she knew it. Sophie was welcome to him. He was a sleaze-ball, a womaniser and a spoilt bastard. He'd been nice to her because he fancied her – but only, she thought, for a fling. When she hadn't come across he'd dumped her, ignored her and gone after an easier target. And Sophie certainly seemed easy.

'Just one more thing,' she said.

'Yes?'

Poppy leant in towards Jake and kissed him back.

'We'll get done for being unprofessional,' said Jake, eventually.

'Bugger unprofessional,' said Poppy. 'Who cares?'

The door to the bar opened and a burst of noise swept across the hall. They both jumped apart guiltily, despite Poppy's defiant words of a second before.

'Time to get back,' she said regretfully. Sod Sophie, she thought, as she headed back towards the bar. She was welcome to Charlie and she could play her little games as much as she wanted. What did Poppy care when she had Jake? Knowing that Jake had fallen for her made her feel warm and fuzzy and safe and happy – joyful even.

'Poppy,' Charlie called over the buzz of chat as she entered. His arm was around Sophie's waist. 'Thought you'd disappeared off somewhere. Let me buy you a drink.'

She ran her eyes over the pair of them. They deserved each other, and if he wanted to set a crap example by flirting with an employee so outrageously, so what? It was his company, although she would do her best to redress the balance and show the students how to be the top-quality hosts their clients would expect. 'Thanks. White wine, please.'

'And what about you, Sophie, same again?'

Sophie drained her glass and belched quietly. 'Oops, manners.' She passed her glass to Charlie.

'Jake?'

'I'm good, thanks.'

Charlie went off to the bar, and Sophie turned her attention to Jake. 'So Jake, how are you? I haven't seen you since Greece, when I woke up in your bed and there you were, gone. Sally told me you'd flown back to England, but you might have said goodbye. I mean, that's no way to treat a lady, now is it? Talk about loving and leaving.'

Poppy felt as if she'd been slapped. Then she remembered, this was Sophie, the arch shit-stirrer. She grinned at Jake to show she understood that this was one of Sophie's wind-up comments, but then she noticed Jake's face. Shock? Horror? Embarrassment? Or was it a mixture of all three? Shit, it was guilt! And he was mouthing 'no' at Sophie. This was no wind-up. Jake and Sophie . . . Sophie and Jake . . .

Sophie was prattling on about the last-night party for the staff in Greece but Poppy barely heard a word. 'Shame you missed it, Pops. It was really phat. They made that punch like they do for the welcome party, only we're never usually allowed to touch it, but this time . . . Well, let's just say everyone got rat-arsed. And I mean everyone.'

'I didn't,' said Jake quietly.

'Shut up,' said Poppy with more force than she'd intended but she was shocked. Shocked and angry. She turned towards Sophie. 'What did you say?'

'What? That everyone got rat-arsed.'

'No, about Jake's bed.'

'I said I slept in his bed. Jealous?'

And Jake had said he'd been sober. He hadn't even the decency to offer the excuse of being rat-arsed, which might have made it marginally less unforgivable. He'd been sober when he'd laid Sophie, and Poppy would never forgive him. No way.

'Is it true?' said Poppy, turning to Jake.

'Yes, but . . .' began Jake.

The earlier anger, which had been simmering just under the surface since her encounter with the pair of them in the office, the anger she thought she'd got over, returned tenfold and boiled over. She felt a whoosh of total fury well up inside her, like lava under the crust of a volcano, and she blew her top. Stuff it. Stuff Sophie, stuff the job, stuff the whole of World-fucking-Fleet. Charlie appeared with the drinks just at that moment. Before Jake could explain, Poppy took both glasses of wine and threw one over Sophie and the other over Jake.

'And if I'd had boiling oil I'd have chucked that over you too,' she shrieked, tears spilling over and running down her face. 'You can shove your job, Charlie Pencombe. I think you stink almost as much as lover-boy here, and as for her' – Poppy jabbed a finger at Sophie – 'words fail me. I can't work with Jake, I can't stand to be in the same room as her, you can't make me so I quit. And, Jake, don't ever think of trying to get in touch with me. I'd rather cut my own tongue out than speak to you.' Then she was gone.

*

'What are you going to do, Poppy?' asked Amy, handing over another tissue and refilling their wine glasses.

They sat in the bay window of Poppy's sailing club, ignored by the other members, who were gathered round the bar. They had realised that Poppy was upset about something and, being blokes, really didn't want to get involved. Occasionally they threw a worried glance in her direction but as she had a female friend with her they knew they were off the hook.

'I don't know,' wailed Poppy between snotty sobs. 'I can't go home because Mum has rented out my room to bloody Charlie, I can't go back to the training school, not after that scene, I've made a complete fool of myself and I've discovered that the man I thought loved me shagged the biggest slapper this side of the international date line. And he assured me there was nothing between them. And I've also discovered that Charlie hits on any woman in WorldFleet and I was nothing special; he just thought I might be easy only Sophie is easier still. How much worse can it get?'

'What? Charlie and Sophie? They had . . . ?'

'Not "had" – having, probably,' snuffled Poppy. 'She was all snuggled up to him when I flounced off. But I don't care about him – he's an arse.' She wiped her eyes and squared her shoulders, feeling better now she'd identified what the real problem was with Charlie.

'Hang on,' said Amy, 'that's not what you said a while back.'

'Well, I thought we might have had something going when I was out in the Med. Then when I met him in his office it was all change. He tried to stick his tongue down my throat and grab my tits just because he'd given me this job.'

'He what?' Amy was aghast.

Poppy nodded. 'Honest. And when I told him to lay off he got all shitty about it.'

'That sounds like sexual harassment.'

'Whatever. But it was worse because I thought he was nice to me because he liked me. Now I realise he was nice to me because he thought I was an easy shag.' Poppy burst into tears again.

'Well, at least you proved you weren't,' said Amy pragmatically.

'But the fact that he *did* puts me in the same league as Sophie.' She blew her nose to try to regain her composure. 'And then there's Jake. We got on so well when we were setting up the school. And then Sophie appears and I find them together. But Jake tells me it's nothing and that he loves me, about two minutes before I find that's a lie because he and Sophie had been at it like rattlesnakes in Greece. Oh, Amy, how could he lie to me? And besides, I mean,' Poppy hiccoughed a sob, 'I mean, what's she got that I haven't?'

'Big knockers, apparently.'

The comment just made Poppy sob louder.

'Oh, Poppy, I didn't mean it. It was a joke.'

Poppy pulled herself together. 'Charlie's a shit, I realise that now. He's a spoilt git who's used to getting his own way, but Jake ... How could he? I mean, with Sophie?'

'Look, just because Jake said he was sober doesn't mean diddly-squat. Blokes say all sorts of things to get themselves out of tight corners, lying bastards that they are.'

'But even Jake's not going to think that it'll make it better to tell me he went with her sober?'

'Hmm, you may have a point there.'

Poppy tossed back the last of her wine. 'I'm having another. You?'

Amy shook her head. 'I've got to drive home so best I don't. And why don't you come with me? I'm sure we can find a bed for you. Mum won't mind.'

Poppy raised her tearstained face. 'Really? You sure? Only I can't go back to the manor and Mum's let my room out,' she wailed again, 'to Charlie.' She blew her nose. 'I've got nowhere to go.'

'Come on, Poppy, let's get back to mine and things won't look so bad in the morning.'

Poppy was awoken by the ringing of her mobile. Blearily she looked at it through the fug of sleep. The display told her it was her mum calling her.

'Hiya,' she answered, stifling a yawn.

'Poppy.' Her mother's tone had Poppy wide awake and alert in a second. There was no mistaking the worry that was being transmitted across the airwaves.

'What is it? Dad?'

'No. It's just . . . I heard . . . Mr Pencombe told me he'd had to let you go.'

'That's not the truth, Mum. I told him to shove it.'

'You did what?'

'Mum, I couldn't stay there a minute longer. I had a blazing row with Jake in front of all the students, I made a complete prat of myself and I never want to see Jake again.' Tears sprang to her eyes at the thought of Jake. She blinked them away. She was not going to waste them on a shit like that.

'Oh. I see.'

Poppy thought she probably didn't but it was too late now.

'Anyway,' Anne continued, 'Mr Pencombe wants a word.'

'Put him on,' she said, suddenly wide awake.

There was a pause and a shuffle, then she heard Charlie say, 'I think you owe me an explanation for the appalling display last night.'

'Do you?' she replied, trying to sound as cool as possible.

'It was hardly professional and it certainly wasn't the sort of behaviour we expect from our senior staff. Especially in front of trainees.'

'No.'

'So what have you got to say for yourself?'

Anger flared in her again. She wasn't going to take this sort of crap. And certainly not from a man who'd tried to grab her tits. 'Considering the behaviour that you demonstrated in your office a few months ago and the display you and Sophie just put on, I don't think you're in a position to cast aspersions.'

'That has got nothing to do with it.'

'I think it's got everything to do with it. What is this, a two-tier society? There's one rule for you and another for the likes of me? You can do what you like with the employees, set any sort of example, and I can't?'

'It's not like that and you know it.'

'Actually, Charlie, I don't think I do. And apart from the fact that I don't take kindly to being mauled by my boss, I

like it even less when I find that colleagues of mine have
. . . have . . .'

'What? I'm assuming you're referring to Sophie and
Jake. So what have they done?'

'It doesn't matter,' mumbled Poppy, realising that she'd
probably gone too far. And besides, what had they done?
She didn't have any right to expect any sort of fidelity from
Jake; it wasn't as if they were engaged or married. Why
shouldn't he have a fling with someone else? Except that
he'd always pretended he loathed the woman, so he'd lied
to her. That was what hurt so much – the deception.

'I'm sorry, I think it does matter and, as I said, I
demand an explanation.'

What, and admit to being jealous of Sophie and
holding a candle for Jake? No way. She thought she'd
rather take the consequences than do that. 'I haven't got
one except that Sophie and Jake have upset me.'

'Upset you? Is that all? And you behaved like that?
Then it's just as well you resigned because if not I'd have
sacked you. I'll have one of the staff pack up your room
and return your possessions to the pub.'

'Thank you.' She was glad she wasn't going to have to
face Jake and Sophie. She thought that if she did she'd
really make sure she did some damage to Sophie and not
just to her ego.

'I'm sorry it had to end this way. You had potential.'

Poppy restrained an audible snort. As what? His bit on
the side? 'Yeah, well, I'm sorry it didn't work out too.' She
ended the call and snapped her phone shut. It was a poxy
job anyway, she thought miserably. Trouble was she was
hardly likely to get a glowing reference out of WorldFleet
after this. Maybe she'd be able to get one from the sailing

club. One from her mum was hardly likely to cut the mustard with a future employer. She really didn't want to spend her life in Polzeal, but that looked the most likely possibility unless she could get another decently paid job.

Jake lay on his bed, staring at the ceiling and feeling utterly low and wretched. Outside his window he could hear rain being whipped against the glass. January and raining – the sailing students were going to get wet and cold today and so was he. Still, the weather matched his mood: bloody miserable.

It was his fault that Poppy had lost her temper; he blamed himself. Knowing what a trouble maker Sophie was he should have kept the two apart. Bugger. And he should have been quicker denying Sophie's hint that there had been something going on between them. The very thought made him shudder, but he'd been as shocked as Poppy by the comment she'd made and so stunned he hadn't known how to respond. He crashed a fist into the palm of his other hand. But too late now. Too late to go back and unpick the mess.

As soon as Poppy had gone Charlie had had a go at him. The party around them had fallen silent as Charlie had bawled him out and then turned to the students and reminded them about expected standards of behaviour in no uncertain terms. It had been a very subdued group that trooped off to bed, too embarrassed to stay any longer in the poisonous atmosphere of the bar.

Jake had tried to phone Poppy later but her mobile was switched off. He phoned the pub but Anne knew nothing of Poppy's whereabouts and was curious as to why she wasn't at the manor. Jake had mumbled something about her slipping out and needing her to answer an urgent question; he hadn't wanted to worry Anne with the truth. No doubt she'd find out soon enough, but it was down to Poppy to tell her. Anne certainly didn't deserve to hear the bad tidings from a third party.

Jake rolled over and looked at his alarm clock. At last the hands told him it was almost seven – nearly time to get up. He pressed the button to cancel the alarm before it rang and swung his legs out of bed. He really wasn't looking forward to today. Yesterday he and Poppy had been really excited about the first day of the course; they'd worked so hard to bring the project in on time, to get all the tutors for the hospitality and the sailing parts of the course gathered and ready to start, to get the equipment in place, to sort it all out, and now Poppy had gone.

'I expect Poppy's room to be cleared and packed by lunchtime,' Charlie had said after supper as he'd stormed off towards the village with Rick following, carrying Charlie's bag as well as his own.

'I'll help you,' said Sophie.

'What?' Jake couldn't believe his ears.

'I said I'll help you.'

He snorted. 'You'll do no such thing. I'm not having you touch Poppy's things.'

'Here we go again,' sneered Sophie. 'Saint fucking Poppy can do no wrong and Jake is worshipping at her shrine. Except she's just fallen off her pedestal, so that's why she's out of a job.'

Jake clenched his hands by his side to stop himself from shaking Sophie. 'Don't you dare talk about her like that. The whole thing is entirely your fault. What possessed you to say that stupid thing about being in my bed?'

'Like I wasn't?'

'Okay, you're right, you were, but alone. The whole night. Which was the bit you forgot to mention.'

Sophie shrugged. 'Come off it. You said yourself that you and Poppy were never an item, so what? So she fancies you on the sly – well, that's her problem. If she wants you she should make a bit of an effort and not expect everyone else to stand back while she makes her mind up.'

At that point Jake turned on his heel and loped upstairs to his room. Half an hour later, while he was lying on his bed, still fully dressed, still fuming about the unfairness of what had happened, there was a knock on his door.

'Come in,' he yelled.

Sophie strolled in.

'Yes,' he said as coldly and as rudely as he could.

'Don't be like that, Jake.'

'Like what?'

She walked over to his bed and sat on the edge beside him. 'All mean and nasty. I've come to apologise.'

'Don't bother.'

'Let me make it up to you.' She ran her hand over his chest. Jake pushed it away.

'Leave me alone.'

'You don't really mean that.'

Jake sat up and gave Sophie a push which tipped her

off the edge of the bed so that she landed in a gangly heap on the floor.

'Yes . . . I . . . do,' he snarled slowly and carefully. 'Now get out.'

'You're a bastard, Jake. You know that? A bastard. You wouldn't know a good time if it came up and poked you in the eye. No wonder your girlfriend drowned. She probably did it deliberately to get away from you.' She flounced out of the room and slammed the door, leaving Jake shaking with anger.

He wondered if Sophie knew about his mum – that she'd committed suicide by drowning herself. And to say that Julie had . . . All the bad feelings he'd had about relationships with women came cascading back, leaving him almost overwhelmed with guilt and despondency and misery.

He'd barely slept all night and now it was morning and things still looked bleak and grim. During the night he'd slowly managed to convince himself, once again, that he wasn't responsible for the death of either his mother or Julie, but he still felt bug-eyed from lack of sleep and completely dejected about Poppy's departure. And how the hell was he supposed to cope without her?

When he got to the dining hall for breakfast one or two of the keener students were already there. He could tell by the way the conversation stopped as he walked in that they'd been discussing the previous night's drama. Jake helped himself to bacon and eggs from the buffet and joined them. He slapped on a smile. 'Looking forward to today?'

The two men in the group, Matt and Paul, looked smug and nodded. 'We're in the kitchens,' said Matt.

'But I've got to go out in this,' complained the girl. Jake glanced at her name badge – Angela. 'I'm going to freeze.'

'You'll be so busy you won't notice the weather.'

Angela didn't look convinced. 'When I joined WorldFleet I thought I'd just be schlepping about in the Med. I didn't join to sail in the Channel in the middle of sodding winter.'

'But you've sailed around the British coast before, so this sort of weather isn't going to come as a complete shock.'

Angela shrugged. 'No, that's true, but I just prefer sailing in nice conditions.'

'Don't we all.'

Some more students came in for their breakfast, followed by Sophie. She shot Jake a filthy look, got some food and sat down as far away from him as possible.

Maybe there is a God after all, he thought. The conversation around the table seemed to be mostly focused on the shitty weather, with no one commenting on the very obvious and smelly elephant in the room – Poppy's departure. Jake finished his breakfast and went off to the office to switch on Poppy's computer, check her diary and emails and make sure there wasn't some administrative pitfall lurking to wreck the opening day.

He was scrolling through the email whilst trying to get hold of one of the sailing instructors on the phone when Charlie ambled through the office door. Jake took his hand off the mouse and replaced the receiver on the rest. He'd get hold of the instructor in a minute, when Charlie had said whatever it was he wanted to. With any luck it would have something to do with a replacement for Poppy – or better still, be an announcement that he'd changed his mind.

'Have you cleared Poppy's room yet?' said Charlie coolly.

Jake shook his head. 'Why?'

'Because I want it done as soon as possible. I'll get someone else on the case.'

'It's all right, I'll do it when I've got the students off to their first session. In fact I was just on the phone to see if the two sailing instructors could manage without me this morning. If they each took an extra two pupils they wouldn't need me.'

'You can take the third boat out. I've got the admin side sorted.'

Jake was taken aback. 'Eh? How come?'

'I asked Sophie if she'd take over. She said she'd be delighted to.'

Jake sat down slowly behind the desk. 'You asked Sophie? You're kidding me.'

'No,' said Charlie. 'I thought about it last night, downloaded her personal file this morning – isn't modern technology a life-saver – and I think she'd be excellent. I asked her a couple of minutes ago and she said yes. Problem?'

Jake took a deep, steadying breath. 'Quite apart from the fact that I wouldn't work with that woman if she was the last person left on earth, I can't think of anyone less appropriate to set an example of the hospitality a company such as this should offer. She was sloppy and often surly with the guests on the *Earth Star*, her cooking skills are mediocre, her morals are questionable, and if she joins the team here then I leave.' He rose again so as to look Charlie in the eye. 'Do I make myself plain?'

'Perfectly. And frankly, I'll be glad to let you go.

Especially after last night. Poppy was easy enough to replace, and I can't think I'll have any difficulty in finding someone to fill your job. Your resignation is accepted. I suggest you clear your room immediately and arrange transport to Truro station. I want you off the premises by lunchtime. Anything you can't carry we'll send on.'

Fuck. Jake felt as though he'd been punched. Still, being on the dole was going to be better than working with Sophie. *Anything* was going to be better than working with Sophie. 'I need to make a call.'

'I'll have the cost docked from your final pay cheque.'

'Forget it. I'll use my mobile.'

'Good.'

The two men glared at each other for a few seconds, then Charlie said, 'Out by lunchtime. The clock is ticking.'

Jake moved round from behind his desk and slammed out of the office. Once in his room he threw as much as he could into his holdall and pulled the zip shut. Then he phoned Poppy to tell her the truth about Sophie and that he had been sacked too rather than work with her. He didn't know if that would be enough to make her think again about what she'd said the night before, but he had to hope. He couldn't bear the thought that she hated him.

Her phone rang a couple of times, then he was redirected to voicemail. She'd blanked him. He sent a text and prayed she didn't delete it without opening it. He contemplated ringing Anne and asking her to pass a message to Poppy to say he'd been fired, but when he said his name Anne hung up on him. He was getting the message: Mr Popular he wasn't.

He phoned his mate Paul in Norwich and asked for a night on his sofa, and then he fixed a taxi to the station in an hour. That left him time to walk to the pub and try to see Poppy herself.

'Yes,' said Dan, through the half-open door of the pub.

'I've come to explain to Poppy. Let me in.'

'One, Poppy's not here, she's staying at a friend's house. And two, she rang to say that if you turned up I should punch your lights out. Given the way she stormed off last night I'd lay a pound to a penny that you'd deserve it if I did. I'm usually a peaceable man but if Poppy wants me to stick up for her I know where my loyalties lie.'

'But she doesn't understand—'

'She said you'd say that and I'm not listening. If you don't clear off I swear I'll lay you out cold.'

Jake opened his mouth again but the door slammed shut. He hammered on it but the thick planks stayed put. Dan wasn't going to listen to his side of the story, so there was no way he could get a message to Poppy except through her phone. And if she didn't want to read it he was screwed. He glanced at his watch; the taxi was due shortly and he didn't have time to go chasing round Cornwall looking for her. Besides, he had no idea where she might be; her friend could live anywhere. This was hopeless.

Poppy put the phone down, crossed the ad out, and dialled the next number she'd identified. She asked for the HR desk and as soon as she was put through she began her carefully rehearsed spiel about her qualifications and her desire for the job on offer. As always she was promised an application form. The trouble was, the application forms had to be returned with references and without anything from WorldFleet there was a two year hole in her CV which meant she never got any further with the process. Mostly companies didn't even tell her she'd failed to make the grade, but she had plenty of letters from those who had. Dozens.

And she'd tried every route she could think of to get a job. She'd applied to hotels, holiday companies, private charter agents, cruise ships, the lot. She'd even looked at jobs for cook-housekeepers, but nothing. It was getting seriously dispiriting. Of course she still had a job at the pub, but now that the B & B opportunities had been halved because her mum couldn't let her room she didn't like to take much in the way of pay. What she needed was a proper job with proper wages, then she could move out in time for the start of the season. Fat chance!

She finished her call and threw her pen on her bed. Swiftly her thumb skated over a couple of buttons.

'Hi, Amy,' she said.

'Hi,' said Amy. 'How's the job hunting going?'

'Don't ask.'

'That bad?'

'Worse.'

'And Jake?'

Poppy sighed and tears pricked the back of her eyes. Jake – that was the thing. She'd buggered things up big time with Jake. She'd been so mad with him for the first couple of days that she'd deleted all trace of him from her mobile phone. And on the few occasions he had tried to call or sent her a text, before he finally gave up, she went into her phone's history and took the number off again. The act made her feel significantly better. She wasn't having her phone sullied by that scumbag's number.

The trouble was, when Charlie had moved out of the pub and she'd been able to return, Dan had told her that Jake had been fired too.

'No. Why? What on earth made Charlie do that?'

'He moved Sophie into your office and Jake refused point blank to work with her.'

Poppy had felt almost sick. 'Charlie did what? The bastard. I can't believe it. The flaming woman seems to be destined to make my life a misery.'

'Listen, love, I wasn't there when it all kicked off but I was chatting to one of the kids from the manor in the pub the other night and they'd overheard a ding-dong of a row in the office. Apparently Jake said he wouldn't work with her if she was the last woman on earth.'

Poppy was confused. But he'd slept with her, hadn't

he? Maybe Sophie had been lying and she'd never given Jake a chance to defend himself. And now she'd lost him.

Amy, impatient with the silence, broke into her thoughts. 'So you still haven't heard from him, I take it.'

'No. And I haven't a clue where he might be. I feel a heel. Oh, Amy, I miss him so much. I wouldn't have reacted like I did if he hadn't meant so much to me, and then I go and wreck everything.'

'Oh, Poppy, he's a grown-up. And he knows where you are. He knows where the pub is. He probably still has your number, so if you're patient he's bound to phone you.'

'But what if he doesn't?' Poppy hoped Amy couldn't hear her heart breaking.

'He will. You said yourself that he'd just said he'd fallen for you. I bet he's thinking of you as much as you are of him.'

'When we were setting up the manor, we got on so well. He just never let me get close – until that last day. And then,' she stopped and swallowed, got herself back under control, 'I blew it.'

'If it's meant to be I'm sure it'll happen. Honest, love.' There was a pause while they both digested this. 'However, I may have something to cheer you up.'

'Shoot.'

'Look, this may be a long shot, but I was talking to a mate the other day and there's a new ships' chandlery opening up in Plymouth in a couple of months. Huge place, apparently, down on the Barbican. And – and this is the best bit – there's flat over the shop. The owner doesn't want it as he's got a house up on the Hoe, and it's too small for the manager as he's got a wife and kids, so he's planning to let it.'

'How come your mate knows? I mean, you're not into sailing and other than me I didn't know you had any friends who were.'

'I don't.' Poppy could hear the shudder in Amy's voice. 'All that cold wet water. Ugh. You have to be mad to be into that and I'm quite sane, thanks, as are most of my friends, apart from Potty-Poppy. Anyway, this mate's dad does shop fitting and he's got the contract for this place in Plymouth. Making a tidy bob or two out of it by all accounts.'

'So there's a chance I might be able to find a job and somewhere to live all in one go.'

'Don't get too excited. It is only shop work and not what you're really after, and the flat is titchy by all accounts.'

'But heck, it's a start. And if I bugger off now Mum can re-advertise for B & Bs and find an extra member of staff before the summer season kicks off and all the best people get snaffled by other places. Can you get me a number or an address or anything?'

'For you I'll get both.'

Jake looked around the exhibitor area at the boat show, at the sea of people thronging the vast space, at the ranks of exhibitors' stands, at the girls handing out goody bags and leaflets, at the sales teams working the crowds gathered round their stalls like purveyors of snake-oil, and wondered if by any stroke of luck, fortune or coincidence he might see Poppy. Not a day went by, and it had been months since he'd last seen her, when he didn't think about her and wonder whether to ring her. But every time he reached for his mobile he remembered the stricken look on her face when Sophie had told her she had slept in his bed.

He'd screwed up another life and he owed it to Poppy to keep away from her. He was poison to women. Every one he'd cared about: his mother, Julie and now Poppy. Morosely he wondered what the opposite of a Midas touch was because whatever it was, he had it. Still, this wasn't going to sell outboard engines. He switched on a smile and approached some people who were taking an interest in the display with a handful of brochures.

He did his spiel, made a recommendation as to the size of engine that would meet their requirements, handed out a brochure and a price list and said goodbye. The instant the couple turned their backs the smile disappeared.

'Well, don't you look like a bleedin' wet weekend.'

Jake spun round. He'd know that voice anywhere. 'Ronnie!'

''Ere, Mick,' she bawled through the crowd. 'Look who I've found!' She turned back and launched into an interrogation while Mick pushed his way through the throng towards them. 'How are you doin', darlin'? And how's the lovely Poppy? And what's more, what are you doing working for this outfit? Got fed up of ferrying the likes of me round the Med?'

Jake ignored her questions. 'What on earth are you doing here? It surely doesn't mean you've got bitten by the sailing bug, does it?'

Ronnie's face lit up with a smile. 'Might do. We 'ad anuvver cruise on the old *Earth Star* this summer. It was blindin'. Not quite as good as the one we had with you and Poppy but smashing just the same. What happened to you? I was expecting you and Pops to be looking after us again and we got a pair of complete strangers. Don't get me wrong, they was very nice and did us proud, but I'd been looking forward to seeing me old muckers from last year again. The skipper said you'd left the company but he didn't know about Poppy. Get bored with the sailing lark, did you?'

Before Jake could answer, Mick managed to join them. He clasped Jake's hand and shook it warmly. 'Good to see ya, Jake. How's tricks?'

'Good, good,' he lied. He spotted some more punters. 'Look, I really want to catch up with you. Are you down here just for the day? If so I've got a break in about an hour. Maybe we could meet for a drink.'

'We're staying here, so why don't we take you out to dinner when you pack up for the day?'

'But I couldn't . . .'

'Why not? Our treat and our pleasure, ain't it, Mick?'

Mick nodded vigorously. 'Besides, we'll be able to pick his brains, won't we, Ron?'

'About what?' said Jake guardedly.

'If you come out to dinner with us, you'll find out.'

'All right then. I'd love to. Where should I meet you?'

'Come to our hotel. We're at the De Vere.'

Jake whistled. 'Not slumming it, then.'

'Certainly not. You know me!' Ronnie cackled cheerfully. 'We'll see you at seven thirty. Okay?'

Jake said it would be perfect. The day was looking up.

33

He got to the hotel on the dot of seven thirty feeling rather underdressed amidst the splendid luxury of the swanky, modern hotel. Even if he hadn't heard of it he would have been able to tell instantly from the amazing sloping glass façade that this was a classy place. He wasn't especially surprised; Ronnie liked things with a touch of bling. He wandered into the climate-controlled lobby trying to look relaxed and at home, but inside he was completely aware that this was not his natural environment. However, no one gave him a second glance despite the fact that his clothes didn't have a single designer label between them. Primark was his shop of choice. He felt even more underdressed when Ronnie, who'd been waiting for him in the lobby, tottered towards him in sky-high heels wearing a gold lamé catsuit.

She hugged Jake to her voluminous body like he was her prodigal son returning and dragged him off to the bar. 'Mick's got the drinks lined up: champagne cocktails. We thought you'd like one of those. Or maybe you'd like several. I know I do!' She giggled.

The bar, opulent, beautifully lit and comfortable, was half filled with Southampton's smart set, businessmen and couples. Across the expanse of luxuriously thick carpet Jake could see Mick on a stool by the bar, the promised champagne cocktails lined up in front of him.

'Jake, me boy,' he yelled across the room as Ronnie and her guest made their entrance. A few of the drinkers glanced round at the man disturbing the subdued hum of quiet conversation with his brash greeting. Mick stood up as Jake approached and shook his hand before passing him his cocktail.

'Ronnie and I are ahead of you here so you need to get this down you pronto.' He passed another glass to his wife.

'Cheers,' she said, clinking her glass against Jake's. 'Now tell me all your news. For starters, what are you doing at the boat show?'

Jake wasn't sure he wanted to go into details about his precipitate departure from WorldFleet. 'I've got a job with a firm that makes outboard motors. It's not great but it pays enough for me to keep on sailing.'

'Talking of sailing, what's with you and WorldFleet?'

'I had a difference of opinion with the boss.'

'Charlie?'

Jake nodded. 'He wanted me to work with someone I felt I couldn't.'

'So does that mean the lovely Poppy never went back to work for them?'

'No, she did.' Jake explained about setting up the training school with her. 'And then we'd just got the first lot of students and one of them was Sophie – remember her?'

Ronnie screwed up her eyes as she thought back. 'Not really. She was only on the yacht for about a day before we went home, but I remember I thought she was a bit of a minx.'

Jake nodded. 'She certainly was that. Anyway, she and Poppy had a bit of a falling out that first evening.'

'Over you,' said Ronnie shrewdly.

Sheepishly Jake nodded. He described the events of the disastrous evening eight months earlier. 'And when I tried to explain she blanked my calls. She obviously hates me so much for what she thinks went on between me and Sophie that she doesn't want anything to do with me,' he finished sadly.

'That's a crying shame. She really liked you, you know. You could tell it by the way she looked at you. Then, of course, Charlie made an appearance an' 'er dad got took poorly ...' Ronnie sniffed. 'Anyway, water under the bridge, I suppose.'

Jake took another sip of his drink. He wasn't sure if he was going to be able to hold himself together if they carried on talking about Poppy. Her rejection of him still hurt more than he could have thought possible. 'So, how are the children?' he asked, grasping at a change of subject.

'Well, Lynette is shacked up with Kyle and expecting 'er second. Jade has been a bit of a handful recently so Mick bought her a flat in Colchester and she's living there. It was that or there would have been blood on the carpet. She'd got to that age, and her moods! And Darren – well, you'll never guess what 'e's been and gone and done.'

A variety of possibilities shot through Jake's mind: armed robbery, drug dealing and drink-driving being just a small selection.

'He's joined the army.'

Jake nearly choked on his drink. 'He's what?'

'I know, we was surprised too. But he loves it. It's been the making of him and when we saw him at his passing out parade in his best uniform, well, I fort I'd just burst with pride.' Ronnie dabbed at her eyes as the memory brought tears to them.

'Well done him,' said Jake enthusiastically. 'Good on him.'

'Anyway, enough of that,' said Mick. 'Just to prove we haven't got you here under false pretences.' He pulled a glossy brochure towards him. 'What do you know about motor yachts?'

'A bit,' said Jake. 'Sailing's my thing, but what do you want to know?'

Mick opened the brochure and flipped it round for Jake to look at. 'What do you think of that?'

Jake stared at the picture of a three-deck yacht then read the accompanying details about the state rooms, the teak sun decks, the tender, and every luxurious finishing touch you could think of. He whistled. 'Amazing. Are you planning on buying it?'

Mick nodded. 'Nice, ain't she?'

Jake shook his head. 'Nice isn't the word. It's fabulous. So . . . I mean . . . How . . .'

'What Jake wants to know,' interrupted Ronnie, 'is how can we afford it?'

'Actually,' said Jake, keeping his face straight, 'what I want to know is which bank did you rob?'

'Cheeky bugger! Mick sold his business. After our hols this summer he had a bit of a scare with his heart. The quack said he could either keep the business or stay alive

– up to him, but he needed to make the decision quick.'

'I'm sorry.'

'Don't be,' said Ronnie. 'He got lucky and had a warning first. Anyway, we already knew someone who we fort might be interested.'

'Handy. Your kids didn't want to take over?'

Ronnie snorted. 'My lot? Work for a living? Anyway, we got hold of this bloke, asked if he wanted it and he was like a rat up a drainpipe.'

'That was useful.'

'Yeah. And we've got Poppy to thank for the intro to this guy.'

'Really?'

'Yeah. I ran into that Charlie when Poppy and I went for a picnic together – you know, when she was teaching me to swim.' Jake nodded. 'And he wanted to know what Mick did and I told him. He said his dad was in business but he needed to diversify. He said you couldn't fail with scrap metal fetching the prices it does. Like he needed to tell me! So he's got the whole shebang now and Mick and I have got lots of lovely free time. Oh, and loads of lovely dosh. So you see, Charlie ain't a complete shit.'

Jake couldn't bring himself to agree there so he said, 'And you want to spend the lovely dosh on a boat and then spend your free time on it somewhere nice and warm.'

'In one,' said Ronnie. She up-ended her glass. 'Get another round in, Mick. A woman could die of thirst here.'

'And you want my advice about what exactly?'

'Well, first, do you think this boat is a good 'un?'

Jake shook his head. 'I can't tell just by looking at it but the manufacturer is a reputable one. They're the sort of Mercedes-Benz equivalent in the yachting world. Not quite as good as Rolls-Royce or Bentley but better than Ford.'

Ronnie nodded enthusiastically. 'Sounds fair. We did look at a couple of pricier ones but there didn't seem to be that much more to show for the extra cash. And you know me – I like a bit of show!'

Jake laughed. Ronnie was so outrageously honest about herself you couldn't help but like her.

'And Mick would be able to sail it easily enough?' she continued.

'I didn't know he knew how.'

'He doesn't, do you, love?' Ronnie gazed fondly at her husband who was passing the order for three more cocktails to the attentive barman.

'Like driving a car, the salesman said,' said Mick over his shoulder.

'Ye-es,' agreed Jake. 'Sort of. Navigating is a bit trickier. There aren't any road signs out at sea.'

'Sat nav,' said Ronnie.

'True. But you still need charts and tide tables and that sort of thing if you want to be sure you're going to miss rocks and reefs and sand bars.'

'Oh.'

'There's loads of courses for that sort of thing. And it's not difficult to learn.'

Mick passed them their new drinks. 'Could you teach us?' he asked.

'Probably. But it might be better to get some sort of recognised qualification. You may find your insurance is a bit steep if you don't have the right ticket.'

'Oh.'

'And there might be stricter regulations in Europe or

the Caribbean. I've only sailed around Greece and when I got the job with WorldFleet I had to produce all my documentation about my qualifications. They took loads of photocopies and after that they handled all the admin to do with me and the *Earth Star* – stuff like dealing with port authorities. And port authorities can be a bit funny about who docks what in their harbours. I never had to touch any of that side of it, that's why I'm not completely sure of my ground, but you ought to check. You don't want to get out there and find your new toy gets impounded.'

'I most certainly don't,' agreed Mick. 'Ron, we're going to have to think about this.'

'Not really,' said Ronnie. 'Why don't we just have Jake here drive it for us?'

'Jake wouldn't want to do that. He's a proper sailor, aren't you?'

'I could be tempted,' said Jake, feeling very tempted indeed. Back at sea, with people he liked, probably on a fair salary and with accommodation thrown in. It was perfect. And he could do some serious saving towards buying a yacht of his own.

'Really?' asked Ronnie. 'Only we don't want nothing with sails or anything, so could you bear it, being the skipper of something like this?'

'I think I could bear it quite easily.'

'Oh, Mick – we're going to have to celebrate this. More cocktails!'

34

The rain swept across the Barbican in a grey veil, spoiling the view from Poppy's bedroom window. October, miserable as sin, short days and long nights beckoning, months till it all began to pick up, and meanwhile she was stuck working in a shop. She should have been able to see the cobbled quayside and the jumble of old houses (the few that were left after the Blitz, which had eradicated most of the rest of the city) and the sleek glass of the modern ones, and the ships and boats at anchor in the harbour. But as it was, the low cloud, bad light and sheeting rain restricted her view to fuzzy pompoms of light from the nearby streetlamps and a few headlights illuminating cones of raindrops as they swept along the street. Life was the pits, she thought.

She sighed. Okay, she was being ungrateful. It was a nice shop that she was stuck in, with nice customers who understood about boats. She was near the sea – right beside it in fact – she had a flat right above her job and she was getting a living wage. Things could be much worse. But when she looked back to what she was doing fifteen months earlier, when she had been so happy, when she thought life couldn't get any better, and compared it to this . . . well, it was a pretty big gap between lifestyles.

She thought about the chandlery, and the hundreds of items that covered just about everything that someone planning to take to the water in a boat could possibly want: flares, life jackets, ropes, cordage, life rafts, sails, sailcloth, pennants, burgees, torches, charts, navigational aids and anything else you cared to name, and a promise that if they didn't stock it they could get almost anything in forty-eight hours, and she felt quite proud, She was the assistant manager of a respected business that had built up a huge database of customers and an equally impressive reputation in just six months. And she was partly responsible. She was justifiably proud of what she and Peter, the manager, had done.

The trouble was, she was also dissatisfied, and walking down the stairs to the shop was becoming more and more of an effort each day. There was nothing wrong about working in the shop – but there was nothing right, either.

Not that it was much better when she had time off. She didn't have a boat she could access and although she could afford to join one of Plymouth's several sailing clubs she had to work most weekends when the majority of club activities took place so it didn't seem worth her while to sign up. And being on her own in a strange city she found that she was pretty lonely. Peter was married with a young family and apart from a knowledge of sailing she had little in common with the other assistants she worked with – certainly not enough to want to spend her spare time with them. Frankly, she wasn't that happy in Plymouth, so her days off tended to be spent isolated in her flat with a radio or the TV for company.

'Get out, meet some blokes,' Amy had said sternly, when Poppy had bewailed her lot. 'For God's sake, there's an artillery regiment stationed there, commandos just up the coast and a dockyard full of hunky sailors. Surely there must be enough single blokes kicking around for even you to find one to your liking.'

Poppy had pointed out that most of them seemed to be stationed in the Middle East and it wasn't as easy as that.

'Excuses, excuses,' had been Amy's brisk reply. 'Just get out there, girlfriend, and hook a man.'

Poppy had tried, but walking into pubs and clubs by herself had proved too daunting. She wasn't the sort to go prowling for men on her own and with no old friends to accompany her and boost her confidence, after two attempts she'd given up and now tended to prefer to spend Saturday nights watching trash TV and eating pizza. How sad did that make her, she thought.

Once a month she got a free weekend so she jumped on a train to Truro to escape back home, see her mum and dad, meet her mates at the sailing club – sadly all either married or ancient or female or all three – catch up with Amy and keep right out of the way of anyone from the manor. She loved those weekends but they only seemed to underline how lonely she was in Plymouth.

She glanced at her watch. Time to get downstairs and get ready to open the shop for the day. She slipped on a waterproof, turned off the light and braced herself to go outside and down the steps to the shop below. As she stepped out of her front door the rain lashed into her face and the wind tugged at her coat. The lower half of her trousers was soaked in seconds. Pissing weather, pissing job, pissing life, she thought angrily as she pulled the door shut behind her with a bang and began to clump down the wooden steps.

She was halfway down when she remembered she'd left her mobile lying on the counter in the kitchen where it had been plugged into the socket to charge. She glanced back up at the door but another squall threw rain into her face like a bucket of water and she decided that if she didn't want to get soaked to the skin then a headlong dash to the shop was the only option. She sprinted down the last of the steps and round the corner to the relative shelter of the porch over the shop entrance. With remarkable dexterity she had the two mortise locks and the Yale dealt with in a matter of seconds. She wrenched open the door and darted inside.

The door slammed shut behind her and the sound of the wind shrieking and thrashing through the masts and halyards outside was muted to a dull whistling roar. Poppy shivered and shook water out of her hair like a dog. She flicked on the lights and raced through to the back of the shop to disable the alarm. Then she got out of her wet waterproof and prepared to face another shift.

The weather was still terrible at lunchtime and she dickered with the idea of missing lunch rather than brave the elements to go back to her flat. Eventually her protesting stomach drove her home. She was heating soup in a pan when she noticed her mobile on the counter. Out of habit she picked it up and flicked it open. A missed call alert greeted her. She pressed a button to find out who had rung. No caller ID but a number she didn't recognise. Sod it, she thought. She wasn't going to spend her precious credit ringing a stranger. She was just about to delete it when she suddenly wondered if it was Jake trying to get hold of her again.

She sat down on one of her kitchen stools and stared at her phone. Should she ring it? He deserved an apology. And if it wasn't Jake she could hang up and no harm would be done. If it was him she could make amends. It was a no-brainer. She hit the button to return the call.

'Hello, Poppy,' shrieked a female voice after the third ring.

'I'm sorry?' Who the f—

'It's me, Ronnie.'

'Ronnie?'

'Remember? Sailing, Greece, Mick and the gang? You taught me to swim.'

'Of course I remember.' How could she forget? 'But how come you've got my number? And why the call?' Poppy knew she sounded less than gracious but she'd been caught on the back foot and she felt completely bewildered.

'You gave me your number so I could send you some snaps I took of the *Earth Star*.'

Oh, yes, she remembered.

'Anyway, I thought I'd give you a call, see how things are. How's your dad?'

'A lot better, thanks. He's back working at the pub with my mum. He's still got a limp and she won't let him change barrels, but other than that he's as good as new.'

'I'm really pleased for you, Poppy. That's good news. And what about you?'

'I'm a shop girl. I work in a place in Plymouth and we sell stuff for boats.'

'That's nice.'

Poppy laughed. 'It isn't really but I've got a flat over the shop, the pay's okay and I'm near the sea. It could be worse.'

'I suppose. Have you heard from Jake?'

'We, er . . . umm – not really. We sort of lost contact earlier this year.'

'That's a shame. He's a nice bloke.'

'Yes,' agreed Poppy. 'It's a real shame.'

The conversation drifted on and when Ronnie eventually rang off Poppy had no idea why she'd called in the first place. It had been nice to catch up and it had brightened her day, but it had all seemed pretty pointless. Oh, well, did there have to be a reason?

Ronnie closed her phone and turned to Mick. 'There, I told you so.'

'Told me what?'

'That Poppy and Jake breaking up was a dreadful mistake for both of them.'

'Did you?'

'For crying out loud, don't you ever listen to nuffink?'

Mick shrugged helplessly. The answer 'not if I can help it' would only get him into worse trouble.

'I told you about the look on Jake's face when he was talking about Poppy, that night we took him out to dinner. I fort he was going to blub. And now I've spoken to Poppy I'm even more certain that those two was a match made in heaven if ever I saw one.'

'But just because they aren't seeing each other doesn't mean they're not seeing someone else. You can't go interfering in their lives.'

'Can't I? We'll see about that.'

'So what you going to do?'

'Not sure yet, but I shall start with the Internet.'

Mick sighed. There was no point in arguing, not when Ronnie had made her mind up. Sometimes he knew what it was like to be that little Chinese guy in Tiananmen Square who stood in front of the tank as it rolled relentlessly towards him – you either gave way or you got flattened.

Ronnie disappeared off to the office and Mick heard her tapping away on the keys of their computer. After about ten minutes she came back into their sitting room armed with a list.

'What do you think?' she demanded as she shoved the piece of paper under Mick's nose.

'About what?'

'These companies. Poppy said she worked for a company that supplies stuff for boats in Plymouth. So I Googled and I found these.'

'And?

'And I'm going to ring each one in turn and ask if I can speak to Poppy.'

'But you've just spoken to her.'

Ronnie raised her eyebrows and muttered, 'God give me strength.' She sighed heavily. 'Yes, but I want to know exactly where she works.'

'Why don't you ring and ask her?'

'Never mind,' said Ronnie. 'Never mind.'

35

'Wow,' said Jake.

'It's good, innit?' said Ronnie.

'It's fantastic. And I can't believe you managed to get it delivered so quickly.' He stared at the huge motor yacht that was lying sedately in the marina near Portsmouth. The ripples made interesting patterns of light and shade on the glossy hull and the tinted glass reflected the clear sky and bright April sunlight with blinding intensity.

'Well, this economic downturn might be a bugger for some but we're laughing, although the poor geezer who ordered this baby thinking he was going to get a fat City bonus probably isn't. When his dosh never came through he had to cancel and the shipbuilders asked us if we'd like to jump the queue and buy it.'

'Handy.'

'Yeah, well the only problem was that it had already been fitted out and the decor ain't necessarily what I would have picked, but it's not bad. And they gave us a huge discount.'

'So silly not to really.'

Ronnie nodded, a broad smile lighting up her face.

'What do your kids think?'

'We've told them that they're welcome to come along and join us on it now and again, but this is our present to us and we don't want them with us all the time.'

Jake could see the sense in that. 'Anyway, I suppose they've all got their own lives to lead these days.'

'Exactly, and they don't want the sort of holidays that old fogeys like us want. Now,' said Ronnie, 'let's go on board and I'll show you round.'

She scampered over the gangplank in her flat deck shoes and stood on the sun deck at the rear of the boat as Jake followed her, her face glowing with pride at being the owner of such a classy vessel. She flung open a door into the saloon and gestured for Jake to precede her.

He whistled. Grey leather seats, a bleached wood floor and matching bleached wood fittings made the room elegant and restful. 'This is lovely,' he said truthfully. Beyond the saloon was a dining room and beyond that was the galley, which had all mod cons and plenty of space.

'And you've got to check out the bridge,' said Ronnie. She led the way back to the saloon and went up a spiral staircase tucked away discreetly in the corner. Jake followed.

'Look at all these dials,' said Ronnie. 'There's more gadgets and gizmos in here than on the bridge of the *Queen Mary*, I swear. What do you fink? I mean, you're going to be the one driving it till Mick learns.'

'I think it's going to be a joy to skipper this.'

'Now then, let me show you the rest of this boat.'

She was obviously bursting with pride, and as Jake

was curious to see exactly how many bangs Ronnie had got for her bucks he was more than happy to follow her through the cabins and staterooms, peer into the en suites, and check out the crew quarters and the engine room. An hour later they were back in the dining room with a couple of charts spread over the table, each of them with a cup of coffee, as they looked at the maps of the Med.

'So where do you want to go? And how long do you want to be away?'

'Well, Mick and I fort we'd like to go back to the Greek islands for the summer and then maybe see a bit of Venice and the south of France. Would that be possible?

'Of course. It'll take a while to drift down the Bay of Biscay and round through the Straits of Gibraltar but it rather depends on whether you want to stop for more than a night in each port or whether you want to crack on. Your boat, your decision.'

'I'll have a word with Mick later.'

'I'm surprised he's not here.'

'He's in Colchester, sorting out Jade's flat, but he's getting the train down here this evening and we're going to spend the night together on board. How exciting will that be!'

'Well, you'll be pleased to know I've handed in my notice so I'm going to be footloose and fancy free at the end of the month. We can leave to go on your travels any time after that.'

'Perfect. Oooh.' Ronnie hugged herself. 'I can't wait. I am so excited!'

*

'You know, it is just so much more exciting arriving at a place by boat than it is by car.'

Ronnie and Mick were both standing on the bridge next to Jake as he guided the yacht into Plymouth Sound.

'And the view of a place from the sea is always so pretty,' said Mick.

'It helps that the sun is shining, but even if it was wet this would be a lovely port.'

'And look at that castle,' said Ronnie. 'I wouldn't mind living there.'

'It's called the Citadel and it's a military barracks,' said Jake.

'Even better then,' said Ronnie with a dirty laugh. 'Full of hunky men in uniform.'

Jake swung the wheel so the motor yacht nosed carefully under the battlements that towered high above them and into the narrow entrance that led to Sutton Harbour.

'And we're all booked in here?' asked Ronnie.

'Yup, all fixed. All we have to do when we arrive is pay for our berth.'

'Good. And we're going to stay here for a couple of days.'

'That's what you asked for, so that's what I arranged.'

'Good.'

With the yacht's engine barely ticking over they crept towards the lock that kept the marina behind it full of water when the tide dropped. It took a while to negotiate that and then they continued to edge towards the rows of pontoons and jetties that made up the marina they were booked into.

Jake had to concentrate hard as he turned the yacht

through a hundred and eighty degrees and then brought the Garvies' prize possession alongside, stern first. Mick had been briefed about jumping on to the jetty and securing the yacht, and with a turn of agility that surprised everyone including himself he did exactly as he'd been told. Jake cut the engines and then joined Mick in making the yacht fast.

Ronnie watched the activity from the sun deck.

'Right then, time for cocktails. You'll join us, won't you, Jake?'

'I'll go to the marina office and pay for the berth first if you don't mind.'

'Can you do an errand for me, then?' asked Ronnie. 'There's a shop here that sells these.' She handed Jake a brochure with some really smart plastic picnic glasses. 'Only I worry about using proper glasses if the weather is a bit dodgy. I don't want broken glass getting trodden into my lovely decks.' She smiled sweetly at Jake. 'I meant to get some before we left but in all the excitement it slipped my mind.'

'No sweat,' said Jake. 'Where's the shop?'

'Don't know exactly but it's called Barbican Yacht Supplies. I rang them to check they'd got these in stock. When I said we'd be here in Sutton Harbour they said it was local.'

'I'll ask where it is when I pay the berthing fee.'

Jake loped off along the jetty to the quayside and Ronnie watched him go. She jiggled up and down nervously. Mick glanced at her through narrowed eyes.

'You're up to something, Ronnie,' he said. 'You've got that look about you.'

'What look?' she said guiltily.

'The one slapped all over your face right now.'

'I don't know what you're talking about.' She hurried off to the bar in the saloon and mixed up some lethal gin and tonics.

Mick took his outside to bask in the evening sunshine, but Ronnie was too nervous to settle. She paced about the beautiful floor like a caged animal, taking sips of her drink and then glancing at her watch. Every now and again she peered out across the quay to see if she could spot Jake returning. Not that she wanted him to. Better that he didn't if her plan was going to come together.

'Come and sit down,' yelled Mick from where he was sprawled on a lounger. 'You're like a cat on hot bricks.'

Ronnie perched on another lounger and tried to look relaxed, but the way she jiggled one leg betrayed the tension inside her.

She saw Jake returning. He was carrying a package so he'd obviously bought the picnic glasses, but that hadn't been the sole object of sending him on the errand. And she could tell just by looking at him that his shopping trip had been completely unremarkable.

'Bugger,' she muttered. That was exactly what she hadn't wanted to happen. She'd have to put Plan B into action. She checked her watch. Too late now – it was almost six and the shop would be shut. She'd have to wait till tomorrow morning.

Jake was swabbing bird lime off the sun deck when Ronnie appeared from her stateroom the next morning.

'Breakfast?' he offered, swilling his mop through the bucket on deck, wringing the water out and then tipping the dirty water over the side.

'I'll fix something for myself in a minute. We're not expecting you to wait on us, you know. Mick and I are perfectly happy to look after ourselves. I wasn't always loaded, remember, and I can roll my sleeves up and get down and dirty with the housework with the best of them.'

'I know. I remember the way you and Mick mucked in when Poppy had to leave so suddenly. But I was just about to sort myself out with something, so if I'm making toast I could bung in a slice or two for you.'

'Go on then, spoil me. Mick'll be along in a minute. He's just having a shower.'

They ambled through to the galley where Ronnie propped herself against a counter and Jake got the bread and orange juice out of the fridge.

'Tell you what,' said Ronnie, 'I'll make the tea.' She bustled about doing that, then said almost casually, 'That shop I sent you to yesterday – nice, was it?'

'I suppose so,' said Jake.

'Big?'

'Fairly. They carry a lot of stock.'

'So you had a good look round.'

'Well, a bit. I couldn't see what you wanted me to get straight away so I asked one of the staff.'

'Helpful, was she?'

'He was quite nice. Didn't really notice.' Jake shrugged. Why on earth was Ronnie so interested?

'I wouldn't mind going and seeing what they've got for myself. I don't suppose you'd come along with me.'

Jake stopped pouring out the orange juice. 'If you really want me to. It isn't hard to find.'

'No, of course not. It's just I was finking of getting a

few bits and pieces for the boat and I fort you might be able to advise me.' She smiled sweetly at Jake.

For some reason that Jake couldn't fathom he was certain he was being manipulated in some way – and not just into a shopping trip he didn't really want to go on. If it wasn't a shopping trip, what on earth was it? Maybe he was just being paranoid. In any case, a faint gut feeling that there was a complete sub-plot lurking beneath the surface wasn't reason enough to refuse a reasonable request from his boss.

An hour later, leaving Mick happily sprawled on a sofa in the saloon with a paper, a mug of tea and a bacon and egg sandwich, Ronnie and Jake set off along the cobbled quay.

'Good job I've got me deck shoes with me. These cobbles'd play havoc with me heels.'

Jake considered the suitability of Ronnie's clothing. The deck shoes were fine, despite their brilliant orange hue. And her penchant for velour tracksuits was fine; he might not appreciate their jewel colours – plum, emerald, fuchsia, tangerine – but they were practical and comfortable and presumably they washed easily. Maybe her jewellery was a bit over the top and her hair and nails weren't going to take any sort of work on deck in bad weather – but then that was what she was employing him for.

They strolled along the quay, Ronnie comparing some of the other boats she passed with her own recent acquisition, Jake admiring the architecture of the old houses around him and the contrast some of the modern ones struck with them, and both of them enjoying the warm May sunshine.

'Here we are,' said Jake, holding open the shop door for Ronnie. She belted in, her eyes darting everywhere. To Jake's puzzlement she didn't seem to take any note of the shelves full of yachting goodies. Instead she shot to the back of the shop and did a lightning tour of the aisles before returning to his side. She looked anxious and confused.

'You sure this is Barbican Yacht Supplies?'

Jake nodded and silently pointed out the pile of carrier bags beside the counter emblazoned with the name.

'I don't understand it,' said Ronnie under her breath.

'I'm not with you,' said Jake, feeling as confused as Ronnie looked.

'Never mind.' Still looking a little bewildered Ronnie went over to a rack of brightly coloured foul-weather clothing and began to push through the hangers. Jake wandered over to a display of self-inflating life rafts and other emergency equipment. As soon as she saw he was engrossed in a bit of browsing of his own, Ronnie abandoned the waterproof jackets and scuttled over to the counter.

'Where's Poppy?' she whispered to the bloke serving.

'Poppy?'

'Yeah, Poppy Sanders. She works here, doesn't she?'

'It's her day off.'

'Day off?' She hadn't thought of that. Damn and blast. And tomorrow they'd be gone, off on their way to the Med. Bum!

The assistant nodded. 'She'll be in again tomorrow.'

Too late. Ronnie supposed she could always ring Poppy, tell her she was in Plymouth, and get her to come and meet them on the yacht, but that would lose the element of surprise. She sighed. She'd go back to the boat and think about it. Maybe surprise was less important than just getting Jake and Poppy together again.

'Are you a friend of Poppy's?' the assistant asked.

'Yeah. Just here for today really. I thought I'd catch up with her. Never mind.' Frustrated, Ronnie turned back to the oilskins.

'Found anything you wanted?' asked Jake, returning to her side.

'Nah, not really.' In fact not at all, as the only thing she'd been looking for turned out to be the one item completely absent from the shop. 'Come on, let's go.'

They said goodbye to the assistant, who was on the phone, and left the shop.

'Look, there's a café,' said Ronnie. 'I could murder a cuppa.'

Jake wasn't fussed but it would be churlish not to join her. They sat at a shiny aluminium table outside on the pavement and waited to get served.

She'd try ringing Poppy's mobile when she was alone but if Poppy had gone to visit friends then there was nothing she'd be able to do about engineering a reunion. Maybe it wasn't meant to be, she thought. She was a firm believer that things happened, or didn't, for a reason.

'A friend? In the shop? Who?' Poppy put the iron back on its stand and moved away from the ironing board to gaze at the wonderful view from her window.

'Poppy, I don't know. I'm the manager here, not the Spanish Inquisition.'

'Well, male or female then? Give me a clue here.'

'Female. Middle-aged, bright green tracksuit—'

'Bottle blond hair?'

'Absolutely.'

'Ronnie!' yelled Poppy. She slammed her phone down, and pausing only to grab her front door keys she raced out of her flat, down the steps and into the shop.

'She left,' said Peter.

'You didn't keep her here?'

'How was I supposed to know you'd want to see her? She didn't look like the sort of person you'd be friends with. I can't imagine her on a boat. Talk about fish out of water!'

'Maybe, but she's a diamond. Which way did she go?'

Peter shrugged. 'I didn't pay attention. But you won't miss that tracksuit.'

Poppy grinned as she wrenched open the door. She remembered Ronnie's taste. She glanced to the right, the way that led to the Hoe. The road was wide and clear, and this early in the morning wasn't crowded with heaps of holidaymakers and tourists. She couldn't see anything obvious – certainly not the flash of fluorescent green that was one of Ronnie's trademark colours. She took a chance on turning left and raced along the quay, glancing in shops and down side streets as she passed. The road took a sharp left to skirt the edge of the old harbour. She saw it – that hideous shade of emerald. It had to be Ronnie at the café about twenty yards ahead. There was a man with her but Poppy could only see his back – not Mick, too slim. Darren, possibly?

'Ronnie,' shouted Poppy, sprinting forward.

Ronnie stood up, a huge smile on her face. 'Poppy,' she yelled back across the rapidly closing gap. 'Poppy, my love, we thought we were going to miss you.' She opened her arms to give Poppy a welcoming hug.

'Hello,' said Jake quietly, just as Poppy was enveloped in Ronnie's embrace.

'Surprise,' chuckled Ronnie happily.

36

Released from Ronnie's podgy arms Poppy sat down unsteadily. Where the hell had Jake sprung from? He'd been out of her life for over a year, and now . . . She felt shocked. And horribly guilty. If she hadn't overreacted he wouldn't have lost his job. And she knew how much it had meant to him. He'd loved working for WorldFleet – it had offered him everything he wanted out of life: the chance to sail, security and somewhere to live. And because of her it had all been taken away from him. He must hate her so much. The thought that he must now despise her had been haunting her since that dreadful day when Dan had told her what had happened, but she'd been able to blank it from her memory because she really thought their paths would never cross again. But now they had and she dreaded his reaction. She wouldn't blame him if he gave her a piece of his mind and then stormed off. It was no more than she deserved.

'Jake,' she said, for want of anything more intelligent. 'It's been a while.'

Ronnie sat down beside her and looked expectantly from one to the other, almost as if she was umpiring a tennis match.

Jake nodded.

She paused, taking in the way he looked. She didn't think he'd changed. Of course it hadn't been long in terms of weeks and months but she'd missed him so much it had seemed like a lifetime. She smiled at him tentatively. Would he smile back? Or did he still hate her? 'So how have you been?'

The corners of his mouth lifted a fraction. 'All right. Doing odd jobs, shacking up with mates. And you?'

'Living here, over the shop – literally.' God, he still looked so fit, thought Poppy. How could she ever have fancied Charlie? But he had gone from her life completely – and good riddance – and Jake was back in, or so she hoped.

'You're looking well.'

'Thanks. So are you.'

The conversation bumped along, neither of them quite knowing what to say, both of them feeling uncomfortable and a little embarrassed and both aware that Ronnie was watching them, willing them not to fall out, wanting them to kiss and make up.

'I'm sorry,' Poppy said after a few more meaningless and banal exchanges.

'What for?'

'Lots of things, but mostly for getting you the sack.'

'You didn't. I told Charlie he could stuff his job.'

'But if I hadn't gone off on one, the whole mess would never have happened.'

'Look, it's not your fault. If anyone was to blame it was Sophie. She was out to make trouble from the instant she got to the manor.'

'I thought she was a minx the moment I clapped eyes on her,' said Ronnie with feeling.

'She certainly was that,' agreed Jake. 'There's

something you need to know, Poppy. I never slept with her. I know you think I did, but I didn't. Honest.'

Poppy shook her head. She didn't want to talk about it. 'It doesn't matter any more.'

'Yes it does, because you think I did.'

'So she lied?'

'Sort of.' But this time Jake hurried on before Poppy had time to react. 'She slept in my bed but I didn't. I slept on the *Earth Star*. She'd had a skinful, she passed out, I needed to put her somewhere and I couldn't find the key to her flat.'

Poppy didn't know what to say. She sighed sadly. 'That makes me feel even worse,' she said quietly. 'If only you'd said something at the time. Why didn't you?' A picture of that whole awful evening flashed into her mind, central to which was Sophie grinning smugly at her revelation about sleeping with Jake. Shit, thought Poppy. She'd been so naïve to take what Sophie had said at face value. Why oh why hadn't she asked Jake if it were true instead of being so angry that she'd just let fly with the wine? She'd been wrong and now she felt sorry and guilty that she'd blamed him. He hadn't lied to her. So it probably meant that his declaration of love was true too. She blinked, not sure if she wanted to laugh or cry.

'I did try,' said Jake, with a bigger smile. 'But when you're mad . . . Let's just say you were impressive.'

Then she remembered the iron. 'Fuck,' she shrieked, leaping to her feet.

'What,' chorused Ronnie and Jake together.

'The iron! I left it on.' She raced off, calling over her shoulder that she'd be back in a minute.

Jake took a deep breath and exhaled slowly. 'So, tell me if I've got this wrong, but this whole charade involving those trips to that shop was to make me run into Poppy.'

Ronnie nodded.

'I knew something was going on but I never guessed that. How did you know she was there?'

'Because I phoned her and she told me – well, not exactly, but close enough for me to track her down.' Ronnie looked inordinately pleased with her sleuthing skills.

'But why didn't you tell me she was here?'

'I wasn't sure how pig-headed the pair of you were. I fort if you guessed or Poppy got wind of what I was up to one or other of you would cry off.'

'She may yet. We don't know she's going to come back even now.'

'She will. Didn't you notice the look on her face when you told her nuffink had gone on between you and Soph?'

Jake shook his head.

'Trust me, babes, that girl is head over heels with you. Now then.' Ronnie's tone became businesslike. 'You know I said I was happy doing the cooking on board?'

Jake nodded.

'Well, I am. But if a better option came along, I wouldn't mind taking a back seat. Why have a dog and bark yourself, is what I always say. So if I were to offer young Poppy a job as cook/cleaner, what would you say?'

'I'd say I think I could manage to work with her again.'

'Good. Right answer. Go to the top of the class. As it's her day off, unless she's got other plans, I suggest me and Mick take you and her out for a slap-up lunch to reacquaint ourselves with each other and then you two can bugger off and kiss and make up. How does that sound?'

'Like a plan. But you don't have to take us out to lunch.'

'We need to discuss terms and conditions. Besides, I doubt if she'll be able to drop everything and join us when we sail tomorrow so there's a lot we need to get sorted today.'

Jake could see that Ronnie wasn't going to budge on the subject of lunch. He might just as well give in now.

Ronnie sat on the sun deck, her foot jiggling nervously once again. She was scanning the throng of trippers and tourists wandering along the Barbican in the balmy May sunshine.

'He's a grown-up,' said Mick. 'The bloke can find his way back here without you watching out for him.'

'But I need to know how he and Poppy got on.'

'For Christ's sake, woman, it's none of your bleeding business.'

Ronnie snorted. Oh yes it was. She'd put a lot of effort into getting these two back together and she wasn't going to let either of them blow it now. She took another slug of her gin. She'd invited them back to the yacht for cocktails and it was almost dinner time. Maybe they'd fallen out again. Maybe Poppy had another bloke. Maybe she'd had second thoughts about the job offer. Maybe the shop wasn't going to let her go.

She saw them.

'Coo-ee,' she shrieked, waving vigorously. The couple paused at the bottom of the gangplank and exchanged a chaste kiss, then Poppy waved at Ronnie and Mick and returned along the quay towards her flat. Ronnie's heart sank.

'What's the matter with her?' she asked before Jake was on board.

'She remembered she's babysitting for her boss tonight. She apologises and says she'll be in touch.'

Ronnie's eyes narrowed. 'Is that the truth?'

'Honest.'

Ronnie went behind the bar in the saloon and got a beer out of the fridge for Jake. He nodded appreciatively so she clicked the cap off and handed it to him.

'So what did you get up to?'

'We went for a walk, talked, sat on the Hoe and watched the world go by.' Jake shrugged. 'This and that.'

This and that? What was that supposed to mean, thought Ronnie. She didn't want details, but at the very least she wanted a hint that the pair had done rather more than canoodle. Actually she wanted to know that a lot more had happened, but that was probably asking too much. A blind person with a limited IQ and no understanding of human nature would have problems missing the fact that Poppy and Jake were destined to be together. The trouble was that Poppy and Jake seemed to need that fact spelling out to them.

This and that. Huh! She could hardly ask him outright how they'd spent every minute of the afternoon. She would just have to be satisfied with what little information Jake was giving her.

She bustled off to the galley to start cooking supper and left Mick admiring the scantily clad girls who caught his eye amongst the locals enjoying the lovely evening by strolling up and down the old harbour wall. Jake was left in the saloon with his memories of the confidences he and Poppy had exchanged and her astoundingly tender response when he'd told her about his past – the awfulness of the deaths of his mother and Julie.

'No wonder you didn't want to commit,' she'd said, her eyes brimming with tears of sympathy.

Jake shook his head. 'And the longer I worked with you the harder it got to come clean. I was afraid you'd think I was after the sympathy vote.'

She'd rested her head on his shoulder. 'Never.'

And they'd held each other and Jake had felt utterly complete and happy – a feeling he didn't think he'd experienced with that intensity even with Julie.

'You've been blaming yourself for all those bad things, but how could it be your fault?'

'I just felt as if it was. I felt so responsible for my mum, and I always thought it was my place, my duty, to make her better.'

'But it wasn't. And Julie's death was a tragedy. Awful, desperate, but an accident.'

'I think I've come to terms with that too. I can move on. And the person I want to move on with is you, Poppy.'

37

A month later the tables were turned and it was Ronnie Garvie waiting outside Arrivals at an airport for Poppy. This time it was Malta International airport and the ultra-modern concourse was pleasantly cool despite the soaring temperatures outside. Through the huge glass windows Ronnie could see sprinklers watering the lush lawn and palms that surrounded the new buildings, the sun being splintered into rainbow colours and the slight breeze moving the misty droplets. The tourist season was beginning to crank up on this tiny island and every few minutes Ronnie could hear the roar of another jet landing or taking off. But she wasn't here to admire the view. She turned back to scan the arriving passengers.

She saw her quarry. 'Poppy,' she screeched.

Poppy, pushing a trolley loaded with a couple of soft holdalls, almost ran towards her.

'I can't believe I'm here. It's been such a whirlwind,' she said, throwing herself into Ronnie's generous embrace.

'You'd better believe it, girl. And wait till you see where we're berthed.'

'I'm sure it's going to be lovely. Sorry I'm a bit late. The flight was delayed.'

'Only a few minutes. I've got a taxi waiting so we'll have you on board in no time.'

'I can't wait.'

Ronnie led the way to a smart Merc parked near the main exit. 'In you get.'

The driver loaded Poppy's possessions and then jumped in. They set off at breakneck speed along a decent bit of highway that seemed to have some sort of stock-car race taking place on it. Horns blared, lights flashed and Poppy hung on to her seat belt as cars seemed to come at them from all directions every time they came to any sort of intersection.

'It's just the locals' way,' Ronnie assured her. 'You'll get used to it, you know.'

Poppy wondered if she'd live long enough to find out.

As they approached a much more built-up area their driver turned off on to a narrower and less busy road and Poppy felt her pulse begin to return to normal, until she remembered that she would be seeing Jake in only a little while. To take her mind off her anticipation she looked about her at the wonderful jumble of houses, the old churches with spires and towers and domes popping up everywhere, the ubiquitous yellow, battered, antique buses, the fortifications and the glimpses of azure sea.

A terrific bang nearly made her jump out of her skin.

'Firework,' said Ronnie calmly. 'They let 'em off at all times of day and night. Any sort of celebration and kaboom.'

'Good,' said Poppy weakly. What with the driving, the prospect of Jake waiting for her and now high explosives, she wasn't sure her heart was going to last much longer.

'Almost there,' said Ronnie. The driver skirted under a massive fortress with huge honey and amber stone walls that surrounded another jumble of churches and houses. The road led down a steep hill and brought them out along a quay to a marina stuffed full with boats of every shape and size. However, like a swan surrounded by ducks and dominating the scene, Poppy could see Ronnie's pride and joy.

'Home sweet home,' said Ronnie. She glanced at her watch. 'And just in time for a sundowner.'

Poppy grinned. She remembered well that the Garvies found any time of day a perfect moment for a swift half or a cocktail.

'Let's get your stuff on board and then you can freshen up while I open the bar. I thought you'd like to take it easy tonight so Mick and I are going out for dinner. Jake said he'd cook a meal for you two – if that's all right with you?'

It sounded perfect. Then she could use the next day to get thoroughly au fait with the yacht. She grabbed her bags from the taxi driver as Ronnie settled the fare and made her way along the jetty and on to the yacht.

'Hello, you,' said Jake softly from the bridge as Poppy climbed on board.

Even though she'd been thinking about Jake almost daily since Ronnie had offered her the job she still wasn't prepared for the sheer rush of pleasure and delight she felt on seeing him again.

'Jake,' she squealed, dropping her bags on the deck.

'Wait there,' said Jake. He disappeared and a moment later he emerged from the saloon. Poppy was so busy being hugged she didn't notice Ronnie squeeze past them, grab Mick and steer him to the other end of the yacht.

'Don't cramp their style,' she instructed as she manoeuvred him right out of Jake and Poppy's way.

'Like I would,' said Mick gruffly.

Ronnie gave the couple several minutes to themselves before she called loudly from the galley, 'I was just going to crack open some fizz. Who'd like a glass?' She then clinked the glasses noisily together on a tray before reappearing on the sun deck.

'Oh good, you're here too, Jake,' she said, feigning surprise. 'Come on, Mick, make yourself useful and get this open.' She handed him the bottle of Krug and held a glass out ready to catch the foaming liquid as the cork popped.

'Here's to happy days,' she toasted when they'd all got a full glass. She smiled fondly at Jake and Poppy. 'Right,' she said to Mick. 'Drink up, I'm famished.'

Mick looked as if he was about to open his mouth to protest, but he shut it again when he caught sight of the look in Ronnie's eye.

'Yeah, right,' he agreed. 'We're off for fish and chips. There's a blinding place on the quay, according to the guide book. Says it does the best fish and chips in Malta. We'll have to see, won't we, Ron?'

'You two finish off the champers. There's another bottle in the fridge if you'd like it.' She grabbed Mick by his upper arm, removed the glass from his hand and almost pushed him off the boat.

The silence after they'd gone was tangible. Then both Jake and Poppy put their own glasses down on the tray and moved back into each other's arms.

*

'This is the life, innit?' said Ronnie, replete on fish and chips and half a litre of a very passable Italian white wine.

'Certainly is,' said Mick contentedly, suppressing a belch. 'Blinding view.'

Ronnie nodded and gazed across the marina at the towering walls of the city of Valetta soaring up into the dusky sky. The low sun had coloured them amber, gold and honey, and behind the walls, the domes and spires of some of the city's countless churches rose higher still. Houses seemed to have been built into the walls as well as on top of them so that the ramparts were pierced in places by colonnades and windows. It was staggeringly beautiful. Directly in front of them were some of the tiny, multicoloured local fishing boats resplendent in yellow, red, green and blue stripes, and behind them were the jetties of the marina and the swanky yachts and pleasure craft that were visiting. The sea, deep, inky blue, was flat calm. Not a ripple spoilt the surface and the reflection of the boats and the walls of the city behind was mirror perfect.

'I ought to take a picture of that,' said Ronnie lazily.

'Definitely one for the album,' agreed Mick.

Ronnie got her digital camera out of her bag. She composed the photo and then zoomed in on their yacht. She began to giggle.

'What's the joke?' said Mick.

'Take a look.' She handed the camera to Mick. 'Point it at our boat.'

He looked at the image on the screen. 'And your point is?'

'Look at the water by the hull.'

'So?'

'So all the other boats are lying quite still in the water.' She drew Mick's attention to the little ripples that were rhythmically and gently radiating out from the hull.

'You think . . . ?'

'They've finally got it together. And about bleedin' time.'

little black dress

**brings you fantastic new books like these
every month – find out more at
www.littleblackdressbooks.com**

**Why not link up with other devoted Little Black
Dress fans on our Facebook group? Simply type
Little Black Dress Books into Facebook to join up.**

**And if you want to be the first
to hear the latest news on all things
Little Black Dress, just send the details below to
littleblackdressmarketing@headline.co.uk
and we'll sign you up to our lovely email
newsletter (and we promise that we won't share
your information with anybody else!).***

Name: _____

Email Address: _____

Date of Birth: _____

Region/Country: _____

What's your favourite Little Black Dress book?

_____

How many Little Black Dress books have you read?_____

*You can be removed from the mailing list at any time

Pick up a *little black dress* – it's a girl thing.

THE FARMER NEEDS A WIFE
Janet Gover
PBO £5.99

Rural romances become all the rage when editor Helen Woodley starts a new magazine column profiling Australia's lovelorn farmers. But a lot of people (and Helen herself) are about to find out that the course of true love ain't ever smooth . . .

It's not all haystacks and pitchforks, ladies – get ready for a scorching outback read!

978 0 7553 4715 5

HIDE YOUR EYES
Alison Gaylin
PBO £5.99

Samantha Leiffer's in big trouble: the chest she saw a sinister man dumping into the Hudson river contained a dead body, meaning she's now a witness in a murder case. It's just as well hot, hard-line detective John Krull is by her side . . .

'Alison Gaylin is my new must-read' Harlen Coben

978 0 7553 4802 2

Pick up a *little black dress* – it's a girl thing.

ITALIAN FOR BEGINNERS
Kristin Harmel
PBO £5.99

Despairing of finding love, Cat Connelly takes up an invitation to go to Italy, where an unexpected friendship, a whirlwind tour of the Eternal City and a surprise encounter show her that the best things in life (and love) are always unexpected . . .

Say 'arrivederci, lonely hearts' with another fabulous page-turner from Kristin Harmel.

978 0 7553 4743 8

THE GIRL MOST LIKELY TO . . .
Susan Donovan
PBO £5.99

Years after walking out of her small town in West Virginia, Kat Cavanaugh's back and looking for apologies – especially from Riley Bohland, the man who broke her heart. But soon Kat's questioning everything she thought she knew about her past . . . and about her future.

978 0 7553 5144 2

A red-hot tale of getting mad, getting even – and getting everything you want!

Pick up a *little black dress* – it's a girl thing.

HANDBAGS AND HOMICIDE
Dorothy Howell
PBO £4.99

Haley didn't actually mean *murder* when she said she'd 'kill for' the latest fashions. But when her department store boss is discovered dead in the store room, fingers are pointed firmly at her! Will gorgeous Ty Cameron believe in her innocence?

978 0 7553 4731 5

A sharp, comic debut combining mystery, romance and shopping – what more could a girl want!

TRULY MADLY YOURS
Rachel Gibson
PBO £4.99

Delaney Shaw has to stay put in the town of Truly, Idaho for an entire year to claim her three-million-dollar inheritance ... At least the other condition of her stepfather's will, that she has nothing to do with sexy bad-boy Nick Allegrezza, sounds more manageable ... doesn't it?

978 0 7553 3744 6

Fall in love with Rachel Gibson and her fabulous, sexy romantic reads!

You can buy any of these other
Little Black Dress titles from your
bookshop or *direct from the publisher*.

FREE P&P AND UK DELIVERY
(Overseas and Ireland £3.50 per book)

TO ORDER SIMPLY CALL THIS NUMBER

01235 400 414

or visit our website: www.headline.co.uk

Prices and availability subject to change without notice.